Merlin's Vow

(The Camelot Inher

Also available in the
Camelot Inheritance series:

The Golden Sword

The Time Smugglers

Merlin's Vow

(The Camelot Inheritance ~ Book 3)

Rosie Morgan

You all have gifts; use them wisely.

Merlin's Vow

ISBN: 978–0–9954982–0-4

This edition first published 2016 by Liscarret Creations

Both the characters and the events in this story are entirely fictional; however the setting is loosely based on the beautiful landscape of the county of Cornwall, Britain.

Illustrations by Rosie Morgan
With those of Dragon by Helen Blenkhorn

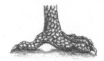

Cover design by Katie Stewart, Magic Owl Design

For three very special people,
Jonah, Faith and Robyn.
I wrote this book for you.

Map of Trezion
and surrounding areas.

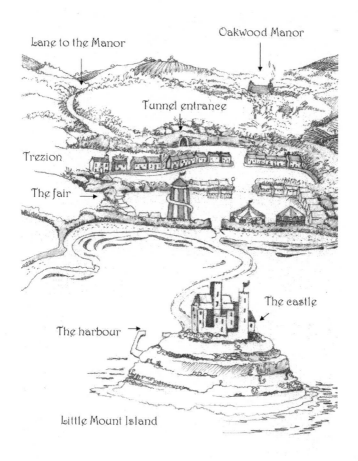

Lane to the Manor

Oakwood Manor

Tunnel entrance

Trezion

The fair

The castle

The harbour

Little Mount Island

Table of Contents

The Beginning

'Man, this is weird!' Nick muttered, holding a tiny dragon to his chest.

Nick and Dragon sat in the cramped bedroom of the house in Lyskeret, where Nick lived with his mum, and watched the book turn its pages. Blurred images flew past – the book was in a hurry.

After the last couple of years he was *fairly* used to having a book with self-turning pages (after all, owning a small green dragon was perhaps more unusual), but he'd never actually been there to see it in action. Normally it waited till he was out.

Dragon wriggled.

'Oh no you don't! You'll damage it.'

The animal struggled, determined to pounce, but Nick had a strong grip. Eventually the creature gave up and laid his chin on Nick's arm, flicking his tail and watching the pages.

The book's pages slowed and stopped. It had reached its chosen chapter.

It started this way.

Nick leant over and examined the opening paragraph.

At the beginning there were three young people: Arthur Penhaligon, Tamar Tamblyn and Nick Borlase.

'Why are you telling me this? I was there, remember.'

The book's page didn't move.

***

On the night-dim road outside Nick's house a shadow materialised. It glanced towards the bedroom window where a small winged shape was briefly silhouetted against the drawn curtains before being caught and disappearing from view. The shadow nodded. He was in the right place. Shivering, he drew his cloak around him, trying to ignore the biting cold.

***

Nick sat on the crumpled bed and rocked his skateboard backward and forward with his toe, deep in thought. Why had that weird teacher given him the book? She could have given it to Tamar; she *liked* reading. He sighed as the book rustled its pages impatiently.

And these three were destined to be Cornwall's Guardians. They had allies and enemies and fought important battles.

Nick was briefly distracted by Dragon snapping at a passing fly but he turned back to the book and did his best to concentrate.

The three were aided by the cat known as Cathe (a leader of cats), Michael and Angela Jolly (a time-resistant brother and sister), and the ancient knight Sir Bedivere.

A fourth Guardian joined the friends; Gawain Kitto, a boy destined to be as great as the others.

The Guardians' enemies were the Crow Man, his colleague the pale-faced Hagarawall, and Matearnas – the woman who wished to be Cornwall's queen.

'But she wasn't the queen 'cause we won,' Nick commented. 'Hey, you haven't mentioned Art's dog.'

If the book could have sighed it would have. Instead, its words rearranged themselves. *With the help of their allies, Matearnas was defeated … aided by Lightning, Arthur's dog.*

'Cool!' Nick was impressed.

A small picture of a black and white collie was quickly drawn in the margin by an unseen hand. Nick wondered if the book was being sarcastic but the page turned quickly. It had more for the boy to read.

By the end of that particular summer the four young people had been knighted as Guardians of Cornwall by the sword Excalibur, and the woman Matearnas was dead.

***

Outside, the wind howled and the shadow pressed back against the wall. A cat – ginger … for now – sauntered towards Nick's gate and sat beside the shadow. The shadow studied the sky: low cloud obscured the stars but above Lyskeret the moon hung, waiting.

***

Nick's bedside light dimmed and the back of his neck prickled. Something was stirring.

'Okay, I'll concentrate.' Dragon wriggled free and launched himself at the desk, landing on a stack of empty cans and pitching them to the floor. Nick winced and exclaimed, 'It's just as well Mum's out!'

So far he'd managed to keep Dragon a secret – although there had been a few near misses. Only the other Guardians knew about him.

Nick sighed and shook his head and turned back to the book.

However, a year later the Crow Man reappeared with a new leader: the Lady of Clehy – the Ice Lady.

He shivered. Michael Jolly had given each of the Guardians miniature swords – gold for Arthur and silver for the other three – to wear around their necks; replica Excaliburs that warmed when they were near someone they could trust and turned cold when someone dangerous was close by. Nick's had cooled at the mere mention of the Ice Lady. He ran his fingers over the chilled metal.

But the Guardians were helped by Michael Jolly and Arthur's Aunt Dywana.

Tamar Tamblyn travelled through time and became the Time Keeper, custodian of the emerald pocket watch, and Nick found a small dragon carved from green stone.

'That's you, Dragon,' Nick said, pointing at the illustration. 'Do you remember Michael waking you up?' The dragon landed on Nick's shoulder and peered at the picture. His portrait gazed back at him. A tiny, pocket-sized dragon.

Finally Arthur Penhaligon was appointed as heir to King Arthur and entrusted with the sword Excalibur and succeeded in defeating Cornwall's enemies.

'You didn't mention Lancelot,' Nick mused remembering Arthur telling him about the knight who'd stepped out of the painting.

He thought for a bit. 'Is it because he wasn't as involved as Bedivere?'

But the book didn't add anything. Maybe Lancelot's story would come later.

He looked up and contemplated a poster of a skateboarder tacked to his wall and considered his friend. No one would guess that the lanky, dark-haired boy – the skateboarder who lived in Castle Close, Lyskeret – was also the new King Arthur.

***

Outside Nick's gate the cat meowed. His transformation was beginning. The shadow Watched his companion trade ginger fur for black, and a small body for extra-large. Cathe's makeover always fascinated him but a voice in his brain interrupted his thoughts.

'The boy has read the book, Viatoris?'

The shadow nodded. 'As far as I can tell, ma'am.'

'Good.'

'Is Servo joining us, ma'am?'

Some miles away a woman put a pen down and stifled the first reply that came to mind. The Writer sighed. Her invisible Watchers were an uneasy double act.

'He will be here, Viatoris.' The Writer paused, tucking a strand of steel-grey hair behind her ear. 'Servo will arrive at the right hour.'

She cast her mind to Viatoris's other assignment a few hundred years away in Italy. Most Watchers were given a single charge to observe but both Viatoris and Servo had been given two assignments. 'Does it go well with the young Leonardo da Vinci?'

Viatoris took a breath but the recitation of Leonardo's achievements was halted before he began.

'Hush! Listen and Watch Viatoris. It is beginning.'

Chapter 1
The First Move

Tamar had been looking forward to helping her sister Morwenna at Trezion's Christmas Fair, but now she wasn't certain that it had been such a good idea.

I shouldn't have come, she thought. *Not by myself.*

Trezion's fair used to be one of the highlights of her year but Tamar's world was different now.

She looked across the sea to the island, the Little Mount, rising out of the shallow Cornish waters like a circular, tiered wedding cake. Trees and gardens decorated the bottom layer, climbing to a fairy-tale castle crowning the top. It wasn't very far from the mainland, probably only a few hundred metres out to sea. People came from all over the world to climb its steep steps to the castle perched on the rocks. Hollywood couldn't come up with anything more enchanting if it tried.

So much history locked up in one tiny, rounded island. So many memories trapped in its stones, waiting to be released.

The lights in the cottages at the foot of the island's hill twinkled. Here and there pockets of smoke hung above the chimneys while, from time to time, a door opened and the night was briefly illuminated as the people went about their daily routines.

Something's wrong, she thought. *It looks normal, but it's not.*

A few months ago, when she'd first been made the Time Keeper, she hadn't been used to the pocket watch's habits, but now she felt its ticking as if it was part of her. It had been whirring and breaking into chimes ever since she'd arrived at Trezion. It only ever did that when it was building itself up to a reveal. Were Cornwall's enemies closing in?

She thought about her encounter with the Ice Lady, whose one touch made her feel as if the blood had frozen in her veins. And then there'd been those meetings with the coal-eyed Crow Man and his pale-haired companion, Hagarawall; but they'd all been defeated by Excalibur and Arthur. Surely they wouldn't come back.

A sickening thought pinged in her brain. *But the Crow Man lost before and came back, didn't he?*

Tamar dug into her pocket. Maybe she should call Arthur. Perhaps being separated from the other Guardians was asking for trouble. It was possible that coming to Trezion while the others were miles away in Lyskeret wasn't the most sensible choice she'd ever made.

'Stupid, stupid girl!' she muttered, and pulled out her phone.

Checking that no one was within earshot, Tamar scrolled to Arthur's name but she hesitated. She could hardly say that she was feeling a bit odd, and that the watch was ticking more than usual, and please would they come and keep her company. Maybe she was imagining things.

Which is when the pile of leaves moved. By itself. Tamar's thumb froze as the leaf pile stilled.

For some seconds neither Tamar nor the leaves stirred. She peered at the little mound, faintly conscious of the activity on the other side of the field and of carols being sung, and she waited. A snowflake drifted towards the ground beside the leaves and another fell and settled on the mound.

Tamar was sure she hadn't been seeing things and she waited and watched until finally an individual leaf gave up – revealing a tiny, black nose.

'Phew, you had me worried!' she exclaimed, waiting for the hedgehog to hurry off. However, instead of scuttling away as most normal hedgehogs would, it allowed the leaves to slide off its back while it looked at her with a pair of beady eyes.

'Hello,' Tamar whispered.

The watch in her pocket ticked a little more loudly as Tamar crouched down and repeated, 'Hello … Can you understand me?'

There was something about the intelligent way it looked at her that made Tamar think it was more than just a normal hedgehog. She wouldn't have been surprised if it had spoken to her.

Animated ticks escaped from her pocket as a voice behind her asked, 'Do you often speak to animals?'

Tamar whipped round and immediately the hedgehog was bustling towards the edge of the field.

A boy, probably a few years older than her, was standing a couple of metres away. He was tall and broad-shouldered and wearing a silver biker's jacket with matching silver leather gloves. And his hair was silver! And he swaggered. Even standing still he swaggered.

There was something about him that made Tamar think of an owl, not a cute owl, more of an eagle owl. If this guy had been a raptor he would be right at the top of the food chain.

'Animals are more polite than some humans,' she retorted, getting to her feet. She could feel herself blushing.

'Do you make a habit of creeping up on people?'

He laughed. 'And do you have other hobbies, apart from talking to hedgehogs?'

'I like hedgehogs. And it's no business of yours what I like doing!'

'Okay, okay.' He paused. He seemed to be considering his next question. 'Are you Morwenna Tamblyn's kid sister?'

Bristling, Tamar answered, 'I'm Wenna's *sister*, yes. Why?'

'Just wondered. You look like her, that's all.'

He said this casually but Tamar was all too familiar with this sort of approach. There was a boy at school who would just 'happen' to be walking home at the same time, or suddenly 'need' to borrow something from her for history or geography; he was so transparent it was painful. For some reason this boy was interested in her, in Tamar, as well.

The watch quietened, like a mouse freezes if a cat is nearby. She wished the silver boy would go away. She wasn't sure how long the watch would be able to hold its ticks.

The boy's tawny eyes blinked and slid towards her pocket. She held her breath, willing the watch to quieten its cogs, when there was a rustling in the hedge.

The boy glanced up and peered into the darkness – his pupils dilated until his eyes were black, ringed with gold.

Tamar had never seen a person's eyes react like that.

A thread of a breeze sprung up and whipped around them, sucking up leaves and dust. The boy frowned and zipped up his jacket.

'Will you be helping on Morwenna's stall?' he asked, keeping watch on the hedge.

'Probably ... some of the time.' She shoved her hand into her pocket and wrapped her fingers around the watch. The metal felt clammy against her palm. 'When it's busy.'

She wished that she could come up with some witty put-down and get rid of him.

'Cool,' he said, a little too nonchalantly. 'In that case we'll probably be seeing a lot of each other. I'm here for the fair too.'

'Oh? Which is your stall?' She couldn't recall seeing him.

'Just one selling the usual sort of thing.'

'What sort of thing? Christmas decorations or Christmas food ...'

'No way! There are enough people here trying to flog ... winter stuff!'

'What's wrong with that?' Tamar asked, puzzled. 'It *is* a Christmas fair! Anyway, what's not to like about Christmas?'

The boy shuddered.

Tamar was intrigued. 'If you hate it so much why come in the first place?'

'Duty,' the boy replied, raking his hair with his fingers.

'Duty?' Tamar repeated. 'Oh, do you mean that your family makes you come?'

'My family?' The boy looked as if the word mystified him.

Tamar was lost. She tried another question. 'Okay, tell me why you don't like Christmas, what's wrong with it?'

'It's hideous.' He shuddered again, as if the word revolted him.

'What's wrong with a bit of happiness and excitement?'

Tamar asked. 'I love it. It's my favourite time of year – after summer.'

'You can keep it.'

A Father Christmas wandered past, complete with black boots, a red, fur-edged suit and a white beard. He glanced towards the two young people, lifted a tin whistle to his lips and very quietly began to play 'The Twelve Days of Christmas'.

The notes drifted towards them, the air swirling as the music grew, and the darkness receded. And Tamar was filled with a cheerfulness that had nothing at all to do with presents. But it appeared to be having the opposite effect on the boy: the longer the music played, the more he tensed, balling his fists.

Tamar flashed a quick look towards the musician, wondering what would happen and wishing that the music could carry on for ever when their eyes met; the man winked, lowered his tin whistle and ambled away.

The boy followed the man's progress across the field until he disappeared into the gloom.

'Ridiculous garbage,' he spat. 'Just a load of old fairy-tales!'

But he was shaking. Whatever the reason, it was clear that he was no fan of Christmas.

'Are you okay?' she asked.

'Course I am,' he snapped and, without warning, leant across and seized a single hair.

'Ow!' Tamar yelled as the hair twanged from her scalp. 'How dare you!'

'Sorry … thought it was a stray hair.'

'That was a really weird thing to do!' She rubbed her head, shaken. 'Didn't your mum teach you any manners … like not to go around creeping up on people, and that it's not okay to pull a stranger's hair out!'

He'd regained his composure and merely shrugged, but Tamar noticed him rub the hair between his fingers and wind it around his gloved forefinger.

'It's only one tiny hair.'

But she thought she heard him add something about the wonders of science.

The boy watched her and continued fiddling with the snatched hair, winding it round and round until it was coiled around his finger. It felt like an ant was crawling over her skull.

'You're odd,' she mumbled, her scalp throbbing.

'I'm not the one who goes around talking to animals, but if you meet any more hedgehogs you can say "hi" from me.' He smirked and flipped his fringe out of his eyes.

And before she was able to deliver a devastating one-liner, he shot her a brief, 'See you,' and was walking away, leaving Tamar boiling and uneasy. Who on earth did he think he was?

'What an idiot,' she said. 'What an arrogant idiot …'

But worry bubbled inside her. She was certain that he'd snatched the hair on purpose: there'd been something in the way he'd examined it before tucking it into his pocket.

'Concentrate on the other stuff,' she told herself firmly. 'Never mind the idiot.'

It was then that she realised the silver sword hanging around her neck had chilled. It only ever did that when there was a threat nearby.

'Tamar,' she whispered, 'you should have got away.'

She looked across the field to the stalls and the rides and did her best to quell the growing anxiety. She could make out the top of the spiralled helter-skelter jutting above the canopy of a striped tent. To her right, a candy-floss stall was parked next to the sweet-chestnut stand, white lights swinging from their canopies, breaking up the darkening winter sky. And just beyond was a stall packed with pink and white sugar canes, giant lollipop spirals and dark chocolate mice.

Tamar caught a waft of spiced, mulled wine and fragments of a carol being sung somewhere on the edge of the fair. It was all so *perfectly* Christmas and yet something was definitely wrong ... and it was more than just the boy.

Which is when the tent appeared – and disappeared.

If she hadn't been inspecting the field, Tamar might never have seen it. In fact she barely had time to register its appearance (a sort of circus pavilion swathed in purple and gold, with a circular roof rising to a point), or to see the familiar figure standing in the open entrance, before both the tent and its occupant were whisked away. The figure had been Angela Jolly.

'Angela?' Tamar stared at the space. The materialising tent had been accompanied by her old friend. 'Okay, this is getting *really* weird now!'

A girl with a cloud of red hair was standing in a gap between two stalls. She was frozen, staring wide-eyed at the space where the tent had been. She flicked a brief look towards Tamar but the second their glances connected she darted away.

Everyone else was carrying on as if nothing had happened. All around her people were hurrying, tying awnings and fastening flickering lights to their stalls.

Tamar frowned, bemused. And then she understood. No one else *had* seen it – apart from the girl.

She worried at a fingernail. 'Now I'm *definitely* going to call the boys.'

But then the watch began to stir, its cogs gathering speed for a reveal. Tamar glanced around. She had to find a private place where nobody could creep up on her.

Her sister was busy at their stall, putting finishing touches to their display of Christmas decorations. Tamar hurried over. 'You don't need me now, do you Wenna?' Her eyes swept the field but there was no sign of the boy.

Morwenna looked up as she rearranged a lacy angel and shook her head. 'No, we're just about done.'

She looked sideways at Tamar. 'Are you okay?'

'Yeah, of course I am.' Tamar shoved her hand into her pocket. Any minute now and the watch would start to chime.

'You don't look okay,' Wenna observed, peering at her. 'You look like you've seen a ghost.'

'No, honestly I'm fine.' She clamped her hand firmly over the watch's casing and began to edge away. 'I'm just a bit cold. It's all this standing around. Perhaps I'll have a look at the other stalls.'

'Hmmm,' Wenna was unconvinced but some banter from the other stallholders distracted her and, before she could be delayed any longer, Tamar slid away.

The moment she was out of Morwenna's sight she plunged her hand into her pocket and drew out the watch.

Its beauty still caught her.

A silver case studded with tiny green emeralds on one side and intricate engravings on the other. But now wasn't the time for admiration.

Her hair fell forward as she examined the watch, veiling it from anyone else who might happen to look her way. Tamar frowned, flashed a quick look around to be certain that she wasn't being watched – and stepped into the shadow of a gnarled oak tree.

Standing under the bare canopy she opened the watch. It still bore its Roman numerals but she recognised the signs of it priming itself to show her its pictures. She edged backwards until her spine was pressed against the rough bark and waited.

Above her the air parted, brushed aside by white feathers. A barn owl flew towards the centre of Tamar's chosen tree. Twigs and bare branches opened, allowing it to land as silently as it had arrived. Then the tree rearranged itself and pulled its twigs back into shape as the bird perched at its heart. The owl inspected the Time Keeper and her watch.

Tamar heard the clicking and humming as the cogs moved up a gear and the face of the watch began to glow, bathing the tree in a soft light as the images took shape.

At first they appeared slowly, a procession of people and places. But within half a minute the watch had got into its stride, flashing one brief image after another. It seemed that the timepiece had decided that the pictures alone weren't enough – it had chosen a sound-track to accompany them.

Tamar was too busy concentrating on the pictures to be interested in the tune but then the notes slithered into her mind and she raised her eyebrows. The watch had picked a carol, one of the oldest carols: 'God rest ye merry, gentlemen, let nothing you dismay ...'

Tamar's brow furrowed as she tried to take in all she was being shown. The pictures were changing so fast that it was like watching a speeded-up film.

People and animals chased each other across the miniature face: a cat, changing from ginger to black; a knight on horseback; a silver-bearded man, hollow cheeked and stooping and leaning on a wooden staff; a magnificent white stallion; a room filled with books; a crow perching on a rooftop ... and a woman dressed from head to toe in black velvet. It might be a rapid message but it was a clear one – Cornwall's allies and enemies were gathering.

The music that had accompanied the pictures died away and the watch quietened as the last of the images faded. Tamar waited until the watch had returned to its normal face and snapped it shut. The whirrs and chimes were replaced by a contented ticking.

It had done its duty for its Keeper.

Tamar leant back and thought about what she'd been shown.

It was starting again and she knew only too well that their enemies meant business. They wouldn't allow anyone to stand in their way. They were bent on the domination of Cornwall. Glancing around, she pulled out her phone and scrolled to Arthur's name. On a branch above her the owl waited.

'Arthur, you've got to get down here,' Tamar said as soon as Arthur answered. She looked around, flicked a strand of dark hair over her shoulder and lowered her voice. 'The watch has warned me.'

'I know.'

'You know! How?'

'The books – both of them, mine and Nick's – they told us some stuff and showed us some pictures.'

'What did they show you?'

'My book showed me the island and some other stuff.' Arthur was still trying to make sense of the second page his book had shown him. 'What did you see?'

Slivers of frozen air slid down her back. She shivered. 'I'll tell you the details when you get here. But it wasn't just the watch.' She paused. 'I saw something else too.'

'What?'

Tamar hesitated. 'Um, look I'd rather tell you when you get here.'

There was silence at the other end.

She scanned the field. There was no sign of the boy or anyone else who might be a threat, but she couldn't take a chance. 'I don't know who's around, Art.'

'It's okay, I get it.'

'Are you all coming?'

'Yeah, course. We told our folks that you and Wenna could do with some help – but I think that Dad guessed there was more to it than that. Anyway, he managed to persuade Mum that it'd be all right if we're together, and Nick's mum said it would be okay as long as we take our phones.'

'And what about Gawain?'

'Yeah, it's sorted with his uncle too.'

'So when are you coming?'

'Tomorrow morning.'

'Tomorrow!'

Arthur pictured Tamar's brown eyes widening. 'Yeah, I know it's not great but there aren't any trains till the morning.'

Tamar sighed. 'Okay, but get the earliest one you can.' She faltered before whispering, 'Art, it showed me *her*, the Ice Lady … and the crow. There were others too but I didn't recognise them.' She paused. 'And I met a really strange boy.'

Arthur was quiet. 'Look, stay near Morwenna. Don't go anywhere by yourself.'

'I'm not stupid!' Tamar fired back.

Arthur held the phone away from his ear and grinned. That was more like the Tamar he knew.

'I know,' he said. 'Only stating the obvious.'

Tamar's temper subsided. 'Sorry. I suppose I was shaken, seeing *them* again.' She clutched her arm, injured earlier that year by the Ice Lady's cronies.

'I'm not surprised. Can you find somewhere for us to stay?'

'What? Oh yeah, I'll sort that.' She was distracted by a movement in the shadows to her left and then by another to her right.

'I've got to go, Art.' She had a sudden, and unusually urgent, need to be close to her sister. 'I'll organise something. See you tomorrow.' Thrusting her phone into her pocket she glanced around again and hurried towards her sister's stall. The branches of the tree swayed as its other guest left its shelter for the cover of the night sky.

Two shadows walked to stand beneath the oak tree where Tamar had been standing a moment before. They stood back, observing the activity and the business. One of them pulled his cloak around him.

'So, the Time Keeper has alerted the other Guardians.'

His companion nodded.

'Have you seen the Guardians' opposition?'

'No Viatoris, I have only just arrived. I was pulled from Egypt without warning.'

The other Watcher looked sharply at his partner. 'You too? I also was given no notice!'

They took in one another's clothes: robes suited to other times and centuries.

The challenge of time travel never became easier.

'So,' Viatoris began, after a cursory inspection of their surroundings, 'how does your other charge, young Joseph, do?'

'He's doing well and is entrusted with much … and yours?'

Viatoris nodded proudly. Servo's heart sank. He knew he shouldn't have asked. There were times his fellow Watcher really irritated him. Anyone would think that it was Viatoris himself who enabled the young Leonardo da Vinci to paint and to invent.

'He is but fifteen,' Viatoris began. Servo stifled a yawn. His colleague folded his arms and leant back against the tree. This could be a long lecture. 'And yet he is already apprenticed in painting … the things he draws! He has even begun sketching ideas of flight, and this when the year is only fourteen hundred and sixty-seven.'

Servo's eyes began to glaze over but a shimmer in front of them, and strains of music better suited to another century, came to his rescue.

'Hush!' he commanded, laying his hand on Viatoris's arm. His colleague frowned, annoyed at the interruption.

'Listen,' Servo continued, cupping his ear.

'I can hear,' Viatoris huffed. But his indignation at being interrupted melted as the dark notes twisted and twirled, rising and falling, towards him. It appeared that they were not the only ones to travel through time to this field in Cornwall.

The music machine with its thief was on its way.

Chapter 2
Time Train

The following morning Tamar sat on the icy grass at the edge of the fair. She wrapped her arms around her legs and rested her chin on her knees. She wished that the boys were there already. Too much was happening too quickly.

An antique barrel organ had appeared late the previous evening, which wasn't particularly significant except no one had seen it arrive, or knew who owned it. So now the stallholders were examining it and admiring its polished wood. Tamar observed them as they studied it and listened as they discussed the scuffed, leather bag hanging at its side and its wheels with their wooden spokes and rims. But her anxiety grew as she realised that not one of them had noticed the absence of any tracks. The ground was soggy beneath its layer of frost. Nothing could be wheeled across the field without leaving a trail.

Perhaps the automaton – the carved figure on top of the organ – distracted them, with its top hat and tail coat. Maybe they were too spellbound by its dark eyes and painted moustache and the way that the eyes appeared to be looking at you wherever you were. However, the most disturbing thing was the way the stallholders accepted its unconventional arrival as soon as they'd touched it.

I wouldn't be surprised if that boy's connected with this, she thought. She watched Morwenna join the small crowd, stroking the inlaid wooden case and running her finger over the silk plush brim of the figure's top hat.

'How do you think it got here?' Tamar asked as her sister walked back towards her.

'What?'

'You know – that thing … the barrel organ or whatever it is.'

Morwenna looked at her blankly.

'Well,' Tamar said, 'it wasn't here yesterday evening.'

'Of course it was!'

'No it wasn't.'

Morwenna nodded. 'Yes it was; don't you remember? It arrived during the afternoon.'

Tamar looked at her sister. Morwenna really did believe that it had been there all along. She glanced uneasily at the barrel organ and the top-hatted automaton leaning on its cane.

I hope the boys get here soon. She pulled her coat around her. Was it her imagination or was it getting colder?

***

Arthur and Nick sat on the bench in Lyskeret station, with Lightning on the platform between their feet. They'd chosen a quiet corner of the platform well away from the other commuters while they waited for Gawain's train to arrive from Pendrym.

They were both holding their bags tightly because their books were restless. It would have been much easier to leave them behind but they never knew when they might be shown another picture. And in Nick's case there was always the added danger of his mum deciding to deep-clean his room.

'I wish I could have left the book at home,' he said. 'But I don't think Mum would cope with a self-opening book.'

Arthur grinned. 'Yeah, me too. Although my mum tends to leave my room alone. She says it's too much of a health hazard 'cause there's stuff all over the floor.'

'That wouldn't stop my mum,' Nick said gloomily. 'She's on a one-woman mission to clean the planet.'

Arthur chuckled. Dragon was adding to Nick's troubles. From time to time a tiny snout protruded from his friend's jacket pocket and Nick glowered.

'You okay mate?' Arthur asked innocently.

'Oh just fine!' Nick erupted. 'Apart from having to deal with a hyperactive dragon and a self-opening book.'

And right on cue the book in Nick's backpack began to shuffle restlessly and the dragon belched. A fine plume of green smoke rose out of the pocket and Nick groaned. 'Seriously mate, there's no way we can get there without *someone* noticing.'

Arthur looked at the groups dotted around the platform. No one seemed particularly interested in them apart from a couple of girls giggling and throwing them sideways glances. He never paid much attention to his looks, barely looking in the mirror to comb his hair, but in the last few months he'd grown quite tall – although Nick was still a head taller – and now girls seemed to like him, which was quite nice but also a bit embarrassing. And he wished they wouldn't keep going on about his brown eyes!

However, he probably wouldn't have noticed the woman sitting in one of the station's cream and green shelters at the far end of the platform, even if he'd seen her.

She had a large shapeless bag at her feet and a worn, leather-bound book resting on her lap. The woman smiled to herself when she heard their quiet conversation. The Writer had to admit that owning a small dragon was challenging in this day and age. Years ago it might have been a different matter. It wouldn't have been such a surprise to meet a Dragon Boy then. She leant back and listened to the rest of the boys' discussion.

'What time is Gawain's train getting in?' Nick asked, pinning his pocket closed.

Arthur looked at his watch. 'Should be here in just a minute.'

'Good, I can't stand much more of this! I'm getting seriously stressed.'

'I know mate,' Arthur said a little more sympathetically, but his attention was divided between their backpacks and the other people gathering on the platform. He lived in a permanent state of alert. He scanned the pre-Christmas travellers crowding onto the platform before checking those waiting on the opposite side of the track. Then he glanced at the sky, at the gulls wheeling and screeching above them, but there was no sign of the crow. They were probably safe … for the moment.

At last a two-carriage train nosed around the bend of the track from Pendrym.

'It's here. Come on,' Nick said.

Brakes squealing, the small train slowed and stopped. It was packed, so it took a while for Gawain to appear. Arthur watched the guard close the door after the last person stepped down, and waited for it to begin its return journey along the single track winding down the valley towards Pendrym.

He wanted to be sure that no one was following his friend. As far as he could see, there was nobody who posed a threat.

Nick's blue eyes widened when he saw Gawain. 'Bringing the kitchen sink as well, mate?'

Struggling with the straps of an enormous bag, Gawain answered, 'Most of this is Uncle Kitto's. He asked me to take it. He said he may come down later.'

'What's in it?'

'Books, books and more books. It weighs a ton!'

'That's what comes of enjoying reading,' Nick said. 'See? I always said it was bad for your health.'

Gawain shook his head and grinned. 'You're a philistine Nick!'

'A fili what?'

'Oh forget it! The Penkernow train will be here soon.' Gawain lowered his voice and ran a hand through his hair. 'We need to find a quiet bit if we can, so that you guys can tell me exactly what the books showed you.'

'But we told you!' Nick exclaimed.

'Yeah, I know, but I've a feeling something's missing.'

Arthur's head snapped up. 'Why? Have you seen anything?'

His friend shook his head and was about to reply when a commotion broke out on the opposite platform. A whirlwind, about a metre high, was spinning through the air, not at ground level but at head height. As the boys watched, the mini-tornado suddenly veered sideways, crossed the tracks and headed straight for them.

In the centre was a single feather.

The moment the whirlwind reached them it died away, dropping its collection of twigs, wrappers and dead leaves at their feet.

The crowds around them laughed, relieved that the freak weather phenomenon had been short-lived, and were quickly chatting and discussing the weather: Britain's favourite topic of conversation.

But Arthur was more interested in the contents of the whirlwind and bent down to retrieve the feather.

'At least it's not black, so it can't be a crow's feather!' Nick said.

Arthur dug into his memory. Ever since the crow had become such an unwelcome part of their lives he'd been interested in birds. It had felt important to know more about them. He sifted through the little knowledge he'd acquired. He was sure he knew this type of feather. Closing his eyes he frowned and a piece of text floated into his mind:

'The feathers of the owl are adapted to break down the turbulence in the air. The comb-like edge of the primary wing feathers are called 'flutings' or 'fimbriae', which accounts for the sound of the owl's flight being muffled.'

Arthur examined the feather and noted the colour. Could it belong to a barn owl? The other two boys were watching him.

Nick said, 'Don't tell me that you know what sort of feather it is!'

'I'm not sure ... but I think I know.'

The Writer sat in the shelter and listened with a small smile: the boy was learning to take note of the important signs. She understood that school-acquired knowledge could have its uses, but so often formal education proved to be restricting rather than enlightening.

An announcement rang out and the waiting crowds began to gather their luggage and shuffle towards the edge of the platform.

A pale-haired figure hung back in the shadows but she saw him. She'd known Hagarawall was there all along but she also knew that, for now at least, the boys and their possessions would be safe.

The London to Penkernow train approached Lyskeret loaded with weary travellers.

'I wonder if we'll be able to find a seat?' Gawain mused as he looked up and down the platform. 'It looks like the world and his wife are trying to get to Penkernow.'

The train slowed and the passengers surged forward.

'Come on!' Nick said, taking the lead. He shrugged his bag onto his back and forged his way through the crowd with Gawain and Arthur trailing behind him.

By the time Arthur and Gawain caught up, Nick was already seated, in triumphant possession of a corner table, but as they got closer Arthur understood why he had the table to himself. Dragon's latest snack appeared to have had an unfortunate side-effect.

'What *have* you been feeding him?' Arthur exclaimed.

Gawain looked around and giggled. 'Well, whatever it is, it's mighty effective, no one's coming near. Bet they think it's you Nick!'

'Yeah, but I don't care. It's usually impossible to get a seat; even this is worth it.' And to make the point he rummaged in his bag for a packet of dried insects and slipped one into his pocket.

'There you go boy, that should keep the hordes at bay.'

A pair of tiny jaws crunched the long-dead creature and the smallest whiff rose out of Nick's pocket.

'See?' Nick said. 'Our very own secret weapon.'

Gawain groaned. 'It's terrible.'

'Yeah,' Arthur agreed, holding his hand over his nose and sliding into the seat. 'That's chemical warfare!'

But the books quietened and the boys began to relax. Lightning sidled under the table and curled up at Arthur's feet.

Nick, sitting across the table from his friends, arranged his long legs, leant back and looked around. He could see down the carriage but no one appeared to be paying them any attention.

A girl of about fifteen was tapping on her phone with black varnished nails while a white-haired lady looked on with undisguised curiosity. Nick was reminded of his own gran. He smiled as he remembered the number of lessons it had taken to teach her to text.

'What else did your book show you, Art?' Gawain asked as he settled his bag on the table in front of him, his amber eyes serious. He leant forward and rested his chin on his hand.

'Apart from the island?'

'Yeah, you told me about that. What was the other picture?'

Arthur hesitated, but neither Nick nor Gawain could have guessed the reason why. He suspected that whatever the book had been trying to show him could happen at any moment. 'Let's wait until we're closer to Penkernow.'

Somewhere in the carriage a child whined and was hushed by its mother. On the platform the station guard raised a yellow disc signalling the train's departure, and with a quiet hum the train left Lyskeret.

The boys watched the small market town disappear to be replaced with steeply sloping fields and dun-coloured cows. Here and there an isolated stone cottage grew out of the surrounding countryside, and squat church towers or slate steeples reached up into the overcast sky.

The train gathered speed as it entered open country and approached the first of the tunnels burrowed beneath Cornwall's hills, and the Writer sat back in her seat and waited.

Hagarawall, standing at the far end of the train, gritted his teeth because he never enjoyed what they were about to experience. He should be used to it by now, but time travel never became easier for him. Popping a hard-boiled sweet into his mouth, he chewed and swallowed, hoping that maybe this time he wouldn't feel sick and his ears wouldn't hurt. He'd been told to follow the young king wherever he went and whatever happened. He sighed.

There was a blast of sound as the driver leant on the horn and the engine rushed into the tunnel. Immediately all the lights went out and the train was plunged into darkness. Not even an emergency light came on to break up the pitch black enveloping them. The train accelerated and Nick was sucked back into his seat. He recognised this feeling from flying to Spain with his dad, only now they were on a train not in a plane.

There was a deafening roar, and it felt as if their chests were being crushed by the sudden increase in power. Not one of them could have measured how long it took, but as fast as it had begun it was over and they were back in the light, travelling at a normal speed.

Arthur opened his eyes, wondering what he might see, and realised that he was right about what his book had been trying to tell him.

It was obvious as they exited the tunnel that their surroundings had changed. And if he needed any further convincing he was wrapped in a fog of travel sickness. Not the usual form brought on by road travel but the more violent form brought on by travelling through time. Arthur recognised it from his first encounter with the Crow Man, when he'd been momentarily transferred from Lyskeret town to Bodmin Moor.

Blearily Arthur catalogued the changes around him. He was still sitting on a train with his friends, but nearly everything else was different. They were no longer travelling in an unlovely plastic and metal tube but were now in the gleaming, wooden carriage of a steam train.

They were alone in a compartment. The seats were padded and upholstered in a crimson, slightly itchy, material, and the window opening was no longer restricted to a tilting flap but instead had a brass sash window set in the exterior door. Above their heads were luggage racks, now stacked with their bags, and the table had disappeared. At the other side of their compartment a windowed corridor ran the length of the train. Lightning still slept at Arthur's feet, and Dragon still fidgeted in Nick's pocket, but apart from that everything was different.

Nick and Gawain were stunned. Neither said a word. And although Arthur had expected something to happen, this was rather more extreme than even he could have guessed.

'What's going on?' Nick asked after a few moments of shocked silence.

Gawain looked to Arthur as if he could come up with the answer.

Their friend frowned and merely said, 'I didn't know it meant this.'

Nick and Gawain glanced at one another. They were both a pale shade of green. Even the few freckles scattered over Gawain's nose appeared to have faded.

At the other end of the train Hagarawall clutched his stomach and leant out of a window taking deep breaths while the Writer, observing his discomfort from a distance, smiled serenely. The boys' enemy wouldn't be troubling them for a while. The weakening of time had some helpful side effects.

A smartly uniformed figure appeared in the corridor outside the boys' compartment and slid the door back.

'Mornin' lads. Can I see your tickets please?'

He took in Lightning, curled up at Arthur's feet.

'Your dog likes travellin' then?'

Arthur nodded dumbly.

'On your way for the Christmas holidays?'

Again Arthur nodded, battling against confusion and sickness. Through the mist clouding his thoughts he realised that the man must be a ticket inspector, so he fumbled through his pockets for his wallet. The ticket, previously a rectangle of orange and cream card, was now thick, yellowed paper torn off a continuous roll. The ticket inspector took it, punched it with the machine slung around his neck, and handed it back to Arthur. The other two silently followed Arthur's example.

The inspector scratched his head under his peaked cap. 'Surprisingly quiet on here considerin' it's only a few days till Christmas. Still, I expect you're glad of it. Least you could get a seat, normally you'd be standin' in the corridor at this time of year.' He leant into the doorframe and continued, 'They give it to snow too, so travel's going to be difficult.'

Nick felt Dragon shift and hurriedly held his hand over his pocket as, in the luggage rack above their heads, a book began to fidget.

Fortunately the ticket inspector didn't notice. 'Still, must get on before we get to the next station.'

Arthur and Gawain nodded.

The inspector began to turn away, ''Ave a good Christmas then lads.' He cast a curious look at their jeans and trainers and doubt chased across his face but it quickly cleared as he added, 'Oh, and enjoy the fancy-dress party. What's the theme? No, let me guess, somethin' to do with the Wild West of America.' And chuckling at his wit, he slid the compartment door closed and moved on to the next carriage.

'Did you *know* this was going to happen?' Nick said.

Gawain's colour was returning. 'Art, give us a clue next time will you?'

'Sorry,' Arthur replied. 'I wasn't certain what it meant and I didn't think it was worth worrying you if I'd got it wrong.'

'No, honestly,' Nick said, 'we'd be happier if we knew!' He looked around. 'So where are we?'

Arthur looked out of the window and remembered what his book had shown him. The scenery looked much the same as it had minutes before, although perhaps there were fewer houses. The train huffed its way over a small road bridge and Arthur caught a quick glimpse of a car, a gleaming vintage machine with a pair of enormous round headlights, nosing along a lane.

Gawain had seen it too. The train, the ticket inspector and the old car, they all added up to being somewhere in the last century.

When Arthur didn't answer, but instead remained glued to the window, Gawain turned to Nick. 'I reckon we must be in the 1930s.'

'What? No! You're kidding.'

Gawain nodded, watching as Nick subsided into silence and his colour drained. Together they listened to the regular clatter of the wheels on the track and watched as plumes of grey smoke floated past the window.

The sky outside darkened and individual snowflakes began to fall.

Arthur observed, 'Looks like it's winter here too.'

'Oh well, that's fine then!' Nick muttered. 'As long as it's Christmas here as well, everything's just perfect.'

'Have you any idea why this happened?' Gawain asked Arthur.

'No ... well not really. Although ... remember what happened to Tamar last summer when she was at Porth Pyra? One minute it was day and she was in our century, and the next it was night and she was a couple of hundred

31

years away. Maybe something's messing up time.' He shrugged. 'I don't know.'

The boys were silent, contemplating the possibility of time being messed up, when a girl of about their age arrived at their compartment and slid open the door.

'I say,' she started without introduction, 'I don't suppose you've seen my little brother?'

The girl sounded as if she'd been plucked straight out of an old black and white movie, and she looked like it too. Although she must have been about fourteen she was wearing a knee-length dress, a navy-blue blazer edged in yellow braid, white ankle socks and flat shoes. Her hair was a straight, shiny bob pulled back from her forehead with a hairband.

'He's called William and he's wearing his school uniform. His blazer is red and blue and his cap is plain blue. Mummy told me to keep an eye on him but he's a little beast, he's always getting lost.' This last word came out like 'lorst'; she sounded like a young Queen Elizabeth.

The boys stared at her and said nothing.

She continued. 'I expect he'll appear soon. It's nearly tea-time and Mummy always packs a picnic when we come down for the Christmas hols. The little monkey is bound to come to light then!'

She paused and surveyed them critically, her head on one side.

'Are you going to a fancy-dress party?' She was eyeing their jeans curiously. She glanced at Nick's blond hair flopping over his eyes. It was much longer than people would have worn it in those days. A book in the luggage rack rustled its pages and Dragon found the remains of an insect in Nick's pocket and began to crunch on his unexpected snack. The girl frowned and the silence expanded as she stared at them and they stared back.

Her frown deepened. 'Are you all going home from school for the hols as well? I've never seen you on this train before. Which school do you go to?'

Gawain looked from Arthur to Nick, who by now was not only deathly pale but also transfixed with this further evidence of their transfer into another time.

He thought quickly. 'No we're not from around here.'

Arthur muttered, 'You could say that again.'

Gawain continued. 'We're going to a friend's party. It's a sort of American theme.' He'd caught her looking at their clothes. No one, early in the last century, would have worn jeans. What's more, the girl would never have heard of comprehensive schools. She was obviously referring to some sort of boarding school.

At that moment a little boy wearing grey, knee-length shorts, a crooked tie and striped blazer, shot past the compartment door.

'William,' she shouted, 'Mummy wants you. Come back!' But her brother was already along the corridor.

'Come and get me, Mary!' he called.

'Oh he's such a menace. He never does what he's told.'

'Don't you think you should go after him before he's grounded?' Gawain asked, keen to rid themselves of their unwelcome guest.

'Yes, you're probably right.' Mary's frown returned. 'Grounded? What do you mean?'

'Oh well grounded means …' Gawain racked his brain in an effort to come up with a reasonable explanation. 'Well it's an American word. We're trying to get into the spirit of the party.' He looked at Arthur and Nick and grinned, 'Aren't we … chaps?'

Nick didn't move. This was way too weird.

'I say,' the girl pondered. '"Grounded." I've never heard that expression before. What did you say it means?'

'I didn't,' Gawain said. 'It's when you're not allowed out for a while.'

'Oh I see! Like being in detention at school.'

Gawain nodded but his attention was abruptly diverted by a book that Mary was holding and all his thoughts of their strange situation were banished. Suddenly getting rid of the girl was less important. Neither Nick nor Arthur could believe his next words.

'Can I have a look at your book?' he asked eagerly.

The girl looked just as surprised as Gawain's friends. 'Why, do you like King Arthur too?'

Gawain nodded.

'Well not exactly "like",' he replied, throwing Arthur a look and a grin, 'but I suppose you could say that I'm one of his followers.'

Then to the amazement of both Arthur and Nick, he reached out and took the book being offered to him.

'*Le Morte d'Arthur* by Sir Thomas Malory,' he read aloud, and reverently opened the book at the first page.

'1928 – Illustrations by Catherine Donaldson. My uncle's been looking for this one.'

The book looked brand new, unspoiled, with the dust-jacket still in place.

'You can buy them easily enough,' Mary said. 'They're not exactly rare.'

'They're pretty rare where I'm from,' Gawain said. He looked at the dedication: *For Mary with our love, Mummy and Daddy*.

The books in his backpack were becoming increasingly restless. It could have been that they felt one of their own nearby or that the time travel had woken them up. Whatever the reason, Arthur was aware of the girl's attention being drawn back to the luggage rack. They had to get rid of her. At that instant Mary's brother rescued them by rushing back past their compartment. This time his sister didn't hesitate.

'Come back *here*, William,' she shouted. 'Sorry I'll be back in a tick, I've got to get him. I'll come back for the book when I've delivered William into Mummy's custody.'

And with that she disappeared down the corridor.

As soon as the girl had gone Nick turned to the other two and said, 'What are we going to *do*? Are we stuck here?'

But Gawain was completely absorbed handling the book as if he'd found a valuable relic, carefully turning the pages to gaze at the illustrations.

'Arthur!' Nick said, becoming more edgy with every turn of the wheels and each wisp of engine smoke that floated past. 'Do you happen to know what happens next?'

'I'm not a fortune-teller!'

'But you had an idea that this was going to happen, didn't you?'

'Yes, but only a blurry idea. It's not like the book showed me everything.'

'What did it show you then?' Gawain asked, suddenly interested.

'It just showed me …'

Arthur was about to go into more detail when the train's whistle sounded, the air filled with smoke and they were plunged into another long, dark tunnel.

Their ears roared and their eyes stung and again their chests felt as if they were being compressed and every breath was being expelled from their bodies; as if they were deep under water, a long, long way down.

Not one of them could have measured the time between entering and leaving the tunnel. It could have been seconds or minutes, but suddenly there was another blast of sound and light and they were expelled into the daylight, once again in a modern carriage with a table in front of them.

Gawain gazed at the book. He hadn't meant to keep it but here it was in the twenty-first century. It wasn't as perfect as it was when he'd first seen it – it was more yellowed and mottled – but in every other way it was the same book that Mary had been reading over eighty years before.

Le Morte d'Arthur had travelled from a 1930s steam train to its diesel-powered offspring.

Further down the carriage the small child continued to whine while, at the other end of the train, Hagarawall cursed and sucked another boiled sweet.

Chapter 3
Snow

Tamar wondered how much longer it would be before the train got in. She knew she shouldn't have come to the station by herself but she needed to see the boys. She'd tried to ignore the barrel organ but every time she'd glanced at it, the puppet's painted eyes were staring at her. It was its fault she was here feeling so vulnerable.

I've seen some creepy stuff, she thought, blowing on her fingers and stamping her feet to keep warm, *but that one wins.*

She'd been trying to help Wenna but she hadn't been able to stop her hands shaking and had dropped a decoration. Wenna had exploded and Tamar had made some excuse about not sleeping well (partly true), and decided to risk meeting the boys. So here she was, by herself.

She glanced along the station platform taking in the small crowd waiting to meet their friends or family. *Bet no one else has a friend with a dragon.* She knotted her scarf. It was really cold. *And I bet no one would guess I'm waiting for the new King Arthur.* She smiled a private smile and then something caught her eye; a scrap of grey skirt and grey eyes. Tamar turned but their owner was already bolting out of the station door. It was the girl who'd seen the tent.

Tamar had never seen such a mane of red hair.

'Blast!' Tamar couldn't risk running after her; the train was due in two minutes.

At least the boy wasn't around. She chewed her lip. *Don't give him head space Tamar Tamblyn, he's not worth it.*

Towards the rear of the station platform, Viatoris adjusted his jacket and cap and shifted the bag containing his cloak onto his other shoulder.

Being pulled from time to time could be trying enough without having to think about appropriate clothing. Now he and Servo always had a bag at the ready. The majority of people would never see them but there was the odd occasion when it was right to be visible. Or when someone managed to catch a glimpse of them.

The Watcher noted the red-head's hasty departure – and her eyes latching onto him.

The girl has the sight. He thought, buttoning his jacket against an icy finger of wind as a crow swept over the station roof.

Viatoris recognised the bird. *Ah, so you're here.* It was Brane's crow; the Crow Man's bird. The Watcher suppressed a sigh; he was meant to be neutral. *And if you're here, your master must be close by.*

A snowflake spiralled towards the metal rails of the track and a gust of freezing wind ushered a feather across the platform floor.

But this wasn't a crow's feather; it belonged to an owl and despite his attempted neutrality, Viatoris smiled. He knew the feather's owner. Maybe the Guardians' enemies weren't going to have things all their own way.

The small crowd waiting on the platform listened to an announcement and picked up their bags.

Tamar looked around and glimpsed a hint of a shape in the shadows, but bizarrely she wasn't alarmed. She was reminded of the two men who'd appeared on the cliff path last summer, who were shadowy but caused them no harm. In fact, she was almost comforted, especially as one very reliable indicator appeared to agree with her: the sword and chain around her neck were warm.

She sighed. Just sometimes it would be nice to be able to live a normal life, but it wasn't going to happen, was it? Her life would never be ordinary. It would always have this level of weirdness going on.

She thrust her hands into her pockets and turned her attention back to the approaching train and tried to remember her life 'before'. There'd been school and hanging about with some of the girls in her class (who mostly talked about boys), and the very occasional holiday.

'Be honest Tamar,' she muttered. 'A lot of it was pretty boring. The *after* is much more interesting.' A snowflake settled on her shoulder and she turned her thoughts back to the *now*. It looked like the boys might have just made it before the bad weather set in.

There was a squeal of brakes and the doors swung open. Lightning sprang from the train but the boys disembarked rather more gingerly. At the other end of the platform Hagarawall mingled with the crowds. He was always pale but now, after his travels, he could have passed for a ghost.

Finally, the Writer stepped onto the station platform and glanced across to see Viatoris, one of her Watchers, blending with the shadows. Their eyes met and unsaid words passed between them, carefully shielded from either Arthur or his adversary.

Viatoris listened and nodded. Then he turned and made his way out of the station, unseen and unheard by those around him. Meanwhile his overseer hung back and watched the Guardians and the crowds around them. Apart from Hagarawall there was little evidence that the teenagers' enemies were ready to make a move quite yet.

The Writer picked up her bag and waited.

She watched Tamar hurry towards her friends and saw her envelop Arthur in a rib-crushing hug as the boy checked the now empty skies.

The Writer smiled to herself. *Cornwall is in good hands.* Then she turned her mind to the cottage that had *so* conveniently become available when she needed it, and in *such* a useful position.

Quietly, the Writer exited the station: an unremarkable grey-haired lady dressed in head-to-foot beige and carrying a nondescript bag. It was the perfect camouflage for someone who preferred to be overlooked.

'Boy, am I glad to see you guys!' Tamar ruffled Lightning's ears. 'You would not believe all the weird stuff that's been going on.'

'Think we might,' Nick said gruffly.

'Yeah, try us,' Gawain agreed.

But Arthur shook his head. 'Let's wait till we get to the fair.' He slung his backpack over his shoulder. 'Besides, it's too cold to hang around.'

It *was* cold. Unusually cold for Cornwall.

Although it was no more than mid-day the light was already dimming. Charcoal-grey clouds scudded across the low horizon and the winter-wind was picking up, scattering dead leaves across the track. The station guard checked the train doors and signalled for the train to leave.

'Hope the driver doesn't get travel-sick,' Nick remarked.

'What?' Tamar asked.

'We'll tell you when we're in the caravan,' Gawain replied. 'It was an interesting ride.'

Tamar didn't say anything. She'd picked up the vibes. Instead she just said, 'You've got an amazing caravan. You'll love it. It's really old, practically an antique!'

She carried on. 'Wenna and I were meant to be sharing it but it'll be better if you guys have it 'cause it's big enough for three. I promised to work more if you guys could stay, so Wenna's managed to borrow a little one that'll just fit two. We'll be fine in it.'

Tamar was so caught up in describing the details of the ancient gypsy caravan with its 'cute' windows and its tiny wood-burning stove that it took a while before she realised that not one of her friends had said a word.

'I thought you'd like it,' she said, puzzled by their muted reaction.

'I'm sure we will,' Gawain responded. 'Look, when we get there we'll tell you what happened, then you'll understand.'

'Let's put it this way,' Nick began, holding his pocket as Dragon attempted to wriggle free. 'I thought that there couldn't be anything more unusual than owning a dragon, but I was wrong.'

'Oh … right.'

The wind whined and Arthur inspected the now empty station platform and the shabby ticket office. He took in the clouds and the muddy, empty fields and then he cocked his head.

'Listen!' He held up his hand.

'What?' Nick asked.

'Can you hear that? I'm sure it's a barn owl.'

And right on cue the distinctive saw-like shriek of the white-faced owl cut through the air.

'Don't you think that you're just a *little* bit obsessed with our feathered friends?' Nick remarked.

Tamar ignored Nick. 'They don't usually call during the day, do they?'

'No, not usually.' Arthur ran his fingers along the edge of the feather he'd picked up in Lyskeret. First the owl's feather and now the call.

'D'you know,' he stated, 'that pretty much the only bird that'll fight a crow is an owl? There are others, but not many.'

'This isn't a school trip!' Nick objected. 'Can we save the lecture till later? I'm freezing.'

'Yeah,' Gawain heaved his bag onto his back. 'Let's go before we get frostbite.'

***

From the refuge of a farm gate the red-headed girl watched the friends ramble down the lane. She observed the bags and the fidgeting books and she caught sight of a tiny snout protruding from Nick's pocket. The girl waited until they were a little way ahead and then she followed, slipping behind trees or parked cars.

Swirls of blue-grey clouds like giant bruises, crept across the winter fields from the sea. The girl's forehead wrinkled and her grey eyes became serious as an icy wind carried a snowflake towards her. If snow came to this part of Cornwall it generally came from the landward side not the sea.

Hagarawall, still sucking a sweet, stood with his arms folded, leaning into the wall outside the station and watched the four Guardians make their way towards the Christmas fair followed by the girl.

A spit of wind carried a couple of snowflakes towards him and he heard one of the station staff call out to a colleague, ''Tis tryin' to snow. Eh Tom, when was the last time we 'ad snow down 'ere?'

Tom mumbled something about it being at least ten years.

'Ten years, eh? 'Ave you seen the forecast? The weatherman on the telly reckons it's goin' to be a cold 'un this year. He was talking about it being a white Christmas.'

Hagarawall looked out to sea. Somewhere beyond the horizon a ship was sailing, its course set for the castle-topped island. And the ship would be carrying his leader, the Lady of Clehy.

So, he thought, *she is already working her weather-magic.*

He rolled a sweet between his fingers. The Lady of Clehy, the Lady of Ice. If these people knew her they would have no doubt about their white Christmas ... but they might worry for the future of their beloved county.

***

Tamar climbed the wooden steps and swung the caravan door open.

'There! A real gypsy caravan.'

The boys looked at one another and then at the date carved in the caravan's frame: 1930, the same era as the steam train. It was beautifully painted and decorated – a real work of art. The wheels were wooden with metal rims, and there were shafts where the horse would have been harnessed. No one said a word as they followed Tamar up the steps and took in the wood-burning stove, the cushioned seats and curtained windows.

Tamar turned around and waited for at least one of them to say 'Thank you', but there was silence.

'Okay.' She pulled the door shut and sat down. 'Tell me what happened.'

Arthur glanced out of the window, at the field packed with stalls and the Christmas trees dotted between them. He looked across to the island, the black sea encircling it and the dark sky pressing low above it. And then he heard the choir start to sing the first of the Christmas songs:

The holly and the ivy
When they are both full grown,
Of all the trees that are in the wood,
The holly bears the crown.
O, the rising of the sun
And the running of the deer,
The playing of the merry organ,
Sweet singing of the choir.

'This could be any time in the last couple of centuries,' he mused.

'What?'

'Well this fair could be happening any time from a few hundred years ago till now, couldn't it? No one would know that it was the twenty-first century. It could be Victorian or the early nineteen hundreds. There's nothing here that looks remotely like our time.'

The other three studied the fair, seeing it through Arthur's eyes.

'Suppose so,' Nick agreed.

'Yeah,' Gawain nodded. 'Well, apart from the lights.'

'It's like everyone's wishing themselves back in another time,' Arthur said.

'But that's what Christmas is about, isn't it?' Nick pointed out. 'It's about how life *should* be, not how it really is.'

'Yeah, I know, it's just … it *feels* wrong. It feels like the more people want another time, the more they weaken our time.' Arthur knew what he meant but it was difficult to explain. He thought he was hearing snatches of conversation too. Deep words, not ordinary words, which could mean that some of their ancient friends were nearby.

44

Nick shrugged. 'Listen mate, after everything that happened on the train it's not surprising you feel weird.'

He got up, turned on a battery-powered lamp swinging from the ceiling and closed the curtains. Checking the door was secure, he sighed. 'At last! There you go boy,' and Dragon was finally allowed to exercise his wings.

'Why? What happened on the train?' Tamar asked, watching Dragon's aerial manoeuvres.

Gawain slung his backpack on the seat and examined his newly acquired book. He felt like he'd stolen it but there was nothing he could do about it now. 'Well,' he began, 'we got on the train as usual and everything was normal but then the train changed to a steam train …'

'And we were somewhere in the nineteen thirties, or at least that's what these two reckon,' Nick added.

'What! You and the train?' Tamar was incredulous. 'No way! What about everyone else, all the other passengers, were they there as well?'

'No, I don't think so. It seemed like it was just us, although there were other, different, people there too.'

Tamar shook her head. It seemed impossible but she knew better than to doubt them. After all, she was the one who'd travelled back in time in the summer, with the man Zephaniah. She wouldn't admit it, but a little bit of her felt jealous and a tiny bit left out.

Nick held out his hand with a dried woodlouse balanced on his palm. Dragon swooped down, swallowed it, and took off again. Nick grinned and looked at his friends. They were all so serious.

'Okay,' he announced, taking charge. 'Time for food and talk: you can tell us what the watch showed you Tamar, and then we'll tell you what happened to us.'

He inspected the cupboards and thrust packets of biscuits and cakes at his friends. Lightning sat up and waited expectantly and Dragon landed neatly on Nick's shoulder. Rustling packets equalled food.

'First of all, has anyone seen the Crow Man or his friends?'

Gawain and Arthur shook their heads and Tamar said, 'Only in the watch.'

'What else did it show you?'

'It was hard to see – some of the pictures were so quick, but I'm sure that the cat was there.'

'The Jolly's cat, the one staying with Dywana?'

Tamar nodded. 'And I saw a knight but I couldn't see who it was.' She paused and added thoughtfully, 'But actually I think he seemed young, much younger than either Lancelot or Bedivere.'

'Anything else?'

'I told you about the weird boy I met didn't I?'

'Yeah, sort of. What was strange about him?'

'Only everything!' She shivered. 'Did I tell you about his hair?'

Arthur shook his head. 'No.'

'It was silver, not grey-silver, real silver! He was creepy …' She launched into a vivid description of their encounter. 'I haven't seen him since. I've no idea which bit of the fair he's working in – if he really *is* working here.'

'So,' Gawain said when Tamar had finished describing the boy, 'we know that the watch is telling us that the Lady of Clehy, the Crow Man and that pale guy, Hagarawall, may be around. The cat could appear and another knight may come as well.'

'Oh, and I had a glimpse of Argo,' Tamar added, recalling the Watch's rapid reveal. 'He was definitely there.'

Arthur had been staring at the floor but as soon as Tamar said Argo's name he leant back and his face softened. His mind went back to the night when he'd been made King Arthur's successor. Without the stallion's timely arrival it might never have happened. Without that midnight ride he might never have been given Excalibur by the Lady of the Lake; or been crowned by that other King Arthur. *And,* he thought, *how many people have had a real conversation with a horse?* It had to rate as one of his more unusual experiences.

Nick was talking. 'So, apart from the cat and Argo, we don't know if any of the others are going to be around to help. No sign of Michael or Angela Jolly or anyone else on our side?'

Tamar shook her head. 'No. No one else I recognised.' She frowned. 'Oh! And I think I saw a room, a bit like an old-fashioned library, but I didn't see anyone in it.'

'More books!' Nick exclaimed, as he held out a hand to the dragon. 'That's just cruelty.'

'Yeah, but it wasn't just the pictures the watch showed me that I wanted to tell you about,' Tamar said, ignoring Nick's comment as she coiled a thread of jet-black hair around her finger. 'There's other stuff too.'

She described her brief sighting of the tent with Angela in the doorway and the unusual arrival of the barrel organ and its effect on the stallholders. 'It's almost as if it wipes their memories of how it arrived as soon as they touch it. It even did it to Wenna!'

Nick pulled a face, 'Weird.'

Gawain turned to Arthur and Nick. 'Have your books shown you anything else?'

'Mine just showed me the island, the one out there,' Nick said, waving in the direction of the island.

'Yeah, mine did too,' Arthur agreed, 'and the train, but nothing else. Definitely no barrel organ or anything.'

Nick leant back against the window and lifted his hand to stroke Dragon's chin and the caravan was filled with the dragon's contented clicks.

With his other hand Nick mimed holding a pipe to his lips and stretched his legs. 'So my dear Watson, it appears we have the mystery of the disappearing tent, the mind-altering barrel organ and the Very Unusual Train.'

Tamar giggled. Nick could never be serious for long.

'Ah, but Holmes,' Gawain continued, elaborating on the Sherlock theme. 'We must not forget … *the Feather*.'

'Ah yes, *the Feather*! A timely reminder Watson. And we know, because of our learned friend here,' Nick gestured towards Arthur, 'that *the Feather* belongs to the species of bird known as … the barn owl!'

By now even Arthur was smiling. Nick was working his own, very special form of magic.

Nick puffed on the imaginary pipe. 'So ladies, or as I should say, lady and gentlemen, not only do we have the unrivalled skills of a small but dangerous fire-breathing dragon …'

He looked meaningfully at Dragon but the tiny creature chose that moment to curl his tail around his snout, close his eyes and begin snoring. And Gawain, Arthur and Tamar were giggling as Nick raised an eyebrow and muttered, 'Even in sleep the rare Malachite can be a serious foe!'

None of them saw a pair of grey eyes at the caravan's window, peering through a space between the curtains.

Or heard the cry of an owl as it flew home to its master.

Chapter 4
Time Slip

Tamar opened her eyes and listened. She heard the quiet ticking of the pocket watch under her pillow (to muffle it if it started to chime), and the busy chatter of the stallholders mingling with scraps of Christmas music. And then a smile grew as she recalled the previous evening and Nick's rendition of Sherlock Holmes and the pure *easiness* of the four of them being together.

She pulled herself up and hugged her knees. It was funny really, Nick used to get on her nerves just by breathing. Maybe he'd changed because of Dragon or perhaps she'd changed because of being the Time Keeper.

'You're over-thinking things, Tamar,' she told herself. 'You just get on better, leave it at that.'

She glanced around the caravan and at Mug Shot's photo propped up on the shelf. She missed him. She'd wanted to bring her dog to the fair but, as Wenna had pointed out, mixing him with candyfloss stalls was a recipe for disaster.

'Bet he's pining for me,' she said, casting her deeper thoughts to one side. 'Maybe I'll give Mum a ring.' But her eye was caught by something sitting next to the photo and the phone call was forgotten.

It was just a plain, cream envelope – which hadn't been there last night. Tamar frowned. Perhaps it was from one of Wenna's boyfriends (she couldn't remember the name of the current one), but somehow she doubted it. She reached out and picked it up.

Elaborate writing curled across the paper. It wasn't for Wenna, it was for her.

Miss Tamar Tamblyn

On the back a red wax seal, indented with the letters 'C' and 'F', sealed the envelope's opening.

'Curious.' She frowned. The pocket watch's ticks grew louder. Maybe it knew who'd sent it.

Opening a drawer, she rooted under mismatched socks and knickers until she found Wenna's pink manicure case.

'I'm just borrowing them,' she muttered, pulling out a pair of scissors and checking the door for her sister's sudden reappearance. She'd be in deep trouble if Wenna caught her borrowing them. She slid a blade along the top edge of the envelope and pulled out a cream card. It was an invitation.

Dr F. Columbarius requests
the pleasure of the company of
Miss Tamar Tamblyn
for afternoon tea
at Oakwood Manor.

Please arrive no later than 3pm.

She turned the card over but it was blank. There were no clues to hint at the whereabouts of the Manor or who this person might be.

'Strange.' She read the card again. 'Who on earth is Dr F. Columbarius?'

But her deliberations were cut short by someone climbing the caravan's steps. Swiftly, Tamar slid the card, envelope and manicure set under her pillow as the door opened and her sister's face appeared.

'Good, you're awake! I could do with some help. It's beginning to get busy out here.' Morwenna held up a covered hanger. 'And you do remember that we're wearing Victorian clothes?'

Tamar nodded. The fair's theme was 'A Victorian Christmas'.

'This was left for you.' Her sister paused. 'It was a bit weird; the woman who delivered it seemed to know who I was but I'm certain I've never met her.' She continued. 'She was called Mrs Beswe …' she stopped and frowned. 'I can't remember her name. Anyway she said it was for you. Did you order it from a fancy-dress shop? I thought I'd said I'd got you an outfit.'

Tamar glossed over the question. She hadn't ordered anything from anywhere.

'Um, yes you did. What did she look like?'

Wenna shrugged. 'Quite round and friendly. I had the impression you might know her …'

Morwenna left the sentence hanging, waiting for her little sister to tell her more, but Tamar didn't say anything. There was no way that she'd let Wenna know that the woman was a complete stranger.

She took the hanger from Morwenna and casually said, 'Oh right, thanks.'

The outfit was encased in the sort of zipped-up, opaque cover used by people to protect a suit or smart dress. The label was a brown rectangular luggage tag, tied with coarse string to the hook of the hanger. Tamar's name was on it, written in the same handwriting that had addressed the cream envelope. Apart from that, there was no clue where it came from.

Morwenna lingered, obviously hoping that Tamar would tell her more, but Tamar just smiled. 'Okay, I'll be out soon. You'd better not leave the stall if it's busy!'

Her sister glanced behind her to the swelling crowds before throwing another curious look towards the mysterious costume.

'Okay. I'll see you in a couple of minutes.' And slowly, and rather reluctantly, she closed the door.

Tamar waited until she was certain that Wenna had gone and tugged the zipper down. First the letter then this.

The protective cover fell open to reveal a layer of tissue paper.

Tamar surveyed the package and her heart thudded.

The outer layer of gossamer-thin paper was not plain white but a rich, midnight-blue sprinkled with flickering silver stars and a full moon. Fine clouds were actually *floating* across its surface.

That's so beautiful! was her first thought, quickly followed by, *Impossible!* But another voice was reminding her of the living, moving map that had led Arthur to Excalibur.

Carefully, and with a slightly shaky hand, she peeled the night paper back to reveal another layer of lighter blue tissue studded with fading stars in a now clear sky. Slowly, Tamar lifted one layer after another, showing the sky's transition from midnight to dawn, until finally just a delicate moon remained on rose-tinted paper.

She took a few moments to gather herself before taking the corner of that last sheet between her thumb and finger to reveal what had been sent.

It was everything that most girls would love – and everything that the packaging had promised.

A golden velvet bodice topping an emerald green skirt lay in the paper. The dress was perfectly suited for winter because the fabric was thick and heavy. However, it wasn't the material or the style that held Tamar transfixed but the elaborate embroidery. Roman numerals, pocket watches, tiny cogs and delicate wheels ran over and around one another on the bodice; planets and constellations shone on the skirt, plunging towards the hem. And a tiny pocket, just big enough for a pocket watch, with a drawstring opening lay hidden in the skirt.

It was a dress for a Time Keeper.

'Oh, my word,' Tamar said breathlessly, as the watch gave a muted tock from under the pillow. 'Who is Mrs Beswe …?'

And then there was another knock on the door.

Tamar had been so absorbed in her package that she hadn't heard the footsteps.

'Hi, can I come in?' Arthur's face appeared round the door.

Tamar nodded and Arthur ushered Lightning up the steps and shut the door behind them.

He didn't look at the dress or the paper. 'Have you had a letter?'

'Yes.'

'Like this?' He held up a cream card embellished with familiar writing.

Tamar nodded again.

The watch chimed, its cogs turning. The Time Keeper and Cornwall's protector together. Perfect.

'We've all had one: Gawain, Nick and me,' Arthur continued. 'We found them in the caravan this morning. The door was locked to stop Dragon escaping, so we've no idea how they got there. We haven't any idea who Dr Columbarius is either.'

Tamar shook her head. 'Neither have I, but look, I got this too. Someone gave it to Wenna this morning.' She held up the dress. 'A lady delivered it to her and said it was for me. She was called a Mrs Bes … something or other. I don't know who she is but she must know who I am: just look at the bodice.'

Arthur took in the embroidered watches and cogs and whistled, his eyes widening. 'A Time Keeper's dress!'

Tamar nodded. 'Exactly, and the wrapping is pretty amazing too.' She displayed the outer layer of tissue paper and together they contemplated the clouds floating in front of the stars.

With his right hand Arthur traced the ornate cogs and wheels sewn on the bodice and thoughtfully took hold of the golden sword hanging around his neck. Instinctively Tamar followed his example. Neither of their swords were cold; a sure sign that both the letters and the dress must have come from a friendly source.

'Well,' Arthur started, 'it looks like we've got an invitation to tea and it seems that you've got a very clever costume designer.'

'Hope she knows my size!'

'I somehow think she might,' he said, and added wryly, ' Sherlock Holmes will be kept busy with this one.'

Lightning scratched at the door.

'Something worrying you boy?'

The dog sat at the door expectantly. Arthur took a step and then turned around. 'Look, we'll find out where Oakwood Manor is and we'll be here at two-thirty to meet up. Do you think Wenna will let you go?'

Tamar nodded. 'As long as I work hard enough till then. After all she's not paying me anything.' She threaded her finger along the embroidery of the dress. 'I wonder if we'll meet the anonymous dressmaker.'

'I wouldn't be surprised,' Arthur replied and opened the door. 'Have fun on the stall.'

'Oh yeah, right. I can't think of anything I'd rather be doing!'

'You know you love it really,' Arthur retorted and, grinning, dodged a screwed-up paper ball and scooted down the steps.

Tamar shook her head but it was good to have Arthur around, it helped to take the edge off the strange stuff. She looked out of the caravan window. Morwenna was deep in conversation with a potential customer while smiling her most dazzling smile. Her sister could sell ice-cream to Polar bears. She watched another customer approach. Morwenna would be kept busy for a while.

'Go for it Tamar,' she told herself, as she locked the door and tugged the curtains closed. She eyed the dress. If she was honest she was a little bit nervous about trying it on. She was certain that the watch's muffled ticks were getting louder which was a sure sign that something was going to happen.

She lifted up the dress and slipped the watch from under her pillow. 'I'd better keep you close. Look, there's a pocket just for you!' and she dropped the dress over her head.

***

She could never say for certain whether what happened next *really* happened or whether it was just an illusion, because what seemed to be happening was that she was spinning through space. And in the seconds before her eyelids took control and slammed closed she thought that she'd glimpsed the curve of the earth as it stretched beneath her and the stars glittering high overhead.

In a far-flung corner of her brain she was dimly aware of the watch chiming, and she thought she could feel the buzz of its cogs turning, but it all felt a long way off. Cold air rushed over her face, as if she was standing right on the edge of a cliff in a gale. Then her knees buckled and she was lying on hard, cold ground.

For quite a long time she lay still with her eyes glued closed, gripping the watch and waiting for her pulse to slow. With her eyes firmly shut she ran through what had just happened. If she kept them closed it could just be possible that she'd had a funny turn and was still in the caravan, with the fair outside the door. But all her senses told her that she was somewhere else entirely.

Finally she muttered, 'Come on Tamar Tamblyn, stop being so pathetic,' and she opened her eyes.

She wasn't in the caravan. She was lying in the centre of a clearing. In a wood. In deep snow.

The dress had settled and spread out around her, a pool of green against sparkling white. Tamar swallowed. She was in a very cold winter-wood and she was alone. The pocket watch gave one contented chime and settled to a quiet tick. It had escorted the Time Keeper on her first independent journey through time.

Tamar took a deep breath and tried to gather her thoughts. She'd wondered if being the Time Keeper might have more to it than merely being the pocket watch's custodian and it looked like she'd got her answer.

She turned her attention to her surroundings.

Wherever she was, it had been snowing heavily, although now a watery sun was making a brave effort to light up the landscape. Blue shadows filled the ripples in the snow and every branch and twig had glistening highlights. Most of the trees were leafless, apart from a few evergreen hollies showing off their red berries.

Tamar propped herself up on an elbow.

Trees surrounded her and it looked like they went on for miles. There was no sign of a track out of the clearing, just a few indistinct paw prints. High in the skeletal canopy birds sang.

'Well my trusty pocket watch,' Tamar began bravely, 'I don't know where we are, or why we are … wherever we are, but I wish I'd been given some warning and I wish I wasn't by myself.' She bit her lip. She felt very alone.

'I could really do with Nick here now. Dragon might warm me up.' Her voice wobbled.

'Why?' she muttered, choking back a sob. 'Why did *I* have to be chosen to be the Time Keeper? Look where it's got me. In a wood, in winter, alone.'

She looked around. There was no clue as to where she was. Gripping a low-growing branch, she pulled herself to her feet and sniffed, shakily wiping away a tear. She shoved the watch deep into the pocket of her dress and pulled the drawstring of the opening extra tight. She couldn't risk losing it. The watch might be her only passport back to the place she knew.

And then something rustled in the undergrowth.

Every nerve in her body jangled. Not only was she without her friends in a strange forest but someone else was there too, and you could bet your bottom dollar that it wouldn't be somebody she knew. Her neck prickled. She could feel eyes watching her.

'Who's there?' Rather annoyingly this came out as more of a squeak than a challenge.

There was silence. That sort of heavy silence when you know somebody is holding their breath and doing their best to stop a cough or sneeze from escaping.

Tamar curled her fingers and dug her nails into her palms and waited. Whoever was there would have to move sooner or later.

'Come on,' she tried to ignore the tremble in her voice. 'I've got all day.'

And now I sound just like a grumpy teacher.

There was a cough, quite a deep cough, from behind the bush. A branch shivered, sprinkling snow onto the ground, but for a few seconds nothing more happened.

Tamar took some deep breaths and put her hands on her hips. She'd seen her sister do this thousands of times and it never failed to deliver that *don't mess with me* message. She waited, because after all she really did have all day.

'Come on,' she repeated, and tapped her foot. She hoped she was succeeding in disguising her terror from whoever was on the other side of the undergrowth. She needn't have worried. She could have won an Oscar for this performance.

A muffled voice babbled from the bushes. 'Don't hurt me, ma'am.'

'Oh for goodness sake,' Tamar exploded, relief flooding through her. Whoever was on the other side of the bushes sounded anything but threatening. 'Do I look like I can hurt anybody?'

'I don't know,' the invisible stranger mumbled. 'But I've never seen you afore and you look like you *could* 'urt me.'

Tamar fixed the bushes with a stern look. 'Well I'm going to get very cross if you don't come out soon and then I won't be responsible for my actions. It's ridiculous talking to a bush!' Now she sounded like an infant teacher.

'I'm not a bush,' the voice protested. 'I'm a 'uman bein'.'

'Well that's something anyway,' Tamar muttered and took a precautionary step back because a foot was emerging, wearing a curiously long ankle boot with an upturned toe. Tamar waited for the foot to be joined by the rest of the body.

Bit by bit, and rather nervously, the stranger appeared. He was very short and obviously a fan of beards (his reached down to his waist), either that or he hated shaving. She estimated that he would probably reach only to her shoulder if he was standing beside her – although she wasn't about to find out. His strange footwear was accompanied by some equally strange clothing: a dull-brown tunic, some sort of leggings and a cloak that looked as if it had seen better days. Actually its owner looked as if he had seen better days too.

Tamar had a sense of déjà vu. The last time she'd encountered someone like this had been when she'd been a prisoner of the Ice Lady. Her fellow prisoner, the one she'd called Hairy Face, had had more than a passing resemblance to this apparition.

The short stranger fiddled with the brown wiry rug that was his beard, and eyed Tamar suspiciously. 'Is you a witch?'

'What?'

'Well, I am told that they come in all shapes and sizes. You can't trust no one. A person might seem normal but you never can tell just by looking at them.'

Tamar bit back a reply about the pot calling the kettle black. 'No! I am not a witch.'

'Are you sure ma'am?' The stranger hesitated. 'Only it looked to me as if one minute you weren't there and the next you was lyin' on the ground.' He took a nervous step back and regarded her warily.

Tamar considered the little man standing in front of her and what had just happened. There was no denying it. She was in a different place and, judging from the stranger's clothes, also in a different time.

Ignoring his questions and observation she asked, 'What year is it?'

The man's eyes narrowed. Maybe this was her way of catching him out. Perhaps she was trying to get him talking and then turn him into a toad or something. 'You don't know?'

She thought quickly. 'Umm, I think I've had a bit of a fall and bumped my head. I may have concussion.'

'Con … what? ' the stranger asked.

'You know, when you hit your head and feel woozy and forget stuff,' Tamar elaborated.

The man frowned, folded his arms and tilted his head. 'Did you fall from a tree?'

'Yes, I climb trees all the time,' Tamar replied sarcastically.

However, the irony of her comment slid over her companion's head and his face cleared. Her sudden appearance was explained, as was her fall. He leant back and assumed a slightly superior expression.

'Climbin' trees is a boys' sport, not one for maidens,' he informed her. 'Women should never try to do such things.'

Tamar frowned but he carried on, blithely unaware of how close he'd come to lighting a fuse. 'I b'aint be sure of the year but our king is Arthur,' he began. 'Our sire won't be far from 'ere. After all, this be 'is home. Tintagel Castle is but a day's ride from these parts.'

Tamar's informant paused, took aim, and spat thoughtfully at an innocent holly bush. 'He and 'is knights are back for the winter. The whole court's here … all the servants and squires and ladies.' He lowered his voice and glanced around nervously. ''Tis said that even 'is wise man, Merlin, is with 'im. An' if 'e's here then you can be sure that somethin's afoot.'

He stopped. He appeared to be listening to something. 'Hush!' he ordered – even though he was the one who'd been speaking. Somewhere in the distance a horn was being blown.

The man swivelled and peered through the trees because the horn was accompanied by frantic barking. Tamar wanted to find out more about where she'd landed, although she had a sneaking suspicion that she knew, but the stranger was distracted by the noises.

'The hunt's comin',' he informed her, his concerns about her origin forgotten. 'Best not be in its way. It could be our king an' his knights an' I don't want to be put in the stocks 'cause I got in the way of their hunt.'

The horn sounded again. It was getting nearer. Tamar heard voices and laughter echoing through the woods. But the most unnerving sound was the bloodthirsty yelping and baying of the hounds. The little stranger was right: it was a hunt and it was heading their way.

By now the bearded stranger was becoming agitated. He started muttering to himself and darting desperate glances at his surroundings, scouring the woods for any way to avoid the hunt's path, when there was a crashing through the snowy undergrowth and a young fox, all eyes and bushy tail, burst into the clearing. Its sides were heaving and its pink tongue lolled from its mouth.

The stranger didn't appear to be in the least bit bothered by the cub's plight, instead he was shouting, 'Come ma'am, quickly! Any moment and they'll be upon us!'

But deaf to the stranger's protestations, Tamar was scooping the trembling cub into her arms. The little man's eyes nearly popped out of his head. He couldn't believe what he was seeing.

Dancing from foot to foot, he began pleading with her. 'Leave the animal ma'am, 'tis only vermin!'

'Don't worry,' she muttered to the fox, 'I'm not leaving you.' There was no way she'd abandon a helpless animal. 'No dog's going to get their teeth into your skin.' And clutching it close to her chest she turned, ignoring the protestations of her new acquaintance.

She heard him shout, 'Ma'am! It ain't worth risking your life for no animal,' but his voice was growing faint as she forced her way through the thicket. She heard a couple more pleas and then presumably he decided to save his own skin because his shouts ceased.

Brambles whipped her face and caught her hair. Thorns snagged her dress and scored her arms. The combination of the snow and the thick undergrowth made any sort of escape almost impossible but she stumbled stubbornly on, over knobbly tree roots and under low-hanging branches.

Tamar was never one to give up at the first obstacle – or the second or the third, come to that – but even her heart plummeted when the horn sounded again.

The hunt was getting closer.

She cursed. The dress was tangled around her feet and ankles and no matter how fast she tried to run, the hunt was gaining on her.

'Darn this dress! Why couldn't I be wearing jeans?'

Another bramble clawed her cheek.

'Ouch!' She swallowed a sob swimming perilously close to the surface.

A deep voice called, 'It went that way. Look! Follow the hounds.'

Another answered, 'Are we to believe your dogs?'

While a third shouted, 'Come Dinadan, stop your jesting!'

Glancing over her shoulder she caught a flash of red and gold and a glimpse of horses' legs through the trees.

So she didn't see the gnarled root rearing up in front of her, or the deep ditch beyond it. A second later and she was falling, slipping, unable to save herself from sliding down an icy bank into a mess of mud and snow and brambles.

She would never be able to accurately describe just how long she lay there clutching the trembling fox and listening to the shouts and barks. It could have been seconds or minutes before the shadow fell over her.

She remembered being vaguely aware of the watch beginning to tick loudly, possibly winding itself up to a chime, while she struggled with the problem of coming between a pack of dogs and their quarry. And she remembered hearing the men's voices. But all those memories were insignificant compared to the moment when she looked up to see the shadow's owner – a tall white-haired man wearing a blue cloak and leaning on a long staff – peering down at her. A deep forehead and bushy white eyebrows overshadowed a pair of calm, grey eyes and beneath the beard the beginnings of a smile on his lips.

'Ah,' he said quietly and appeared to be listening to something.

The watch was working itself up ready to chime, but the man held up a slender finger and frowned and the watch quietened.

'Not quite yet,' the white-haired man instructed. 'Soon, but not yet.'

He gazed at her and stroked his long white beard but didn't offer to help her out of the ditch. He took in the trembling cub and again said, 'Ah.'

Tamar was shivering. She was very, very cold. And muddy … and scratched. Something wet dribbled down her cheek. She brushed at it before clamping her arms back around the cub and glancing at the back of her hand; it was streaked with blood. Deep welts had sprung up along her arms and the dress, which had been so beautiful, was muddied and torn.

'So,' the stranger began thoughtfully. 'So, you were trying to escape the hunt.' He flashed a look towards the noise and frowned.

It can be difficult attempting to describe certain events, especially those which, even if you witness them, don't seem quite real. This was one of those events because the frown appeared to coincide with the noise of the fast-approaching dogs and horses being sent on a different track. Tamar, watching the man's face as the yelps and barks faded into the distance, saw the frown disappear.

'I suppose,' the man began, ignoring the disappearance of the hunt, 'that this is the first of our meetings, although it may have occurred in the wrong order. Time is such a tricky concept.'

The woods had returned to their normal state with the dogs' barks replaced by birdsong.

'I apologise for the manner of our meeting. It didn't go entirely to plan. On occasion time can become a little muddled. The past and present have a habit of overlapping, of entwining.'

Tamar's eyes widened. She'd heard Michael Jolly use a very similar phrase.

The fox wriggled as a robin hopped off a branch and flew into the ditch to land at Tamar's feet.

Watching the robin hop and peck, the stranger murmured, 'Yes I know, I won't keep her long.'

And Tamar remembered that other time when she'd encountered a robin. It had been on the cliff path near Porth Talant in the summer, when a little red-breasted bird had guided Nick to the green stone dragon.

The stranger watched her and nodded. 'Many people underestimate the intelligence of animals and birds. Personally I have never found them lacking.'

Tamar didn't know who this man was. This man who used Michael Jolly's words and appeared to have control over the pocket watch; a man who seemed to be able to redirect a pack of dogs with a frown. But the sword was warm around her neck.

Finally she found her voice. 'Who are you?'

The man regarded her seriously. 'Now that is a question I often ask myself, but if it is a name you ask for, I have several. Some call me Myrddin Emrys and others Merlinus. There are those who refer to me only as the wise man.' He smiled, his eyes becoming a deep blue. 'But that is perhaps a misnomer. Maybe Miss Tamblyn, you can find your own name for me.'

Tamar's heart skipped a beat. If she hadn't felt quite so cold and if the fox hadn't felt quite so real she could have been in a dream. 'Merlin?' she whispered.

The white-haired man smiled; he didn't agree or disagree. Instead he looked at the sky and remarked, 'It is getting late. The moon is rising and soon these woods will be dark.'

Her rescuer was right. The weak winter sun was already setting and the temperature in the snowy ditch was rapidly dropping. Tamar realised that she hadn't noticed the biting cold of midwinter creep up on her, turning her fingertips blue. Sitting at the bottom of a mud-and-snow ditch in December is not to be recommended if you want to avoid frostbite.

'I hope that the next time we meet it will be in happier circumstances,' the white-bearded man said. 'But maybe you will be better prepared for our meeting as a result of this one. However, I do apologise for this journey being somewhat … um, haphazard.'

The robin fluttered out of the ditch.

The stranger smiled and instructed, 'Don't worry about the fox; I'll ensure his safety.' He reached down and took the cub from her arms before nodding towards Tamar's pocket and adding, '*Now* you may go.'

And as the world began to turn he promised, 'Until the next time Miss Tamblyn.'

From the depths of her pocket the watch chimed triumphantly and Tamar was spinning as the stranger commanded, 'Take her straight back. No detours please.'

His voice was fading. 'Oh and Miss Tamblyn, due to the vagaries of time you will find that the dress will be as good as new when you, er … land.'

And there were flashes and sparks as stars and planets hurtled past because this time she didn't close her eyes. After all, if you are a Time Keeper you have to be able to cope with the travelling that comes with the job.

Chapter 5
Memory Thief

'Come on boy!' Nick commanded the dragon. 'Time for a snooze.' He opened his jacket pocket and waited. This always took a while.

'You're going to have to train him better than this,' Gawain commented. 'It would give most people heart failure to walk in on a small flying reptile.'

'Have you ever trained a rare Malachite?' Nick retorted. 'It's all about mind-games, not like teaching a dog to catch a ball.' He glanced down at Lightning. 'No offence mate.'

Arthur felt rumbles of discontent roll through his mind. Lightning was decidedly unimpressed.

The dragon's owner rustled a wrapper in his pocket. The creature flicked his tail from side to side as he perched on the curtain rail and blinked a couple of times, considering his next move.

'Come on,' Nick coaxed him. 'Nice dead spider. Really crispy legs. You know you like them.'

Arthur grinned as he pushed their books and bags into the back of a grubby cupboard hidden under a seat and swung the door closed. He threw a few cushions on the floor in front of it and slung a couple of blankets onto the pile to add to the mess and sat back on his heels to survey the effect. He hoped it would be enough to fool any burglars into thinking that there wasn't anything valuable stashed in the caravan.

The dragon couldn't contain himself any longer and with a tiny chirrup-roar launched himself at Nick's open pocket and the spider's legs.

'At last!' Gawain breathed. 'Perhaps now we'll be able to find out who delivered those invitations. I was beginning to think we'd be stuck here all day.'

He grabbed his jacket from the seat and shrugged it on, pulling up the zip against the biting cold.

'Ready?' Arthur asked Nick.

'Ready,' Nick confirmed, and gripped his pocket, ensuring that Dragon couldn't escape.

'Right, come on.'

Gawain led the way down the rickety steps followed by Nick and Arthur with Lightning at his heels. Arthur locked the door behind them, wishing that there was something more powerful than an ordinary lock to keep other people out. Especially other people like the Crow Man. It was then that he caught sight of a carving above the door. He hadn't seen it yesterday.

A barn owl peered at him, its feathers and feet and eyes beautifully carved and, illogically, his spirits lifted. The owl, sometimes-enemy of the crow.

'Okay guys, let's grab something to eat, I'm starving,' Nick said, steering them towards the sweet-chestnut stall. 'We can start here.'

'Chestnuts? You must be desperate!' Gawain said.

'Not desperate – just hungry.'

'Nothing new there then.' Gawain grinned. 'I bet ten minutes after you were born you were ordering food.'

Nick sniffed and addressed his pocket and the sleeping dragon. 'He calls himself my friend,' he said, sighing dramatically.

Arthur glanced around, only partially tuned into the conversation. Everything about the fair was perfect – just a little too perfect; a little too close to the past it was imitating. Nick and Gawain forged ahead, ignoring anything that didn't involve food, but Arthur wasn't hungry. His head was too full of their invitations and Tamar's mysterious gift and the train journey. He trailed behind his friends barely registering their banter, on the lookout for anyone who might be a threat.

A figure stepped behind a tree. It was unlikely that he'd be seen but Viatoris, the Watcher, didn't want to risk being spotted. He surveyed the field, wondering when the Guardians' enemies would make their move.

Hagarawall couldn't be far away and the Ice Lady must be making her way here; she was already organising the weather. Last time she'd arrived in Cornwall it had been summer but, he thought grimly, she was better suited to winter. He listened to the wind and took in the grey of the sea fusing with the heavy sky. And then he heard it – the first note of a minor key.

In the shadows, Viatoris's knuckles whitened at the dark music; it was an earworm of the worst sort – and the Watcher knew who'd designed it.

He frowned and Watched the boys approach the barrel organ. They slowed, stopping a couple of metres short of the instrument. Arthur laid his hand on Lightning's head and the dog sat, ears back.

'The mysteriously arriving barrel organ,' Gawain said thoughtfully.

Nick nodded, food temporarily forgotten.

The handle at the side of the box rotated, churning out the tinny music and the automaton came to life, bowing and twirling its wooden cane. The music rose on the wind, whirling and spinning and dipping and diving, pulling its unwary audience in. Teenagers, families with toddlers, and mums with babies, sauntered and ran towards the box with its top-hatted performer.

'Man, that's weird,' Nick murmured, as the mechanical puppet bent and doffed his hat and the main performance began.

'Like something out of a horror movie,' Gawain agreed.

Arthur nodded towards two small curly-haired children, a boy and a girl, who were sidling forward. 'Let's watch these two.'

The girl was older than her brother, probably about six, and doing her best to hold her little brother back. However, in a blink of an eye he'd slipped from her grasp and darted towards the barrel organ. But she grabbed him, 'Don't touch it Sam! I don't like it.'

The boys watched the children's mother catch up with them and heard her say, 'It's all right Kate, it can't hurt him. It's only a puppet – it's just a piece of painted wood. Look, I'll touch it.' And she stood up and brushed the carved face with her finger.

'She shouldn't have done that,' Gawain whispered. 'That kid was right.'

The little girl began to cry, 'It's horrible … I *hate* it Mummy. Look at its eyes, they're watching you.'

Her sobs were growing louder and her mother looked around, embarrassed. With a strained smile she repeated, 'Come on Kate, it's only a puppet.'

But the little girl was tugging at her mother's hand. 'No, come on, *please.*'

'This isn't like you!' her mother exclaimed.

However, Sam was surveying the barrel organ, weighing up whether to touch it, but before he had the chance his mother caught his hand and was leading him away. Fortunately for him, his sister had won.

The music stopped and the automaton slowed and bowed and leant on its cane. Job done. More memories caught. The Ice Lady liked memories, they could be useful.

The friends watched the audience drift away. None of them saw the boy wearing a silver jacket standing beside the candyfloss stall, or his satisfied smile when the children's mother touched the automaton.

'What d'you reckon it does?' Nick mused, stroking the sleeping dragon in his pocket.

Arthur ran his finger under the chain around his neck and felt the sword. The gold had chilled.

'Maybe it just blots out memories or something,' he shrugged. 'I don't know.'

Gawain said, 'Yeah, I bet it's something to do with thoughts and minds.'

Nick stopped stroking Dragon. 'D'you remember the stuff I told you about what the Ice Lady did to me before she kidnapped Tamar?'

He glanced about him, checking that no one was within earshot. 'That was all about mind control wasn't it? She managed to change what I could see and smell just by looking at me. I mean, one minute I was in Porth Pyra in Cornwall in summer surrounded by people, and the next it was like I was totally alone in a pine forest in winter. And I hadn't moved.'

In the shadow of the candyfloss stall the boy's smile grew.

Nick shuddered as he remembered the frost creeping into his bones. 'Man! That was evil.'

'What can we do about it?' Gawain asked, studying the wooden box with its moustachioed automaton.

'Well, there's no way we can touch it …' Arthur said, as the handle on the barrel organ began to turn. 'We don't know how dangerous it is, do we?'

The automaton was coming to life again. Fixing them with a glassy stare it bowed, twirled its cane and started its routine. The music rose in the frosty air, summoning a new audience. And the watching boy leant forward and examined the spectators crowding around the contraption.

'Come on, let's go,' Nick urged, keen to be away from the machine. 'There's nothing we can do about it right now.'

Gawain and Arthur studied the device and wondered about its purpose because, as Arthur's dad always said, 'Knowledge is power.' However, Mr Penhaligon probably hadn't been thinking about mysteriously appearing barrel organs at the time.

Arthur stroked Lightning and considered their options. 'Yeah, you're probably right. Maybe we'll find more out later. Let's have a quick look at the island and then find out where we're meant to be going for tea.'

The silver-haired boy watched them meander down the field but he stayed where he was, close to the barrel organ.

'Wonder who Dr Colum … thingy is,' Nick said. 'Hope he or she doesn't mind dragons!'

Despite their worries over the sinister cane-twirling automaton, Gawain and Arthur grinned.

'Only let him eat fresh spiders, then you can explain he's helping to cut down on cobwebs,' Gawain suggested dryly.

Nick rolled his eyes. 'If only life was so simple!'

'Hey,' Arthur said, 'surely anyone who delivers invitations to locked caravans can cope with dragons?'

'Maybe,' Nick agreed, but he didn't sound convinced.

They ignored the stalls crammed with wooden toys and handmade sweets until finally Nick found one selling hot dogs. 'Breakfast!'

'Anyone would think you hadn't eaten for days,' Gawain said.

'I'm a growing lad,' Nick retorted. 'Want one?'

'Yeah, go on then.'

'D'you want one, Arthur?'

Arthur shook his head. He wasn't hungry.

He scanned the fair as Nick and Gawain loaded their hot dogs with ketchup and onions. 'I wonder if Tamar's with Wenna.'

Nick, a head taller than the other two, took a bite and turned and peered above the crowds. 'Are they selling Christmas decorations?'

'Yeah, Wenna's been making stuff for months.'

'Got more patience than me,' Nick muttered, craning his neck. 'Hey, isn't that Wenna's stall over there, the one with loads of angels and things?' He waved towards the other side of the field.

Following the direction of the half-eaten hot dog, Arthur swivelled round and spotted Tamar. She was serving a customer but her usual sparkle seemed to have deserted her. She looked up and, seeing them, summoned a wan smile but unfortunately Morwenna had seen them too. The last thing she needed was Tamar's friends messing about near her stall.

'Come on guys,' Nick said, taking in Morwenna's expression. 'Let's make ourselves scarce; we can see Tamar later. The greater Tamblyn doesn't look too happy to see us.'

Gawain protested. 'She's not that bad.'

'Don't you believe it,' Nick retorted. 'She likes you but she could turn me to stone with one look. Come on, let's go to the beach before I'm traded for a boulder.'

But it wasn't Morwenna that worried Arthur, it was Tamar. Something had happened to her. It was written all over her face and, worryingly, she was surrounded by a sort of weird shimmery effect.

He frowned and caught her eye and raised his eyebrow in an, *'Are you okay?'* look.

She nodded and mouthed, 'Tell you later.'

He hesitated. He wasn't convinced. But she jerked her head towards Gawain and Nick, who were already wandering down the field, and mimed an urgent, 'Go on!' She obviously didn't want to discuss it now.

A brass band struck up, trumpets blending with trombones and cornets, and a school choir began to sing:

> *'God rest ye merry, gentlemen,*
> *Let nothing you dismay ...'*

Arthur sighed and reluctantly turned away. Digging his hands into his pockets and whistling to Lightning, he followed his friends and wondered what had happened – and the reason for that sepia glow.

Suppose she'll tell me later, he thought. He didn't notice any of the stalls: the mince pies being warmed by a rotund stallholder or the spiced wine being heated, and tested, by a particularly red-faced man. Instead, he mooched down the slope towards the sea and told himself: *And anyway, whatever's happened she's okay now, isn't she?*

Lightning whined, sensing Arthur's concern.

'I'm okay, mate, but I'd like to know what's happened to her,' Arthur said. 'I'm just going to have to be patient, aren't I?'

He looked up. Nick and Gawain were at the bottom of the field, waiting for him by a wooden caravan similar to the one they were staying in except this one appeared to double up as a stall. Instead of a counter, a hinged flap displayed the owner's wares: a selection of carved toys and wooden ornaments.

A chestnut-coloured carthorse was tethered behind the caravan, tearing at the muddied grass, but as they approached it stopped grazing and lifted its great head. There was something in the intelligent way it looked at them that reminded Arthur of Argo, the horse that had carried him and Excalibur from the lake to the coast, and the only horse he'd ever met capable of its own horsey sort of deep talking.

The stallholder was small and wiry and perched on a low stool, whittling wood while he whistled. A crimson-lined, threadbare jacket hung over his shoulders; his trousers were patched and his leather boots were cracked and holed.

The woodworker appeared to be unaware of the boys lingering nearby; he didn't even stop work when Arthur picked up a whistle.

Arthur held it and turned it over, inspecting it as his brain made connections. 'Did you make this?'

The man nodded but continued his whittling.

'I was given something like this a while ago …'

The stallholder didn't make any comment but his hands slowed.

'The person who gave it to me was called Michael Jolly.' Arthur watched the stallholder for any reaction.

The woodcarver stopped whistling, and Gawain noticed a slight tremor start in his hands, but still he didn't look up – although he did put the knife down.

'Useful in times of trouble; folks can 'ear that whistle for miles, 'specially on a clear night,' the woodcarver observed, speaking for the first time. 'People sometimes like to give them to folks who might need them. To folks who might need a bit of extra protection because they're more special than most.'

Finally he looked up and a pair of black, pebble eyes fastened onto Arthur.

Gawain frowned. There was something about this man that didn't quite chime with this century; almost as if he didn't really belong in it.

'What's your name lad?' the woodcarver asked, his eyes fixed on Arthur.

Dragon shifted in Nick's pocket and belched softly, but the man's gaze didn't waver. Gawain checked his sword and chain; they weren't quite at blood heat but neither were they cold.

Arthur's eyes flicked from the man to the carved whistle. He turned it over. Then he glanced towards a box of walking sticks at the man's side.

'Did you make those too?'

The man nodded.

Arthur put the whistle down and picked up one of the sticks. It was extremely long, so probably only useful to someone who was very tall. The head, or handle, was a leaping dolphin made from smooth, varnished wood.

'What sort of wood is it?'

'Hazel,' the man replied shortly.

Arthur stroked the wood and thought about the first time he'd encountered someone with a walking stick like this. It had been on the moors close to Lyskeret two summers ago when his life had taken an unexpected left turn and veered towards the mythical.

That person had been the other-worldly Michael Jolly: the man who had rescued him from the clutches of Matearnas and ensured that it was Arthur, not the mad woman, who inherited King Arthur's crown. Was there a connection between the two men?

Arthur met the woodcarver's eyes. He regarded him thoughtfully and glanced towards his handiwork.

'Why do you use hazel?'

The man pondered on his reply. 'Hazel has many uses … but p'raps it's best known for givin' a little extra knowledge to some folks.'

'What else does it do?'

''Tis said to help find water.'

Gawain watched the interchange with interest. Arthur was checking out the guy.

Arthur fiddled with the other sticks rammed into the box. All the handles were modelled on animals or birds. He picked one that was a cat sitting upright with its tail wrapped around its body.

'Careful with that one lad, 'tain't no ordinary stick!' the woodman exclaimed sharply. 'You could 'urt someone.'

Arthur examined it curiously. 'Why. What is it?'

'Give it 'ere; I'll show you.'

He held out his hand and took it. Then he fiddled with the handle and slid the stick apart revealing a steel blade. 'It's a sword cane.'

'I've seen one of those on telly!' Nick exclaimed. 'Wasn't Dr Watson supposed to have one? You know … the guy who worked with Sherlock Holmes.'

'Looks like it could do some serious damage,' Gawain commented.

'Sherlock Holmes?' The woodcarver shook his head. 'Dunno lad.' He slid the blade back into the polished wooden case with a click.

'Impressive,' Gawain was fascinated.

Arthur watched the carver replace the stick in the box with the other canes and lovingly stroke the wooden handle. Something about that action decided him.

'I'm Arthur Penhaligon.'

And at last the woodcarver's face broke into a wide smile, radiating grubby wrinkles.

'Well, after all these miles …' he began, 'and all that travelling.' Nick was certain that he heard him add, 'and all those years.'

And the woodcarver was thrusting a calloused hand into Arthur's, crushing him with an iron grip.

'So *you* be the sire! I could see it in your eyes,' he said, pumping Arthur's hand. ''Tis an honour … a long-awaited honour. I was promised that we would meet but I was never told the day or the hour. And I was told that it would be another Arthur with a family name close to that of our king, but I didn't expect one so young!'

Finally he loosened his grip and let Arthur have his hand back, his smile was already disappearing. He scanned the busy field and the vast, grey sky. The carthorse whinnied and its master muttered, 'I know, Marth, I know. I 'ad hoped that we'd meet at a better time and in a better place …'

He was becoming distracted.

'The others are close,' he said, and cast another hasty look across the field. 'You must be on your guard.'

Lowering his voice he added, 'They're coming. It won't be long before they're all here.'

He looked wistful. 'I would wish us to talk longer and for you to tell me 'ow you came to be king, but that will 'ave to wait.'

A sliver of wind carrying freeze-dried leaves curled around them.

Somewhere far off an owl screeched, and in the gloomy shadows Viatoris listened.

The woodcarver shivered and retrieved his knife. Glancing furtively around he whispered, 'Sire, the whistle, the one you were given, 'ave you still got it?'

Arthur nodded. It was in his backpack in the caravan.

'Probably best to keep it close to you. You never know when it'll come in 'andy.' He held Arthur's gaze for a moment longer. 'They're special. I don't make many, just one or two when they're needed.'

Nick's pocket rustled as Dragon made himself comfortable. Wordlessly the woodman reached into a box under the table and pulled out a brown paper bag. 'Might find that useful, lad,' he said, holding it out to Nick.

Nick looked uncertainly at the bag. 'Thanks.'

The man picked up his carving and lowered his head and hunched his back. 'You'd better be on your way,' he urged. 'They could arrive at any time.'

'Who might?' Arthur asked.

'You know 'em, sire. You know 'em. Those that are led by *her*.'

Grasping the knife, he shaved at the wood with a shaking hand, 'You must go, sire.' Despite the cold, beads of sweat stood out on his forehead.

Arthur wanted to ask him more about his connection with Michael Jolly and what else he knew of their opposition, but the woodcarver's anxiety was catching.

'All right, but maybe we can talk later. We're staying in the top field.'

But the woodcarver wasn't listening. He was beyond conversation, darting rapid looks over his shoulder and towards the sea and the cloud-filled sky.

Zipping his jacket up to his chin, Arthur turned on his heel, thrust his hands deep into his pockets and began to walk away. Why was the woodcarver so worried about them being seen together?

Gawain scanned the crowded field and the other stalls. He couldn't see any of their known enemies.

But that's the problem, isn't it? he thought grimly. *That's where they've got the upper hand. They know us, but we don't know all of them.*

He'd begun to follow Arthur when the woodcarver tossed a, '*Comero weeth*', 'Take care', in his direction.

And deep words were seeping into Arthur's brain urging, '*Tereba nessa*, sire.' (Till the next time, sire.)

When Nick opened the bag he found a selection of dried insects perfectly suited to a tiny, fiery dragon.

Chapter 6
The Unhappiness of Stone

'Weird,' Nick muttered as he opened the bag and drew out a shrivelled insect. He examined it with the expert eye of a dragon minder and slid it into his pocket.

The boys sat on the rocks at the edge of the beach. The tide was in so they couldn't walk to the island. In summer small boats ferried day-trippers when the tide was high, but in winter only a few boats operated.

'How do you think he knew about Dragon?' Nick asked, as muffled crunching rose from his pocket.

'Or the whistle,' Arthur added, contemplating the possible link with Michael Jolly. He didn't comment on the woodcarver's deep words, unheard by his friends, which had filtered into his mind.

'Don't know,' Gawain leant back against the rocks. 'But he seemed okay.' He considered the caravan and the carvings. 'I know he was a bit strange but I think he's all right. I mean, I think we can trust him. He seemed cool.'

'Cool!' Nick exclaimed.

'Yeah, he seems like a nice guy.'

'Only someone,' Nick objected, 'who lives in a house with books that open their own pages could describe that guy as cool!'

Arthur agreed. 'Yeah, I might go with interesting, but "cool"?' He shook his head. 'Not really mate.'

Gawain grinned ruefully. 'Suppose it's having been brought up by Uncle Kitto, it sort of blunts your take on normality.'

'Too right it does!' Nick said. 'Perhaps you should spend more time with ordinary people.'

'What, like us?' Arthur suggested wryly. 'We hardly qualify!'

'I wonder what he meant by "the others"?' Gawain picked up a pebble, turning it over in his hand.

Arthur shrugged. 'Probably the usual suspects, although we sort of know that already.'

They considered the trio who'd almost succeeded in ripping Cornwall from their grasp the previous summer: the Crow Man, Hagarawall and the Lady of Clehy. And Arthur thought of Matearnas, who'd died rather than forfeit the rule of Cornwall.

But Nick could never be quiet for long. 'What was that dress-thing that Tamar was wearing?'

'The "dress-thing", as you so eloquently put it, was a gift,' Arthur replied, his mind still full of their unseen enemies. 'It arrived this morning.'

'Who gave it to her?'

Arthur stroked Lightning. 'It was given to Morwenna by a woman but she couldn't remember her name. All Tamar knows is that it was Mrs Bes… something or other.'

'Last time I saw Tamar in a dress was at the Porth Pyra festival. I can't think of another time I've seen her wear one.' Nick gave another insect to the dragon in his pocket.

'Oh yeah, come to think of it there was that time when we had that fancy-dress dance at school. Man, that was something else. D'you remember what Mr Trelove was wearing?'

He turned to share the joke with his friends, but his grin disappeared when he saw a little girl of about five or six with grey, serious eyes standing a few metres away, scrutinising them while she swung her doll and sucked her thumb. The toy was a replica of her owner, right down to her jade-green dress and her blue-buttoned boots.

In a cleft in the rocks, Viatoris Watched and listened as the girl broke her silence.

'It's going to happen in a minute,' she stated without introduction.

The boys gazed at her.

'Any minute now.'

Mystified, Nick asked, 'What's going to happen?'

She turned to look at him, her eyes becoming darker. 'The island, it's going to call out.'

'What?'

'It does it when it's unhappy.'

'The island … unhappy?'

She nodded. 'It's because they're away. It doesn't like it when they're away. It's not safe.'

By now even Nick was mute.

The girl swung her doll and traced a shape in the sand with her foot. 'The island's never safe when the keepers are away on holiday.'

Arthur had been frowning, trying to work out what she meant, but now his face cleared. 'Oh, do you mean the owners?'

The little girl shook her head emphatically. 'No. The family who live in the castle are just the *keepers*. No one can own land, silly! The land belongs to itself. It just needs people to protect it.' Pinning Arthur with a sharp look she added, 'People like you.'

Viatoris shifted, his interest stirred by this child who could see more than most. He was reminded of his other charge in Italy so many centuries away, the young da Vinci.

'What do you mean?' Arthur asked.

But the child just looked at the sea. 'Watch!' she commanded.

Nick frowned but did as she said, and saw the ripples begin and heard the rumbling start. The sky darkened and the watery sun disappeared.

'See?' the girl said. 'I told you: the island's unhappy.' She hugged her doll and sucked her thumb, with her head on one side as she considered the view.

There wasn't much to see, apart from the ripples as the ground beneath the sea trembled, but they all heard the rumbling. The few people walking stopped and looked out to sea. Seagulls took to the air, swooping and calling to one another. On the sand, shells shivered and hair-line cracks stole up the beach; a small-scale earthquake.

Lightning whined and, in Nick's pocket, Dragon tensed. An icy hand clutched Nick's heart and squeezed. He couldn't take his eyes off the island. He swallowed. Something bad was preparing itself. For a second he felt Dragon's fear mingle with his own.

Deep words slithered into Arthur's head. Some silver, others purple, a few dark grey. It was as if a discussion was being conducted behind closed doors so that all Arthur could hear was the tone of the conversation rather than the exact words. He couldn't make out the individual voices so he probably wasn't meant to hear what was being said, but he remembered his Aunt Dywana telling him that sometimes, if the person doing the deep talking was on the edge of some emotion like anger, the words might seep out and be overheard.

But as suddenly as it had begun, the rumbling and the discussion – or argument – stopped. The winter sun reappeared and the birds quietened, no longer disturbed by the island's grumblings. The boys watched the sand settle, dusting over the cracks, and considered the island and its castle. Eventually, the little girl spoke again.

'It's all right now,' she pronounced, 'but it needs help because *she's* coming.'

A pair of solemn eyes bore into Arthur. 'You mustn't let her control it. People have been trying to control it for hundreds of years, Daddy says. He says it's like it's a stepping stone. Once they've got the island they think they can have all Kernow.'

Her speech finished, she stuck her thumb back in her mouth and cuddled her doll.

The boys were quiet. Even Dragon was still.

'Gwen!'

The little girl glanced towards the top of the beach.

'Gwen, come on,' the voice commanded impatiently. 'You know we've got to practise.'

Arthur caught a glimpse of a red-headed girl wearing a long, grey skirt and holding a top hat.

The little girl surveyed her caller, took her thumb out of her mouth and announced, 'That's my sister.' And without another word wandered up the beach, her wooden doll dangling from her hand, pausing from time to time to inspect a particularly interesting stone or shell.

A sharp wind seized a handful of sand, flung it into the air and mixed it with a few snowflakes.

Snow on a beach is a rare phenomenon – especially in Cornwall. Arthur shivered. The boys studied the island; it looked normal but they knew not to trust appearances.

'How can a *place* be unhappy?' Nick mused, trying to push the dread away. He was reminded of the Ice Lady's effect on him, that feeling of hopelessness she'd projected into his mind. What he'd been describing to his friends as they'd watched the barrel organ was happening to him again. He shivered and stroked Dragon.

'Dunno,' Arthur replied, Lightning's silky fur warm beneath his fingers. 'But remember when I put the sword back in the statue's hand – you know, the angel-statue that was guarding Cornwall? Remember how there was that sort of rumbling as if the land was settling. Even the sea calmed down didn't it?'

'And there is that legend about the giant of this island,' Gawain added. 'Maybe it's something to do with that.'

'Man!' Nick remarked, shaking his head. 'An unhappy island with a giant. That takes weirdness to new levels.'

'Yeah, but it's not a real, living giant.'

'Oh *really*?' Nick said. 'That's okay then. Just an unhappy island and a once-upon-a-time sort of giant. I'm feeling better already.'

Listening to their conversation, disguised by the winter shadows, Viatoris smiled.

Gawain began to explain, 'There's a legend about a giant who used to live on this island.'

'Oh yeah,' Arthur said. 'Didn't he used to come off the island and eat people's sheep and cows and things?'

Nick focused on the island. 'Thought I was the one with the big appetite!'

'Anyway, he was supposed to have been killed by a boy ...'

'And everyone lived happily ever after,' Nick finished. 'Well mate, that sounds fine to me as long as we all get to live happily ever after too!'

Gawain checked the sword hanging around his neck. It was a little chilly but that could be the weather.

'Come on,' Nick said. 'Let's try and find out where Oakwood Manor is – I've had enough of this beach. And let's steer clear of weird kids.'

'I think I'll pick up Michael's whistle from the caravan,' Arthur said, thinking of the words of the woodcarver. 'You never know, it might come in handy.'

They checked the sky but it was reassuringly empty, with just a few seagulls soaring and dipping on the icy wind.

Viatoris shrunk back into the rock, but as they passed the fissure Gawain caught a movement out of the corner of his eye. He stopped and peered into the rocky crevice. He thought he could make out a vague shape but the light was bad and it was difficult to be sure.

The Watcher held his breath and pinched his nose and sniffed. A sneeze was building. But Nick called and Gawain turned away and Viatoris breathed out ... and managed to stifle the sneeze. *Darn this Cornish winter; a cold is all I need!*

Holding a hankie over his nose, he edged out of the fissure and saw the boys walk up the slipway leading to the village road. Satisfied that they would be making their way to the fair he relaxed and scanned the beach and cliffs for anyone who might be of interest, which is when he saw a familiar silhouette. Viatoris froze.

A man was standing on a spit of land that jutted into the sea. The Watcher noted the broad-brimmed hat, the long coat being whipped by the wind, and the crow hopping from rock to rock. It was Brane, the one the Guardians called 'the Crow Man'.

He cast a hurried look over his shoulder towards the cobbled slipway to reassure himself that the boys had already gone. Fortunately, their enemy had missed them by minutes.

Viatoris stood perfectly still, but as he Watched he realised that the Crow Man's attention wasn't focused on the beach but on the sea. He was studying the horizon. It was quite likely that Brane had seen the Guardians and yet he'd ignored them. Why would he do that?

Then he understood.

The Crow Man was waiting for the Lady of Clehy. She'd come by sea before, when she'd tried and failed to claim Cornwall. She must be arriving by sea again.

An icy gust snatched at Viatoris's collar and dropped a stray snowflake on his cheek. He wiped it away and dug in his pockets for his gloves.

So, he thought, *she's on her way and she's bringing her winter with her.*

He looked at the sand being swept along the beach. He saw the few snowflakes, the promise of the deep cold that only she could deliver, and he shivered. This was just the beginning.

And then he became aware of Brane's black eyes on him. Brane could see the Watchers and he always used it to his advantage; taunting them with a look or a glance. Knowing that they weren't permitted to intervene – no matter what may happen.

Sure enough Brane lifted a mocking finger to the brim of his hat, saluted the Watcher and smiled and bowed. Then he looked to the skies and concentrated. A split second later and a bolt of blinding lightning lit the beach and a pulse of thunder rumbled above them.

He was making a point.

Maybe he'd been surprised by the strength of Arthur's allies at the beginning, but things were different now. He'd known that the Watcher had been observing him but the Lady of Clehy would soon be arriving … and then they'd claim the island and Cornwall's crown for themselves.

***

Tamar handed the change to a customer, checked the time on her wrist watch and turned to her sister. 'Will it be okay if I go soon, Wenna?'

Morwenna finished wrapping an elaborate bow around a package and considered Tamar. 'Is something up?'

Tamar busied herself rearranging their display, carefully avoiding Morwenna's eyes. In her head she said, *No, nothing it all – I'm totally used to paper with designs that move and a dress that makes me travel through space.*

But aloud she said, 'No, it's just that I said that I'd meet the boys soon.'

'Did you now ... and without asking me!'

'Oh come on Wenna! You know I don't want to be paid.'

Morwenna's eyes narrowed. 'Oh I see, because you're being so generous with your time you're going to leave me by myself!'

Tamar recognised the warning signals: Morwenna's hands were on her hips and her cheeks had two bright dots of colour.

'No,' she reasoned. 'I like helping you, it just seems a bit mean to leave the boys alone.'

'You mean that they're not old enough to look after themselves?'

'You know I don't mean that! Oh Wenna *please* can I go?'

Something in Tamar's tone registered with her sister and she began to calm down.

Sighing, Morwenna glanced around. 'I suppose I could ask Becky to help, she's not working today. But if she can't, I really will need you here.'

'Oh thanks Wenna! I'll go and find her,' Tamar offered before her sister could change her mind. 'Back in a minute.' Tamar darted away, unaware of a pale-haired man lounging against an oak tree watching her.

Hagarawall saw Tamar catch up with an older girl and engage her in earnest conversation before leading her back to her sister's stall. He was interested that the Time Keeper appeared to be so animated, and that she kept glancing at her watch.

A voice in his ear muttered, 'I've got a strand of her hair.'

Hagarawall jumped and cursed. 'Cador, will you stop creeping up on me?'

'I didn't need to creep, you weren't listening,' the silver-haired youth retorted. 'You know Mother's always reminding you to use your ears.'

Hagarawall bit back the reply that came to mind because it wouldn't do to insult the Lady of Clehy's son; instead he asked, 'Why her hair?'

Cador yawned. 'It could be useful.'

'Useful?'

The boy surveyed his companion. 'Don't you know *anything*?'

Hagarawall looked blank.

'Mother might be able to use it in some way. She might be able to find out more about the little Time Keeper from this hair.' The boy paused. 'But things like that never occur to you, do they?' Arrogance dripped from every word.

Hagarawall rammed his hands into his pockets. He'd love to punch the boy. It would almost be worth the ice-touch of his mother.

Cador continued, 'Haven't you heard the saying that knowledge is power?' He put his arm around the older man's shoulder and squeezed. 'But maybe in your case that's expecting too much – knowledge I mean.'

And smirking he turned and strode away leaving Hagarawall fuming. That boy did it every time. He knew just how to wind him up. The pale man felt in his pocket for a sweet, popped it in his mouth and crushed it.

He watched the paper fall to the ground and settle on the mud while insults and retorts leapt to mind. Then a glint caught his eye. Trying to ignore his boiling rage, Hagarawall brushed the object with his boot and bent over to get a closer look. It was the rim of an old coin. He picked it up. It was a Roman coin. Another glint winked a few feet to his left and then another to his right, and Hagarawall's frown cleared.

Ah … the ground is waking. He dug into his pocket and pulled out a second sweet. *Its memories are being pushed to the surface.*

He took in the roasted chestnuts, the toffee apples and the candyfloss stall. He listened to the band and the choir and watched the stallholders in their long dresses and suits, and he smelt the spiced wine.

Hagarawall shook his head. *You're all making it so easy.* Every one of them was playing their part in calling out to the past and weakening the present.

Hagarawall smiled.

The boy hadn't noticed any of this.

His mother might have filled him with notions of his own superiority but they were totally misplaced. And then he looked towards Morwenna's stall and his heart sank.

He'd been so wrapped up with his conversation with Cador and his own thoughts that he'd lost sight of the girl!

Frantically he scanned the field and the stalls but the Time Keeper had disappeared.

He cursed and melted into the shadows.

***

'How did you find out where the Manor is?' Tamar asked as they walked up the lane past the tightly packed cottages. She'd succeeded in persuading the ever-amenable Becky to take her place at Morwenna's stall and had swapped the dress for jeans – thankfully without any side effects.

Smoke drifted above the slate roofs and, although it was only early afternoon, lights already shone from the cottage windows. Arthur glanced over his shoulder. The lane wound up the hill from the centre of the village, steeply pitched roofs framing the grey silhouette of the island. The cobbled causeway glistened in the fading light, revealed by the now-low tide.

He scanned the lane and the sky but they were alone; only gulls flew above them.

'Great detective work,' Nick began, grinning.

'Yeah, Sherlock couldn't have done better,' Gawain agreed. 'Especially if he'd asked someone and they'd given him directions.'

There was a scrabbling in Nick's pocket and a dragon snout emerged. 'Get back in!'

Tamar giggled and glanced around. The lane was deserted. *Now* she could tell them. 'Something happened to me this morning.'

Arthur looked at her seriously. 'I thought so!'

Nick stopped. 'Not something else?'

Tamar nodded. 'Keep walking.'

She waited until they'd gone a few more paces and checked that they were still alone.

'It was after you left my caravan Art, just after I'd shown you the dress. Did you tell the others about it?'

'Yeah, well not about the packaging and stuff.'

A bird flapped in the branches above them and Tamar jumped and grabbed Gawain's arm. 'Sorry, I think I'm a bit on edge.'

'I'm not surprised,' Gawain replied, 'but don't do that again or I'll be black and blue.'

They watched the blackbird fly down the valley before walking on. 'Well, I was about to put the dress on when I remembered the pocket watch … boy, I'm glad I did!'

'Why? What happened?' Nick asked.

'Well, you know you guys and the train? It was a bit like that, only instead of staying in the caravan I was sort of travelling through space. I could even see the stars and stuff. It was terrifying.'

For once even Nick didn't comment.

Arthur digested Tamar's story. A couple of years ago he would never have believed it. Now it was just one more thing to log. 'Where did you end up?'

'In a wood.'

'That's not very exciting,' Nick complained.

'It was exciting enough for me!'

'Go on,' Arthur urged. 'What happened when you got there?'

'Well at first not much, but then I heard something move behind a bush.'

And Tamar described the snowy clearing and the little man, and hearing the hunt echo through the woods and trying to rescue the fox cub. Finally she came to her meeting with the blue-robed stranger.

'He was amazing. He knew all about me.' She frowned. 'Yeah, and you know I think he even knew about the dress, and I'm pretty sure he stopped the hunt from coming our way *and* he seemed to be able to control the pocket watch.'

At last she had the luxury of remembering their conversation – or rather her monosyllabic replies to his observations.

'And I think … I think he was called,' she hesitated, 'I think he was called Merlin.'

Arthur's stomach flipped. They'd been on a time train and Tamar had been on a time journey. Anything was possible.

Eventually Nick whispered, 'Wow … the real Merlin?'

Tamar nodded.

They carried on walking, kicking at the dried leaves, lost in their thoughts. From the outside they looked like a normal group of teenagers out for a walk with their collie dog a few days before Christmas, perhaps discussing what presents they hoped to get. No one would guess that they were thinking about the problems of time travel and the existence of a mythical wizard.

Arthur looked up from the leaves at his feet. 'Tamar, I think we're almost there. There's loads I want to know but we'd better bring you up to speed on what happened to us.'

'Something happened to you too?'

Arthur nodded as he ran a now automatic precautionary check of the skies and listened for any unusual rustlings. Then, beginning with the barrel organ and the woodcarver, he quietly summarised the morning's events.

Tamar pondered on the girl's words about the island's unhappiness. 'I wonder what she meant.'

Above them a pale-feathered bird silently spread its wings and flew away.

Nick shrugged. 'Dunno. She lost me!'

Gawain cast a sideways look at him and grinned. 'That's not exactly difficult though, is it?'

Nick shook his head. 'It's just one insult after another! Hey, this must be the boundary wall the guy told us about.'

The wall was a couple of metres high, solidly built from granite and topped with slate: Cornwall's stones.

Ferns grew out of the cracks, moss clung to its side, and at the base of the wall were occasional openings about the size of a small animal.

Tamar looked back and realised that they must have been walking beside it for a while. 'Wow. Whoever owns this place must be rich.' It reminded her of the sort of places that her mum sometimes took her to: houses that had belonged to Lord or Lady somebody or other.

They walked along the lane in silence, with the wall to their right and a Cornish stone hedge sprouting holly and prickly hawthorn to their left, and wondered who would be waiting for them.

The road – rarely used, judging by the line of grass running along its centre – curved, following the side of the hill.

They turned a corner and were confronted by a pair of imposing wrought-iron gates and Arthur was filled with a sickening déjà vu. A couple of pillars, topped by statues, bracketed the gates. The last time he'd seen anything like that had been outside the Granite House where he'd been caught by the Crow Man.

But these statues were different; they looked as if they'd only recently been installed. One was a barn owl and the other was a king wearing a crown. Arthur ran his fingers over the metal sword and chain tucked under his T-shirt. The gold was warm.

'Would you look at those gates!' Tamar exclaimed.

'Stunning,' Gawain agreed, tracing the ironwork. In both gates a circle of dolphins weaved around one another; in the left gate the circle framed a stallion jumping over an elegant F, while the right circle enclosed a cat winding round a curling C.

Arthur touched the C and the gates began to quiver. Then both gates creaked and swung open. There was no evidence of any electric sensors and they couldn't see any monitors but perhaps these gates didn't need them.

The Guardians looked at one another and then back towards the gates which were now fully open.

Finally Nick broke the silence. 'Come on then! It's no good just standing looking at each other. Let's find out why we're here.'

Chapter 7
Oakwood Manor

Brown leaves spun over the grass.

Servo Watched through the gates. He wasn't allowed to enter the grounds, which was a shame. He would have loved to witness what he was certain would be an interesting encounter. Scouring the sky the Watcher noted that there was no sign of the bird when his thoughts were interrupted by a rush of warm wind.

He was being called to Egypt.

This is most trying! He heaved his bag onto his shoulder and turned from the gates. *How can I possibly be expected to do either job properly?*

Checking the lane to ensure that he was alone he stepped into the shadows. There was the smallest of crackles followed by a barely perceptible *woomph* and Servo was back in ancient Egypt – wearing an anorak and a woolly hat. He rolled his eyes, slid the bag off his back and sidled into a conveniently shady alley.

***

Meanwhile, the Guardians wandered along the drive, wondering at their surroundings. Already the sun was low in the sky, long shadows criss-crossing the frost-white grass. It was a Christmas card in the making.

All you need now, Tamar thought, *is some snow and a robin*. And right on cue there was a snatch of red feathers and a glistening snowflake. Tamar smiled and surveyed the grounds and its forest of oak trees. *This place must be really old.* If a unicorn had trotted out of the woods she wouldn't have been surprised. It oozed magic.

But Arthur's thoughts were darker. The last time he'd entered a walled garden had been at the Granite House when he'd been captured by the Crow Man and Matearnas. *At least I'm not by myself this time*, he thought and cannoned straight into Nick's stationary back.

'Wow guys, would you look at that?'

'Sorry mate, miles away,' Arthur apologised. 'Boy! That's some house.'

'Oh my word!' Tamar exclaimed, all thoughts of Christmas cards banished.

They'd found Oakwood Manor.

'I didn't think people still lived in houses like this,' Gawain said.

An imposing, dark-stoned manor house lay ahead of them. Smoke rose from the tall chimneys and a gentle light spilled from the elegant windows. This was a perfect Christmas house.

'I bet they don't do their own cleaning …' Nick began.

'What?' Dragged from his dark thoughts, Arthur exclaimed, 'Only you'd think of that!'

'Yeah but that's what Mum always says when she watches one of those property things on telly,' Nick protested. 'As soon as it's got more than three bedrooms she starts going on about who has to clean it.'

And immediately they were giggling as Nick did his hurt, '*Now* what've I said?' expression.

'Brilliant!' Gawain said, snorting. 'He sees a manor and talks about cleaning!'

'Mate, how d'you do it?' Arthur giggled. 'You're a one-off.'

'Ow!' Tamar clutched her stomach. She took a breath but the giggling began again. 'Ow, my sides are hurting.'

Nick looked mildly offended. 'Honestly, with friends like you lot who needs enemies?'

'Sorry,' Gawain grinned.

'Try and say that without smiling,' Nick said.

Gawain shook his head, another laugh building. Instead he gestured towards the house, 'Pretty impressive, though, isn't it?'

It was *very* impressive, and old and rambling. The gravelled drive ran up to the entrance and to a couple of white pillars supporting a grand porch. Beneath the porch a flight of wide stone steps rose to the front door. Unusually, a couple of statues stood on the extreme left and right corners of the roof. One was a stag the other was a unicorn. Tamar did a double-take and took in a third statue, on the porch roof. It was a stone cat. An exact copy of the cat that had protected them from the Crow Man.

Slowly, they approached the steps. They weren't laughing now.

'Your call, I reckon,' Gawain said to Arthur, nodding his head towards the oak door and a brass bell. Arthur paused.

'Go on mate,' Nick encouraged him.

Arthur ran his fingers over the chain around his neck. 'Okay …' He had no idea who, or what, would be on the other side of the door but his gold sword was warm. His friends hung back and waited as Arthur cautiously climbed the steps.

Finally, taking a deep breath and with his heart drumming, he swung the rope hanging from the bell and a bass note broke the silence. Arthur shot a nervous glance over his shoulder and Tamar attempted an encouraging smile but her eyes were like saucers.

Deep in the house there was movement and then shuffling footsteps approached and a key rattled in the lock and Arthur turned back to face whatever was on the other side of the door. The handle turned and the door creaked open to reveal a plump face surrounded by tight, grey curls.

'Good,' the smiling face said, 'you're on time. The Doctor can't be doin' with folks who aren't punctual.'

The door opened wider to reveal a large woman wiping her hands on a towel and wearing a flowery apron. Dustings of flour decorated her cheeks and nose. She folded her arms and stood back.

'Not wearin' your dress then?' she said to Tamar. 'Pity. Never mind. Maybe you'll 'ave a chance another time.'

'Oh!' Tamar exclaimed, finding her voice. 'Are you Mrs Bes … ?'

'Mrs Beswetherick, yes. I'm the Doctor's housekeeper. Someone has to look after him, he'd never manage to feed 'imself.'

Tamar wanted to find out more about the dress but the housekeeper was obviously not going to waste time discussing clothes. She had much more important things on her mind. Instead she held the door open and urged them inside. 'Come on. He's waiting for you.'

Somewhere a dog barked and Lightning whined in reply.

Seeing them hesitate she puffed, ''Tis cold, come in. 'Tis hard enough keepin' this place warm without folks dithering on the doorstep.'

Nick felt Dragon fidgeting in his pocket and slipped him a snack as they filed in. He had a feeling that Mrs

Beswetherick wouldn't take kindly to a lively flame-thrower.

'Now, which of you likes cherry cake and who prefers chocolate?'

But without waiting for an answer she'd heaved the door shut and started off down the hallway.

'Come on,' she ordered. 'Don't stand there gawpin', he's waiting for you.'

But it was hard not to stare.

The floor of the hall was tiled in terracotta red and burnt umber with the occasional splash of deep blue. Being tiled wasn't unusual because the halls of most big house are tiled, but this design was unlike anything Tamar had seen in other old houses. In her experience they were all dull patterns, but here dolphins swam, cats prowled and owls flew. A dog similar to Lightning was in one corner, a dragon breathed tessellated fire in another and the centrepiece was a magnificent white stag.

It's like the statue on the roof, she thought. *And that dragon looks just like Nick's dragon.* She glanced at Nick, wondering if he'd noticed, but he was gazing at some gold-framed paintings hanging above the staircase.

Nick wasn't usually into art but these pictures were different. One painting was of a knight on a horse, another was of a woman's hand rising out of a lake (holding a sword), and a third was a bearded man with an owl on his shoulder.

Meanwhile Arthur was staring at a suit of armour at the foot of the stairs. He was horribly reminded of the hall in Matearnas's house where he'd been held prisoner. There'd been a suit of armour there too.

'Needs dusting,' Mrs Beswetherick commented, catching the direction of Arthur's gaze. 'Cobwebs everywhere.'

Another bark echoed along the corridors and Lightning took off, feet skidding.

'Sorry,' Arthur said, tearing his eyes from the armour. 'He's normally really good.'

But Mrs Beswetherick was already sweeping along the tiled passage. 'This way … come on.'

They followed, catching tantalising glimpses of rooms filled with statues and armour. There were no overhead lights just iron candle-holders with flickering candles set into the walls.

One candle spluttered as they passed and she tossed it an irritated glance. 'Why the man can't 'ave normal lights like the rest of us, I don't know.'

Turning a corner she flung a pair of imposing double doors apart and announced, 'Your guests, Doctor.'

Chapter 8
Dr Columbarius

'He spends nearly all 'is time in here,' she muttered. 'Books and books and more books. Never lets me dust 'em; they must be filthy. Years and years of dust, imagine!'

A voice from a fireside chair interrupted her with a, '*Thank* you Mrs Beswetherick. I trust that your tea will live up to its usual high standard.' The voice continued, 'Mrs B's cakes are delicious. One never forgets the first bite.'

'Hummphh,' Mrs Beswetherick replied. 'Think you can get round me like that, Doctor? Toast and home-made strawberry jam, cherry cake and chocolate cake?'

'Marvellous – a tea fit for a king! Could you close the door behind you?'

And their guide, with her grumbles and un-dusted books forgotten, left the room with her employer's compliments ringing in her ears.

'Come in, come in.'

Ceiling-high wooden shelves stacked with books ran the length of the walls. Some of the books, which hadn't moved a page when they'd entered, began to rustle. It was like a class when their teacher leaves the room. Gawain thought of his Uncle Kitto. He'd be in his element.

He momentarily forgot his host and wandered over to a shelf to examine some books that he suspected were both rare and valuable. Most of the books sat quietly like normal books but one, bound in royal-blue leather, was more restless than the rest. Then he realised: *Self-openers! This must be where ours came from.*

He glanced at the chair holding their host but was unable to tear himself from the shelves and that one particularly fidgety book. He reached up, pulled it from the shelf and it flipped open. (It had been waiting a *very* long time.)

Meanwhile a barn owl perched on the highest shelf watching the newcomers with night-vision eyes. Tamar returned the owl's stare and thought about her dog; Mug Shot would be beside himself if her mum had an owl in the house. (Wenna's parrot was bad enough!) The owl blinked and refocused on a dead mouse gripped in its talons as a hedgehog emerged from beneath the lowest shelf and scuttled towards the fire.

Tamar's eyes widened. *A library with an owl and a hedgehog …* But then she thought, *Although it might make libraries more interesting!*

A deep chuckle rose from the chair and its occupant nodded as he caught the thought.

But Nick hadn't noticed the owl, the hedgehog or the books.

When they'd first come in the ceiling had been white but as soon as Mrs Beswetherick left it had begun to ripple, exchanging solid plaster for a cold, winter sky. The similarity with a real sky was impressive.

Nick tilted his head. 'Man, that's some effect.'

The figure sitting in the leather armchair, steepled his fingers under his chin and smiled to himself.

And then Nick saw a shooting star flash across the early evening sky and disappear beyond the top of the wall. 'No way!' Nick's mouth dropped open and the owl, which until now had been busy with the mouse, fluffed its feathers, spread its wings and silently flew up into the ceiling-sky and away over the library wall – dropping the remains of its dinner at Nick's feet.

However, Arthur was only dimly aware of the books and the ceiling. He'd flicked a brief glance at Lightning curled up in front of the fire next to another dog (which looked suspiciously like Fly, Michael Jolly's dog), as a piece of text swam in front of his eyes:

'There is a small species of falcon, the Latin name for which is falco columbarius, however the common name for the bird is a merlin.'

And a long-limbed, slightly stooped, figure unfolded itself from the fireside chair and gently rested an open book on a side table. He stood silhouetted before slowly walking towards Arthur. He was wearing a plum-coloured velvet jacket over a white shirt and a golden cravat. He could have walked out of the pages of a Sherlock Holmes novel – apart from his shoulder-length white hair.

'Ah, Arthur,' their host said and, peering over a pair of reading spectacles, fixed him with a hard look.

Arthur's heart pumped. An irrational hope had been growing for the last couple of years, ever since he'd been knighted by that legendary sword. Common sense told him that this man was supposed to be a myth. But so was Excalibur … *and* King Arthur *and* Sir Bedivere.

He took in the wide brow and the high, hollow cheeks, the long, white hair and trimmed beard, but it was the man's eyes that caught him.

Eyes that had travelled through time and space, seen war and peace and everything in between.

'Ah …' was all Falco Columbarius said, as he looked at the young man in front of him. And the world slowly turned as he recalled that first meeting long centuries ago with another young man. Another future king.

Dr Columbarius smiled. 'You know who I am, then?'

All Arthur could manage was a nod. He remembered the once King Arthur asking him the same question on the night he'd bequeathed him the care of Cornwall and entrusted him with Excalibur. It was the same then – that gut feeling.

'Arthur,' Dr Columbarius began, the smile growing, 'you and your fellow Guardians are most welcome.'

He glanced at Gawain, immersed in his chosen book, and at Nick, craning his neck to see where the owl might have gone with his hand clamped over Dragon's pocket.

Doctor Columbarius caught Tamar's eye and smiled as the silence was shattered by a yell.

'Ow, Dragon! How many times? No fire when you're in my pocket!' Smoke billowed from Nick's jacket. '*Now* look what you've done!'

A black-edged hole had appeared in Nick's pocket framing a long snout. Dragon was desperate to get out.

Their host chuckled and watched the antics of the creature and its owner. Then he raised an eyebrow and the ceiling was restored to solid white plaster just as the door opened to reveal Mrs Beswetherick with a tray and a ginger and white cat at her side.

It stalked ahead of her, casually rubbing against the Guardians' legs as it sauntered towards the fire.

Gawain and Tamar exchanged glances.

Cathe had turned up again.

Arthur watched the creature settle by the fire, a further confirmation of their host's credibility. He wondered if Mrs Beswetherick had ever witnessed the shift in Cathe from a household pet to a wild beast. Somehow he doubted it.

'Ah, tea. Over by the fire if you would be so kind Mrs Beswetherick.' Their host rubbed his hands together and indicated a low table in front of the fire.

Mrs Beswetherick swept towards the stone fireplace, set the cakes on serving plates and arranged the scones and a pot of tea on the slate hearth.

'There you are Doctor,' she declared, standing back to admire her handiwork. 'Cherry cake and chocolate cake and toast, jam ...'

'Wonderful, thank you.'

Dragon quietened as Nick held his hand over the damaged pocket.

Mrs Beswetherick glanced towards the window and the darkening sky. 'They do give it for snow,' she stated. 'The forecast said it would be comin' in later.'

A vast Christmas tree stood in the far corner of the room lit by real candles. Nick happened to be the only one looking at it when a candle sizzled and some pine needles caught fire and flared.

He shot a panicked look towards their host but Falco Columbarius immediately caught his eye, winked, and glared at the tree while smoothly continuing the conversation.

'Do they indeed? Snow in Cornwall. How unusual,' he replied, watching as the flame was extinguished before Nick's startled eyes and behind the housekeeper's back.

'So don't you go keepin' these young people here late. I know as how you like to talk Doctor, but we don't want them stranded, now do we?'

'Indeed we don't Mrs B,' their host agreed, smiling at Nick. 'Speaking of which, we'll be perfectly fine if you want to be getting back to Mr Beswetherick. I expect you must be busy with your preparations for Christmas.'

'Well I do have a fair bit to do,' she agreed, wiping her

hands on her apron. 'Will you be all right to take the tray back to the kitchen?'

Falco Columbarius twinkled. 'I think we can manage that. Now off you go. You've worked quite hard enough for one day.'

'Well, if you're sure Doctor. The Christmas pudding is ready but I've still got the cake to ice and the mince pies to bake. The turkey is all plucked and cleaned but I have the whole family comin' so I'll 'ave to make sure we've got enough vegetables. There's my son Charlie an' his wife an' their two young 'uns, and then there's my Jess an' her 'ubby and baby, an' of course ...'

By now Doctor Columbarius was steering the housekeeper to the door as she continued to list her never-ending family.

'Mind you Doctor, Charlie's two aren't any trouble ...'

'I'm sure they're not Mrs B. Will you be all right to see yourself out?'

'Course I can see myself out! But don't forget what I was saying about the weather.'

'Would I dare?'

She shot him a glance and left.

'Well now,' their host exclaimed, closing the door. 'Tea, I think.'

He walked towards the fire, turned and, grasping his hands behind his back, surveyed his guests.

'Come and sit,' he said. 'We'll have brief introductions and then we'll eat.'

He paused. 'You can allow the dragon out, he'll be quite safe. I'm not expecting any callers.'

Their host strode over to the windows and pulled the curtains together, blotting out the dusky evening.

Nick heaved a sigh of relief and opened his pocket wide enough to allow Dragon to scrabble out. They watched the creature flex his wings and circumnavigate the ceiling, inspecting it for stray insects. Then Falco Columbarius reached out to a shelf which held not only books but a fascinating assortment of glass-lidded jars.

Choosing one, he held it up to the light and rattled it. The jar was filled with dead beetles. Their host tipped one out and held it in the palm of his hand.

Dragon surveyed the open hand suspiciously but eventually swooped on the snack.

'That's unusual,' Nick said, slightly jealous. 'Normally he'll only take food from me.'

'It's not me he likes, it's the beetle. These are a favourite.' Falco stroked the animal under his chin and Dragon stretched his neck and they heard a sound they'd never heard before: a dragon singing.

Dr Columbarius explained: 'The rare Malachite. The dragon song can be the most beautiful sound in the whole world or be the saddest song you've ever heard. It has the power to make you feel happier than you've ever felt, or to plunge you into the darkest despair.'

And at that moment, with the dragon blissfully happy and safe and close to Nick, the person it loved most of all (in its own tiny-dragon way), the song was beautiful.

Falco turned to Nick and, holding out his hand, transferred the dragon to his rightful owner. 'You found him on the path between Porth Talant and Porth Pyra?'

Nick nodded and their host smiled, satisfied. 'Good. That is how it was intended to be.'

He observed the once-stone dragon crunch another beetle and fly up to a high shelf.

'You've done well with him,' their host remarked. 'It's no easy task looking after a Malachite dragon.'

Tamar looked at Nick. He was glowing. It wasn't often that he received a compliment.

For a few moments Doctor Columbarius was lost in thought but then he gathered himself. 'I'm forgetting my manners, please, do make yourselves at home.'

He took his place in front of the fire and stood facing them, waiting for his guests to make themselves comfortable.

Nick chose a leather armchair and leant back to keep an eye on Dragon, while Gawain, Arthur and Tamar sat on the rug next to the dogs.

Their host smiled again, his eyes twinkling. 'I must thank you for coming in answer to my rather peremptory invitations. It was rude of me not to have introduced myself beforehand but time is not on our side ... so the usual social niceties had to be forgone.'

Nick's expression was a picture. This man was a walking dictionary.

'As you will have ascertained, I'm Doctor Falco Columbarius. I'm not a medical doctor, merely one who studies what many would consider less useful subjects, such as astronomy, archaeology, horology, our many languages and our planet's history. I do have other disciplines ...' their host gestured to the books lining the walls, 'but I don't wish to bore you before we start.'

He glanced at the book that Gawain was holding. Dr Columbarius took in the title and his smile grew as he considered the book and the boy. How very clever of them to find one another.

'Perhaps we'll do away with any unnecessary formalities, after all I know you and now you know me.'

Nick frowned. It was true that Falco Columbarius had known about Dragon, and he'd seen Cathe wrap himself around the doctor's legs, but that was all he knew about this man. How was *anyone* able to put out a fire with a glance – or have a ceiling which could be a sky?

'But we don't know you, do we?' he said. 'And to be honest this is all a bit weird.'

Tamar was horrified. 'Nick!'

'Well,' Nick declared, 'it's true!'

'No, no your friend is quite right to question me Tamar,' their host agreed. 'I sometimes forget that our journeys are different, that we move to our destinations along varying paths.'

He turned to Nick.

'Maybe I should add that we have mutual friends in Michael and Angela Jolly and that I have visited them in their cottage high on the moors near your home town.'

The dog lying next to Lightning yawned and stretched. Nick recognised him: it was Fly – Michael Jolly's dog. He cleared his throat.

'Perhaps I should also mention that Kitto Cornish and I have been friends for … well, for a very long time.'

'You have?' Gawain asked, astonished.

Dr Columbarius nodded. 'His shop is well known in certain circles for its treasures.'

Then Nick realised that the sword around his neck had been warm from the moment they'd walked through the gates. If he'd put his brain into gear he would have noticed. He'd put his foot in it again. A blush spread from his neck to his ears.

Dr Columbarius waited, watching Nick's face as these thoughts ran into one another.

Seeing the boy's embarrassment, he ran a finger along the frame of a painting and suggested, 'But you're right, Nick. It might be an idea for you to tell me something of your experiences and then we can discover where our stories meet.'

Their host was helping him to save face.

Nick hesitated. 'Well,' he began uncertainly, 'we met

Michael and Angela Jolly a couple of years ago ...' He trailed off, acutely embarrassed.

Arthur picked up on Nick's awkwardness. His friend hated being put on the spot. 'That was just after the storm and the Crow Man wasn't it?'

Nick nodded gratefully and Gawain chipped in. 'I hadn't met you then.'

'No, we didn't really get to know you until we were commissioned.'

And then they were reminiscing and cataloguing the people and animals and situations they'd encountered in the last couple of years; but Tamar was silent. She was darned if she was going to help Nick out when he'd been so rude to their host.

Instead she studied the painting above the fire.

Another white stag.

There was the one on the roof and that other one in the tiled hallway. She nibbled a fingernail and wondered what could be so important about a stag and silently considered their host, now sitting in his armchair, as he smiled and nodded and encouraged the boys. She was lost in thought, piecing the connections together, when Falco Columbarius glanced at her and flicked a meaningful look towards a clock quietly ticking on the wall.

She swallowed. She had a horrible feeling that the doctor had somehow read her thoughts and all the mean stuff she was thinking about Nick. But following his mute instruction she turned to examine the clock, and her watch did a little hiccup-tick in her pocket as her heart beat a little faster.

Hanging on the wall was a splendid pendulum clock. Unlike most clocks the face was a flat ring just wide enough for the numerals. Inside the ring, the brass cogs which would usually be hidden from view, gleamed and rotated, interlocking and turning in perfect harmony. And now Tamar knew without a doubt where her dress, with the embroidered cogs spinning across the velvet bodice, had come from. She was right. This man knew all about them – and that she was the Time Keeper. And then a realisation hit her smack on.

Of course! This is the guy I met in the woods this morning!

It was the man who'd quietened the watch and sent the hunt away. His beard was trimmed now, not trailing over his chest, and he was wearing different clothes, but he was definitely the same person. And if she was right, that person was Merlin.

She was vaguely aware of the boys talking and the fire crackling and the hedgehog in a warm corner close to the hearth, but her mind was in overdrive. Then she caught sight of an engraving on the clock's pendulum. It was her name. Her heart lurched and she turned back to find Dr Columbarius watching her.

The conversation had moved on. The boys had brought their host up to date with the events of the morning – the barrel organ, the woodcarver and the mini-earthquake – and were moving on to the relatively mundane matters of how to look after a Malachite dragon and the best way to cope with time travel.

Tamar waited for a lull in the conversation. 'Um, thanks for the dress and everything.'

Their host smiled. 'My pleasure. I trust it was restored to its former state when you arrived back?'

Tamar nodded and he smiled, satisfied, and gestured towards the table. 'And *now* it's time for tea.'

Nick didn't need a second invitation; he'd been eyeing the table for the past few minutes. So his mouth was full when they heard the crash against the window and the scrabbling high on the roof above them.

Chapter 9
First move

Falco Columbarius didn't appear to hurry towards the window.

There was the crash and then he was pulling the curtains apart, slipping his fingers under the window frame and sliding it up. A blast of icy air swept the room – accompanied by several black feathers.

The doctor stood back to reveal his owl teetering on the window ledge. 'Come in Tyto.'

The owl blinked and waddled over the sill, proudly displaying a dark feather in its beak, while Arthur retrieved a feather which had landed at his feet. He looked up as the owl dropped the feather in its master's open hand and again another piece of text swam in front of his eyes.

'Crows have few natural enemies; however, some birds of prey may attack these birds. The owl could be considered the crow's most well-known adversary.'

Dr Columbarius shot him a sharp-eyed look and deep words penetrated Arthur's mind. Although they weren't specific they were congratulating him on his research and on the accuracy of his deduction. The owl had seen off a crow – and it was unlikely to be just any crow.

Dragon swooped towards the open window but their host slid it down, foiling the tiny creature's escape plan.

Falco stared into the dusk, his fingers gripping the window sill. Gawain was the only one who saw the white shape melt into the woods. The man turned around, his back to the window and surveyed his guests.

'That was a stag wasn't it?' Gawain stated.

The doctor nodded.

'A stag?' Arthur was puzzled.

'A white one. A white stag.'

Tamar looked from Arthur to Gawain. 'Okay ... so apart from them being rare, what's so important about a white stag?'

'Well, I'd always thought it was just a superstition,' Gawain began, stroking the spine of the book.

'Go on,' Tamar said.

'Well there are a couple of ideas,' Gawain began, darting an uncertain look at Dr Columbarius. 'One is that a white stag would appear if someone was trespassing somewhere special.'

Falco nodded.

'And the other idea?' Nick asked, monitoring Dragon approach Tyto on her shelf.

Gawain was quiet for a few seconds before he continued. 'Well, the other theory or legend is to do with,' he swallowed, 'is to do with King Arthur.'

Nick considered Arthur, his friend since infant school. 'Could it be to do with you then?' Nick asked.

Arthur looked at Falco Columbarius. The man was leaning back against the window with his arms folded. He nodded at the boy, his eyes fathomless, encouraging him to speak.

'Umm, yes, it could be.' Arthur began. 'But when the white stag appeared it wasn't just about King Arthur ... it could be the signal that a quest was about to start that would involve all the knights.'

Doctor Columbarius glanced towards the shelf where Tyto was perched. Dragon had sidled close to her and the owl was surveying him suspiciously.

'*Comero weeth*,' Falco muttered, just as Tyto let out an impatient screech.

'Dragon, come here!' Nick commanded, but the dragon didn't need to be told. A grumpy owl is a match even for a small fire-breathing dragon.

'Is there such a thing as a quest in the twenty-first century?' Tamar asked the doctor.

'Are there such things as travelling through time or miniature dragons, Miss Tamblyn?'

'Oh! I see what you mean.'

'So, if there's going to be a quest ...' Gawain began.

'Will it involve us?' Nick finished.

The doctor considered the stag's reappearance.

Events were moving at a more rapid pace than even he'd anticipated. Falco stroked his beard and surveyed the four young people in front of him.

'I think it will Nick, each one of you and probably others too.'

His gaze swept over Gawain, whose birth and parentage had been kept a carefully guarded secret. He watched as the lanky boy ran his fingers through his dark, tousled hair, a habit inherited from his father and his great-great-grandfather. He took in those amber eyes flecked with gold, so like the eyes of the boy's mother, and contemplated Gawain's ability to perceive things beyond the visible world. Another trait passed on from his mother. She would be proud of the person her son had become. Falco made a mental note to congratulate Kitto Cornish on the way he'd raised him.

'Gawain, I'm going to give you this.' He picked out a walking stick from several clustered in an umbrella stand. 'You might have seen one before.'

Gawain put the book down.

'As I think you already know, its appearance is deceptive. There's a lot more to it than meets the eye.'

'Is it a sword cane?' Gawain held it carefully.

Their host nodded. 'Open it. Press the top, the part that's carved like an owl.'

Gingerly, Gawain did as he was instructed and immediately the top sprang apart.

'Always choose where and how to use it. It's a lethal weapon and should never fall into the wrong hands. Respect it and it will serve you well.'

Gawain slid the sword out of its casing. The blade was razor sharp and almost perfect. But near the top of the blade, close to its handle, there were a series of tiny notches in the metal. Gawain ran the tip of his finger over them. Straight away shouts filled the room and blood-curdling screams echoed off the walls and Dragon darted up to the ceiling.

Dr Columbarius rushed forward and seized the sword. 'Quiet memories!' He ordered. 'I'll have none of that. You must obey your new owner.'

The shouts and screams faded and Dragon flew back to his master.

'Wow!' Nick exclaimed. 'Now that's what I call a secret weapon. Just deafen your enemies.'

'What did I do?' Gawain asked, shaken.

'I should have warned you,' Falco said. 'The sword has memories. Each one of those marks is a fight. The sword was re-living them. Your touch brought them to life.'

He held out the sword to Gawain.

'It's safe now. Unless you want them, the memories will remain silent. However, if you should ever wish to use them just pass your finger over the notches and the sword will understand you. You are its master now.'

'Cool!' Nick was impressed. 'That's some sword cane. I bet Dr Watson didn't have one like that.'

'No he didn't. His was rather more ordinary, which is what you would expect.'

Gawain slipped the blade back into the casing. 'I've no idea how to use a sword.'

'It will come to you. After all it is in your blood.'

'In my blood?'

'I'll explain later,' Falco Columbarius said. 'Time is pressing. Sometimes it can be very insistent, almost rude. Don't you agree Miss Tamblyn?'

Tamar nodded, all too aware of the pocket watch and its abilities.

But while Falco Columbarius talked, a part of him was studying Nick. With training this young man could be an excellent knight.

And of course there was the girl, the Time Keeper. He'd watched her struggle to keep her quick temper under control, her brown eyes flashing at Nick, but he'd also seen her speedy analysis of the clock and the way that she'd silently observed his first encounter with Arthur. She too could be trained in the art of sword play.

'It's going to be dangerous isn't it?' Deep words knocked on Falco's mind. Arthur was looking at him.

Only the truth could be spoken between deep speakers. Falco replied reluctantly, 'I wish I could tell you otherwise.'

'Shouldn't I be armed then?'

'You will have Excalibur. It will find you when the time is right. In the meantime use the deep words. You know how much pain can be inflicted if they are used with power.'

Falco watched Arthur turning the black feather between his fingers. No one would guess that he was engaged in conversation.

'I've never used it to hurt anybody – except a skeleton. And nor should you under normal circumstances, but we live in interesting times.'

Tyto had settled, preening her feathers, while the hedgehog lay curled in a tight ball in her usual corner. Both dogs were once again splayed out in front of the fire when another feather floated down the chimney to land and flare in the heart of the flames. The light in the room dimmed and the temperature dropped.

The doctor took a breath and said, aloud this time, 'It appears we will not be allowed too much time together this afternoon.' The wind whistled.

'They're close, aren't they?' Arthur asked, also resuming normal conversation.

Their host nodded grimly, his eyes clouding. 'They are, Arthur, and it's getting dark outside. We cannot risk a night walk. They like the dark. They're at their strongest when they work with the night and of course we're only just past the winter solstice.'

'They're pretty strong any time!' Nick said, thinking of their various encounters with the Crow Man, Hagarawall and the Ice Lady.

'True,' Falco Columbarius agreed. 'However, we mustn't play into their hands. There's much to discuss but we all have work to do.'

He glanced at a grandfather clock standing in a dark corner and the room stilled: the hands on the clocks halted, the flames froze, and the light dimmed. Briefly, their host fixed each Guardian with an intense look.

And immediately Arthur was on a galloping horse, sword in hand, as a great sense of loss corkscrewed its way into his soul. Tamar stood in a muddy field surrounded by tents and horses and people, while Gawain's world was filled with squealing brakes and panicked cries and sirens mixed with flashing lights. Falco Columbarius's face was grim, remembering the night that had made Gawain an orphan as a baby – however, the future would begin to show itself soon.

But Nick didn't see anything. He just felt a dark despair mixed with minor notes. And, although he'd never heard it before, he knew it was the song of a dying dragon.

Dr Columbarius blinked. It was as he thought. He sighed. Gathering himself he glanced at the clock and fixed a smile on his face as the ticks resumed and the flames danced. And the Guardians' dreams, or nightmares, were instantly forgotten.

Arthur got to his feet. 'We'd better go then.'

'Yes but not the way you came, although it would be perfectly safe while you were in the grounds of my house because only those who are invited may set foot here. There's a different way we can take that will deliver you into the heart of the village. As soon as you get there you must hurry to the fair.'

The doctor pulled a blue cloak off the back of one of the chairs. Swinging it over his shoulders, he said, 'I will guide you to the gate.'

He looked at his owl perched on the shelf and instructed, 'Tyto, keep guard whilst I'm gone.'

The owl blinked.

'And don't go to sleep!'

Gesturing to the dragon curled up on Nick's shoulder he suggested, 'I should tuck him well away. This walk may be a little too interesting for him.'

Falco Columbarius turned towards an alcove on the right-hand side of the fire. He retrieved a large brass key from his trouser pocket and slotted it into a hole in the wall.

This wall wasn't plastered or painted. It was plain, grey stone. The moment the key turned, the stone wall juddered and a low arched door, which hadn't been visible before, swung open.

Their host plucked a candle from a holder next to the door and a staff from the umbrella stand and turned to his guests. 'A centuries-old escape route. You will not be the first to benefit from the forethought of its architect.'

He glanced at Gawain. 'Take the sword cane Gawain, it may be of use to you.'

And then he turned, ducking his head under the low stone frame, and led the way into the corridor. The candle flickered. 'There is a handle on the inside of the door. Whoever is last through, please be kind enough to close it.'

'You go first,' Nick said to Arthur. 'We'll follow our glorious leader.'

Arthur shook his head and followed Falco.

Tamar was last. The cat sped through the doorway as she grasped the iron handle – the metal was warm.

The floor, walls and roof of the corridor were stone. It was more of a tunnel than a corridor, but it also had the same self-lighting candles set into the wall that had lit them to the library. This was fortunate because although the first couple of metres were level, very quickly the floor began to fall away.

'Mind your step,' Falco Columbarius called over his shoulder. 'The floor becomes steeper, there's quite a drop from my house to the village so the path has to tunnel under the hill, and it's damp so it can be slippery. There's a rope handle strung along the wall. Hold onto that and you should be fine.'

Lightning's legs slid and slithered on the damp rock. The dog fought for control but he came perilously close to tripping Arthur.

'Careful!' Arthur exclaimed, hopping to the side.

Lightning whined and deep dog-words trickled into Arthur's brain. He was doing his best.

Meanwhile, Gawain was having his own problems. He'd hung the sword cane through a loop on his belt but with every step he took it swung around and whipped his legs.

They mostly walked in silence apart from the odd, 'No! Stay in my pocket,' from Nick, and the occasional, 'Ow!' from Gawain. Now and then a drop of water would drip down their necks and then there would be a, 'Yuck, that's disgusting!'

Cobwebs swayed from the roof and candles flickered, sending long shadows up the walls. From time to time their guide would mutter quiet words – Arthur would have given anything to know who Falco Columbarius was talking to; it could have been any one of their allies.

Eventually, after what seemed like a long time, the floor began to level out and the air felt fresher. And at last the slippery stone gave way to a cobbled path, but the roof was lower down here and Nick, who was the tallest and didn't know its layout, yelped. 'What's that!'

He brushed his head; something was tangled in his hair.

Fine tree roots dangled through the now-earth ceiling. Tamar began to giggle but then their host turned, his cloak swirling, and pulled the hood over his head plunging his hollow-cheeked face into shadow. They'd reached the end of the tunnel.

'You must make haste. They will know of our meeting and will be even more determined to find you.'

Dr Columbarius paused before pinning each one of them with those far-seeing eyes. 'There are others who are going to be summoned to our cause but we are not all yet assembled. There are some who still need to be brought here.'

And as he said this he looked directly at Tamar and the watch's ticks quickened in her pocket. *At last!* the pocket watch ticked. *More travel.*

A sudden pain caught Falco between his ribs as his gaze took in Nick. He knew only too well what that feeling promised but he gathered himself enough to say, 'Nick, you must keep your dragon close to you. Whatever happens, don't allow yourselves to become separated.'

Then he turned, shielding his face from the Guardians. 'We'll meet again soon. *Tereba nessa.* Till the next time.'

He pushed the door and the cat slipped past his legs. 'Remember that although the grounds of Oakwood Manor are secured against uninvited guests, both this door, and the gates, will know you.'

Falco risked a quick smile and inspected the lane.

He caught sight of the Writer's workers, Servo and Viatoris, waiting further up the street. Glancing at Servo's feet he noticed that the Watcher was wearing sandals. He must have been to his other assignment in Egypt. However, apart from these silent observers, the street was quiet.

Cathe padded down the lane towards the fair and Dr Columbarius was a little comforted. No doubt the cat would have his own supporters close by.

Falco ushered them through the little wooden door, briefly touching their heads as they passed, a sort of blessing, and sent deep words of encouragement to Arthur. 'Remember you're never alone … and keep that whistle to hand.'

Arthur's head jerked up. He hadn't mentioned the whistle. It was tucked under his shirt against his chest.

But out loud their host was saying, *'Tenestatha, comero weeth.'* ('Goodnight, take care.')

It was almost dark, the last hint of daylight disappearing beneath glowering, black clouds. Snowflakes rose and fell on the strengthening wind and a white carpet replaced the slate-grey of the road and roofs. Mrs Beswetherick's prediction had been right.

They'd arrived in the centre of the village, far from the other way into Oakwood Manor. Arthur cast a quick look over his shoulder to see their cloaked friend stooped in the low doorway, supported by a wooden staff and lit by a single candle. The door of the tunnel was set into a wall, which was itself set into a low, tree-covered hill. Further up and down the lane, the hill dropped down behind the wall and the stone border of Oakwood Manor curved away, to be replaced by cottages.

Again deep words slid into his brain and Arthur answered, carefully shielding the words and adding the name that he had been longing to say. 'I'll be careful … Merlin.'

Chapter 10
Rozen for Red

Rozen Tregenza watched the Guardians slip out of the tunnel from the shelter of the cottage doorway. She'd glimpsed the hooded figure close the door behind Arthur. She'd also seen a cat slip out and make its way towards the fair and was aware of a couple of dark shapes higher up the lane, although she couldn't quite make them out. (She thought that one of them may have been the man – or nearly man – who had been at the station before the boys had arrived, but for some reason they didn't bother her; they felt sort of neutral.)

She'd considered her dad's warnings, and his pleas for her to be careful, but she knew she hadn't a choice.

'And I am fourteen,' she thought. 'I'm old enough to make my own decisions.'

She thought about her father, always nervously on the lookout for their enemies. Playing it safe didn't necessarily mean being happy. Perhaps being prepared to risk everything would be a relief after living in the shadows.

The girl hesitated for a moment before firmly clamping a grey silk top hat over her red curls and stepping out of the doorway. 'It's now or never, Rozen,' she told herself sternly. 'No second thoughts.' Arthur and his friends had already walked quite a way down the lane.

'Come on,' she ordered herself as she buttoned her grey jacket and tucked her scarf around her neck. 'It's time to make a commitment.'

Overhead a barn owl floated in the darkening sky, while in the window of a nearby cottage a pale-faced witness held a pen and waited.

'Tamar,' Rozen called as loudly as she dared. 'Tamar, stop!' And she ran down the lane towards the group.

As soon as they saw her they were on the defensive. She saw Gawain fiddle with a cane strung through his belt as they moved together: four against one.

'It's okay,' she said, holding out her hands, palms up. 'I'm on your side.' She glanced at the cane. 'You can keep the sword cane in its case.'

Gawain frowned. How did she know it was a sword cane?

They took in the girl's top hat perched over a mass of red corkscrew curls, her grey jacket nipped in at the waist, and long grey skirt. Even her eyes were grey.

She blurted, 'They're really close … those men and that boy, and they know where you've been.' She held on to her hat, pressing it firmly over her hair. Its occupant wasn't happy.

Arthur asked, 'Oh, and where have we been?'

'And how come you know my name?' Tamar added.

After their meeting with Dr Columbarius and his hints of what may lie in wait they were even more on edge.

'I heard you talking at the fair,' the girl replied quickly.

She didn't look like a threat but anything was possible.

'Look, there's no time for this!' she said. 'I don't think they've gone far.'

No one budged.

'Oh, okay then. I'm Rozen Tregenza and my dad's here. I think you met him this morning. He carves wood and stuff.' She pointed at Gawain's sword cane. 'He makes things like that, and whistles, and other bits and pieces.'

Still no one spoke.

'His stall is an old caravan and we've got a horse.' She caught them looking at her clothes. 'I do an act – this is my costume.' She felt like shouting at them. What else could she say to convince them?

And then a movement in Nick's pocket caught her eye. 'And he knows what small dragons like to eat.'

At last Arthur's frown began to disappear and Gawain's hold on the cane relaxed.

'Now I know where I've seen you,' Arthur began. 'You're that little girl's sister aren't you? The one we met on the beach this morning.'

'D'you mean the weird kid?' Nick blurted out.

'Yeah, the one who told us about the island being unhappy.'

Rozen nodded. 'That's my sister.'

Arthur stroked Lightning, calming him, and looked at Rozen. 'She told us some pretty bizarre things.' He hesitated before adding, 'Um, I don't mean this in a rude way, but she's not quite normal is she?'

Rozen shook her head. 'Suppose not. Though to be honest none of my family are.'

The boys thought of their encounter with her father, the woodcarver. That part was certainly true.

'Gwen can *see* stuff but she hasn't learnt *how* to tell people what she sees. We've been trying to teach her to break things to folks more gently but she always jumps right in at the deep end. It really worries some people.'

'No kidding!' Nick exclaimed.

'She doesn't mean to,' Rozen objected. 'She's only little; she just says it as it is.

'Well perhaps you could teach her more quickly. It's

pretty weird, especially for ordinary people who aren't used to fortune-tellers,' Nick suggested.

'You guys hardly class as ordinary,' Rozen said. 'Anyone who's been invited to Oakwood Manor has to be unusual.' At which point Dragon poked his snout out of his master's pocket. She raised her eyebrows. 'See?'

Tamar was frowning as she examined the girl's red hair and long skirt and then her face cleared. 'You're the girl who saw the tent appear!' Her eyes narrowed. 'And weren't you at the station?'

'Yeah.'

'Well, all of that stuff may be true but how do we know that you're on our side and not just spying on us?' Nick asked. 'What proof have you got?'

'And,' Tamar added, 'if you're really on our side, why did you keep running away?'

'I'm here now aren't I?' Rozen countered. There wasn't time for this. They'd spent too much time talking already. 'Your swords,' she offered, 'are they cold or warm?'

Immediately each of the Guardians had their hands at their throats and looked at one another. Nick nodded at Arthur. And Tamar, feeling the pocket watch's excited ticks, stated, 'The watch seems to think that she's okay too.'

'How d'you know about the swords?' Arthur began. But seeing the girl's desperate expression he said, 'Okay never mind, we'll talk later.'

The girl peered down the lane winding its way through the cottages towards the sea. Somehow the men had covered their footprints even though it could only have been a few minutes since they'd hurried away. Although the snow was falling, it wasn't falling fast enough to cover such large indents. How had they done that? She couldn't waste another minute.

'That man – Brane, the guy with the crow – was further up the lane near where you came out. He was with the others.' She paused. 'They were all waiting. I heard them talking. They were discussing whether to stay but the pale guy with the dog …'

'Hagarawall?' Arthur suggested.

'Yeah, him. He said it wasn't a good idea to be close to Dr Columbarius's grounds.'

'Who else was here,' Tamar asked, 'apart from Brane and Hagarawall and the dog?'

'That boy, the one with the silvery hair and the silver jacket.'

'I wondered if he was one of them.'

'Was a woman here?' Arthur asked.

The girl shook her head.

'That's something anyway,' Gawain muttered.

'I wonder how long they've been around,' Arthur mused. 'Not just here in the lane – in Trezion.'

'Well the pale guy came down on the same train as you,' Rozen informed him.

'He did?'

Rozen nodded.

There was a stunned silence. For some reason they all thought that they would have seen their enemies as soon as they arrived. Tamar shuddered. The boy had crept up on her so quietly that she hadn't noticed him until he'd spoken. She thought about the way he'd looked at her pocket; he must have known the watch was there. And then she remembered him snatching her hair.

A dull, sick feeling lodged in her throat. He could have so easily overpowered her and taken the watch. But then she recalled the whistle-playing Father Christmas and the boy's fear. The Father Christmas had come to her rescue.

'So what do we do now?' Nick asked.

'A good question …' a voice drawled.

Tamar spun around. The silver-haired boy had done it again: crept up on them without any warning. Only this time he was accompanied by a white dog which they all recognised. It was Matearnas's albino hound. It appeared to have found a new owner.

***

In her cottage the Writer surveyed the scene.

She took in the snow-covered lane and the tightly packed cottages with their curtains drawn against the night. All their inhabitants would either be tucked up in front of fires watching their televisions or down at the fair. No one would be likely to interrupt them.

She turned her attention back to the silver-haired boy. Cador was taking things into his own hands again, calling the shots ahead of his mother's followers. She imagined Hagarawall's frustration and allowed herself a satisfied smile.

She watched Rozen fiddle with her hat. It had taken guts for the girl to throw in her lot with the young king and the Guardians.

The Writer's hands were still, folded on the desk in front of her. A pair of round spectacles hung on their string around her neck as she pondered on the young people. The quilled pen sat on the desk and the ink pot waited, but soon the Writing would begin. She had that dull ache in her ear lobe which always preceded a momentous event.

Something was going to happen to the Guardians.

***

'Maybe,' Cador continued, 'you could bring everything to its inevitable conclusion.'

Nick gripped Dragon's scaly back. The creature's tail was twitching. Gawain fiddled with the sword cane's clasp, desperate to release it from the case.

'Which is?' Arthur asked, his hand on Lightning's head as the dog gave a low growl. The whistle lay ready beneath his shirt.

'Do I need to spell it out to you?'

'Yes you do.' The sword around Arthur's neck was cold, and was getting colder.

The boy flicked a snowflake off his silver jacket. 'Don't you love snow? Isn't winter so much better than summer?'

'What are you getting at?'

'You can't guess?'

And Tamar was taken back to the previous summer in Porth Pyra when she'd been captured by the Lady of Clehy. She remembered the ice seeping into her veins from the woman's touch. This boy was something to do with her – with the Ice Lady. But then she recalled the discussion she'd had with the boy about Christmas, and the effect just speaking the word had on him.

'Winter's okay, but personally I prefer Christmas,' she burst out, hoping she was right. She watched for a reaction and saw the barely suppressed shudder. Deep in her pocket the watch's ticks quietened.

Nick looked at her as if she'd completely lost it. 'What?'

'I like *Christmas*,' Tamar repeated.

'Oh,' said Rozen after a pause, picking up on the stress on the word. 'So do I, *Christmas* is the best time of year. I love *Christmas* cake …'

'And *Christmas* presents …' Tamar added, throwing Rozen a grateful look.

'Yes, and what about *Christmas* trees? They're lovely, especially when the lights are on.'

'What's your favourite part of *Christmas*?' Tamar asked the boys innocently, but they were just looking at her and Rozen as if they'd gone mad.

'Come on, you must have a best bit of *Christmas*,' she urged, because with every mention of the word, the boy's complexion had paled.

Cador managed to say, 'Forget it Miss Tamblyn, that won't work!' but he looked sick.

However, a voice from the shadows declared, 'Perhaps they really are as stupid as they appear.' A crow hopped into the centre of the lane followed by its master. 'Maybe we'll be forced to spell it out to them.'

Brane walked to the side of the silver-haired boy and, summoning the crow to his shoulder, bowed ironically, his coal-black eyes fixed on Arthur. 'We meet again, *sire*.'

And despite all that he had learnt, and even though he had his friends at his side, Arthur was immediately back in Station Road in Lyskeret making his first encounter with the Crow Man. His stomach lurched and the whistle lay forgotten. Every time they met, Brane succeeded in reducing him to a quivering wreck.

The crow gave one harsh 'caw' and Brane said, 'I know. Have patience.'

He informed Arthur, 'The bird is impatient because he knows that one of your number carries something glittering which is rightfully ours. Apart, that is, from your kingship.'

'My "kingship", as you put it, was given to me by King Arthur. You know that. You were there when the Lady of the Lake gave me the sword and when the king passed his crown on to me.' Arthur replied. 'And apart from Excalibur, which even you can see isn't here, we don't have anything "glittering".'

'Oh but you do,' a voice said behind them. And Hagarawall stepped from a side alley to stand directly behind Tamar. 'And I think you know what it is.'

The pocket watch was as close to silent as it could be. The tiny machine was doing its best to hold its ticks.

Lightning whined but Arthur said, 'No, not yet.'

'Everything we've got has been given to us for *us* to use,' Tamar interrupted, her fingers wrapped around the watch in her pocket. 'Not for you or anyone else.'

Arthur and his friends were standing in a line across the narrow lane with Nick on the outside, Gawain next to him and then Arthur and Tamar. Rozen had been facing them but with Cador's appearance she'd positioned herself beside Tamar. So now the five of them were hemmed in between two rows of ancient cottages with the Crow Man and Cador and the dog in front of them and Hagarawall at their back. It wasn't a good position to be in.

Hagarawall took a step forward. 'It would be better for everyone Miss Tamblyn, if you gave us the timepiece immediately. That way no one needs to get hurt.'

She could feel his breath on her neck.

'No one,' she began, more boldly than she felt, 'no one will ever take it from me. I'm its custodian and my name's inscribed on it. *I'm* the Time Keeper.' The watch ticked gratefully. 'Maybe your mistress is hoping that the damage it did to her can be un-done, but that won't happen.'

Her voice shook. She took a deep breath and met the Crow Man's eyes.

'The injury it inflicted on the Lady of Clehy was her own fault.'

Her palm vibrated to the watch's ticks.

'No one else will have it until the next Time Keeper takes over.'

The Crow Man clapped slowly. 'A commendable speech Miss Tamblyn. But words are only words.' He paused. 'Don't they say that actions speak louder than words?'

'They do indeed,' Gawain chipped in, swiftly slipping the sword out of its case. What did he have to do to make the memories shout? He cursed; he'd completely forgotten.

From her window the Writer watched and murmured, 'Blood will out.'

And Gawain had the sword raised and was at Tamar's side as Arthur shouted, 'Lightning, attack!'

Rozen raised her hat, declaring, 'All for one …' and released a falcon from her up-ended silk topper. The bird took to the skies before spinning around to come plunging back to earth with the crow in its sights.

Nick was about to let Dragon go when Tamar pulled the watch out of her pocket and shouted, 'No! Stop!'

They froze and Arthur said, 'What are you doing, Tamblyn?'

But Tamar had fixed the Crow Man with a determined stare. 'You know what happens if the wrong person touches it don't you? Remember what happened to your precious Lady.'

Without taking her eyes off Brane and the boy she said to her friends, 'Gawain, I don't think that this is the right battle; I don't think it's meant to be here. Not yet anyway. Rozen, call your bird to you.'

She advanced towards the Crow Man, trying to ignore Hagarawall behind her, trusting that when it came to it he wouldn't have the courage to touch the timepiece, and whispered, 'Maybe if you try to take it the same thing will happen to you. Perhaps *your* hands will wrinkle and *your* hair will turn grey.'

Arthur wasn't sure about this. It was a gamble.

Tamar's heart was beating faster than the pocket watch's terrified ticks.

'Maybe,' she continued, 'maybe it won't stop at that. Perhaps your skin and muscle will wither and all that will be left will be your skeleton – and a skeleton crow.'

She watched the Crow Man's eyes dart between the watch and Arthur and saw the tightening of his jaw. He was weighing up the risks. But she was aware of something else happening too. It felt like electricity was flowing above her.

A flicker of silver caught her eye. Gawain hadn't sheathed the sword. And she noticed that although Rozen had called her falcon back, it was still perched on her arm. None of them knew whether the watch would have the same power over the Crow Man.

Arthur watched Brane. He was certain he could feel deep words zinging between their enemies, and then words escaped from Cador. He couldn't have been taught how to avoid them bleeding into space. He heard, 'Why wait?' from the boy before it was buried in a barrage of purples and browns and blacks. They were having a furious argument, although you'd never know it unless you were a deep speaker.

'Why not make our move now?' Cador was suggesting. 'They are together. None of their other supporters are here; it could be the perfect chance.'

But the Crow Man was saying, 'No, the girl and her watch could be dangerous. Remember what injury she inflicted on the Lady with that timepiece.'

Hagarawall didn't need reminding. Within seconds wrinkles and veins had appeared on her hands and her beautiful blonde hair had been exchanged for a dull grey. Now the Lady of Clehy wore velvet gloves at all times.

In the cottage the quilled pen leapt up and dipped itself into the ink. Red words spilled across the page. The Writer read the words as they sprawled across the paper and Servo's voice knocked on her mind.

'Ma'am,' he began, 'do we have to merely stand and Watch?'

She shook her head, returning a sharp reprimand. Both the Watchers knew that absolutely no interference was permitted. Events had to be allowed to unfold in their natural order. She focused on the mottled paper and then glanced out of the window to see the events being written about taking place in front of her.

Hagarawall was glancing around checking that they were unobserved, before making his move. Sending deep words to Brane and Cador, he stepped from behind Tamar towards Nick.

And Arthur was clutching his head and crumpling as the Crow Man and Cador fired a volley of white-hot curses towards the young king's brain. They were supporting Hagarawall's initiative and proving that deep words could indeed be used to powerful effect.

Gawain raised his sword again, fumbling with the blade but it was already too late. Their enemies had out-manoeuvred them.

They'd been so busy concentrating on Tamar, the watch and the Crow Man that none of Arthur's allies had noticed Hagarawall station himself behind Nick.

None of them had seen Hagarawall wrap his arm around Nick's neck and pull Dragon out of his pocket.

Nick was tall but Hagarawall was taller and stronger. The man squeezed Dragon's neck and the tiny beast squealed, his tail flicking.

Hagarawall smiled as Nick's friends turned and he saw their horrified expressions.

He began to edge backwards, dragging his captive with him. 'Maybe the watch can do damage Miss Tamblyn, but can you imagine the injury I can inflict on this creature?' And grinning, he squeezed Dragon's neck again, keeping the snout facing forward so no fire could reach him. This time Dragon didn't squeal but simply hung between his captor's fingers.

'If you try to help your friend I'm very much afraid that this creature will have to be sacrificed ... which would be a shame. Don't you agree?'

Hagarawall hissed in Nick's ear, 'Now, Dragon Boy, which would *you* prefer – to be rescued or to keep your pet alive?'

Nick didn't say a word but his friends watched his colour drain.

Hagarawall tightened his hold on his prisoner's neck and took another couple of steps backwards, forcing his captive to stumble with him.

Gawain still had the sword at the ready as he watched Hagarawall pull Nick's head back but he knew what he would say. If he'd been able to speak there was no way he'd want them to risk harming Dragon. One more squeeze and the creature's neck could be broken.

Gawain hurriedly gestured to Rozen to put the bird away and cast a quick look towards Tamar who was almost as pale as Nick.

There was no way she'd put Dragon in danger.

Arthur dragged himself to his feet. The salvo of deep words had left his head stinging and he felt horribly sick. So much for his ability to use the deep speech against his enemies. He'd crumbled at the first word.

'This is all wrong,' he said, swallowing the bile in his throat.

He looked up and caught the imploring look in Nick's eyes. He wished he could send deep words to his friend but instead he just had to stand and watch Nick being dragged down the lane while Dragon hung in Hagarawall's hand. He spun around to shout at Brane and Cador, but no one was there. They'd faded into the night. All that was left were their rapidly disappearing footprints.

Hagarawall's voice echoed off the cottage walls. 'Don't try to follow us. We'll know if you attempt to find us and then I'm very much afraid that someone – or something – will have to pay.'

Rozen and the Guardians and their king stood frozen, immobilised by the threat ringing along the lane.

'You can't do this!' Arthur shouted, but his words were muffled by the falling snow.

Rozen watched the footprints disappear. Even before they'd been filled by snow they'd begun to fade. Gawain slipped the sword back into the cane. They'd been outwitted.

Chapter 11
Time and Uncle Kitto

Eventually Rozen broke the silence. 'I'm so sorry ...'

No one responded.

Snow crystals settled on their hair. Lightning whined and the watch's hands quivered.

'What?' Tamar mumbled.

'I should have known that would happen, or at least sensed them nearby.'

Gawain looked up from studying his feet. 'So should I.'

Rozen and Gawain gazed at one another and Arthur stared into the middle distance – and at last remembered the whistle.

'This shouldn't have been allowed to happen,' Tamar said to no one in particular. 'Why wasn't Cathe here? Or Michael and Angela, or Dr Columbarius? There are all these people – and animals – who are meant to be on our side and not a single one of them showed up!'

A second later her shoulders sagged. 'But it's all my fault isn't it? I shouldn't have stopped you using the sword, Gawain.' She felt sick.

She had first-hand knowledge of how their enemies worked and now Nick and Dragon would as well. This whole horrible mess was her fault. 'What are we going to do?'

***

From her window the Writer looked on, the pen had quietened and the ink was drying. She glanced up the lane, away from the little group towards where her Watchers should be. Viatoris was alone.

'Where's Servo?' she asked sharply. He *would* choose now to disappear.

'He's with the boy and the dragon,' Viatoris replied, his thoughts interrupted by her question. 'He took it on himself to go with them.'

The Writer's eyebrows arched. 'Did he indeed?'

Viatoris added, 'He expects all to be quiet in Egypt for a while, ma'am; he felt it imperative that he accompany those others.'

She was quietly impressed. 'That's good, but I will need you here.'

Viatoris bowed. 'Of course, ma'am.'

Then she commanded, 'Hush – Watch!' as a snow-flecked figure strode down the lane with a dog at his side.

***

Rozen considered Arthur and Gawain and Tamar. She'd only just met them and yet this catastrophe had happened. No matter what Tamar said, she felt responsible. She could have done something earlier but she hadn't. She stroked the falcon and the bird's head swivelled as it regarded her. She couldn't imagine having it threatened as Dragon had been threatened.

And Gawain's mind was full of the memories he generally tried to forget: his own vicious kidnapping by the Crow Man. Brutality ran in Brane's blood, and now Nick was his captive. He looked past the cottages and felt wretched - and then he realised something else.

Not one curtain had twitched throughout their

encounter – even though there'd been enough shouting to have most people at their front doors. Somehow the Crow Man had organised that too, just as he'd arranged the beach at Porth Talant to empty last summer. Blankly, he stared up the lane, and then he focused and peered through the snow. There could only be one man who strode out like that; hope glimmered.

'Michael? Is that you?'

Snow swirled, obscuring the figure.

'Arthur, is that Michael?' Flakes eddied and swam in front of their eyes.

Arthur pulled himself out of his reverie and stared. 'I'm not sure.' He narrowed his eyes. A tall, broad-shouldered figure with a head of shoulder-length white hair was striding towards them, his long coat flapping. 'I think it might be!'

And sure enough Lightning took off, tail whipping, towards the other dog. Fly had left Oakwood Manor.

'It is,' Gawain said. 'It's definitely him!' And straight away Arthur and Gawain were pounding up the lane towards their old friend, but Tamar didn't move. She was waiting for him to reach her.

Rozen was intrigued by the stranger, by his height and authority and charisma, so it was only when Tamar spoke that she registered that the Time Keeper wasn't as happy as the boys.

'Where were you?' Tamar exploded as soon as he was near enough to hear her.

Her voice was shaking. 'Where were you when we needed you? They've got Nick and they've got Dragon and you weren't here. No one was here. It was just us and we couldn't stop them. It's no good you turning up now, it's too late! For all we know they might have killed Dragon.'

She swallowed and tried to blink back the tears but for once she didn't care who saw her crying. The only one who might have given her grief was in their enemies' hands.

'Tamar,' Arthur began hesitantly, shocked by the outburst. 'Tamar, it isn't his fault.'

The man's eyes, profoundly blue under white brows, were troubled. He held up a hand and said, 'No Arthur, she 'as every right to ask these questions.'

Tamar gathered herself. 'Why weren't you here? You might have saved him like you saved Arthur.' She bit her lip. 'I know some of it's my fault but …'

Gawain and Arthur exchanged looks.

'If you'd got here a few minutes earlier none of this might have happened. Nick and Dragon might still be with us, not being dragged away to some horrible prison.'

She glanced at Arthur and Gawain and Rozen. 'Well it's true! How could we be expected to stand up against them? There's no way we could have won.'

'Tamar,' Michael began slowly, 'you've every reason to be angry.' He sighed. 'And you may be right, but we must go to a place where we can talk freely.'

He put his arm around her hunched shoulders. 'If Nick and Dragon are to be helped we must move carefully.'

Tamar didn't say anything. It was hopeless.

'You 'ave a caravan?'

Arthur nodded.

Michael looked out to sea. A tall-masted ship, silhouetted on the horizon, was sailing towards the island. There was no time to lose.

'When we're there Tamar, I'll tell you more, but not 'ere.' He glanced around. 'Although they've gone they could return.' He glanced at Rozen. So the woodwright's daughter had thrown in her lot with the young king and the Guardians. Her father wouldn't be happy. 'Will you come too?'

Rozen hesitated, unsure whether it was okay for her to be included but Arthur made up her mind for her. 'You've got to come, Rozen. We're going to need everybody's help.'

Michael nodded and without another word, led the way, striding down the hill towards the fair with Fly and Lightning at his side. Arthur shot an apologetic look at his friends and jogged after Michael. There was stuff he needed to know.

'Are you okay?' Gawain asked Tamar awkwardly.

'Of course she's not okay!' Rozen retorted. But seeing his miserable expression she relented and quickly changed the subject, defending both Tamar and Gawain's feelings. 'That guy, is he an old friend of yours?'

Gawain nodded and Tamar mumbled, 'Something like that.'

'And you guys ... have you known each other long?'

Tamar sniffed and pulled out a hanky. 'Well, Nick, Arthur and me ... we've been friends since we started school.' She blew her nose noisily. 'And we've been friends with Gawain for a couple of years.'

She watched him struggling to walk with the sword cane slapping against his legs. Normally she'd be giggling.

'Yeah,' he said. 'We met the summer when we were made ...' he looked uncertainly at Tamar.

'When we were made Guardians,' she finished quietly.

Rozen's falcon clung to her arm, occasionally flapping its wings to maintain its balance.

They walked on in silence. Usually Tamar could be relied upon to keep the conversation flowing but not now.

'Unusual pet,' Gawain commented desperately. *What an inane remark,* he thought. *Talk about stating the bloody obvious!*

'Unusual weapon,' Rozen parried, indicating the sword cane.

'Touché!'

But to Gawain's relief there wasn't time for any more conversation – inane or not – because they'd arrived at the road running along the side of the field containing the fair and caught up with Michael and Arthur.

Shouts and laughter drifted over the hedge towards them and melodic notes mingled with the snowflakes.

Gawain cast a worried look at Tamar.

She was withdrawing into herself. She looked awful. Normally she was, well, attractive. But now her nose was pink and her eyes were red-rimmed. All he wanted was to give her a big hug.

He sighed and turned his attention to Michael and Arthur. They were waiting beside a Belisha beacon: a flashing yellow ball on top of a tall, black and white striped pole. Its twin was on the opposite side of the road.

'We'll go on to Arthur and Gawain's caravan in a minute,' Michael began as soon as they'd caught up.

'It's Nick's caravan too,' Tamar mumbled.

'I know, Tamar.' He seemed to be on the point of going into more detail but instead said, 'However, first I've some business 'ere.'

He turned to the crossing with its yellow flashing beacons and stared intently at the nearest one. 'Ah, this must be the place.'

'I thought we were going straight to the caravan.' Arthur couldn't understand why on earth Michael would waste a second.

'We are Arthur, very soon. But first another of our number 'as to join us.'

The snow had obliterated the black and white markings of the pedestrian crossing but the beacons still flashed on either side of the road. Michael reached out to the one closest and touched its metal pole.

'You may not 'ave noticed, but only a few of these remain,' he began conversationally and stroked the metal, his fingers delicately searching for the right place. 'Their inventor was a Mr Belisha. He designed them in the last century to mark safe crossings on roads; to alert drivers that folk might be in the road and to allow them to cross in safety.'

His fingers stilled and he studied the pole.

'Ah, I was right, this is the place.' He allowed himself a small smile; the first time he'd smiled since they'd met. Grasping the pole's metal casing, he twisted.

The beacon continued to flash.

'This is one of time's weaker spots,' he explained. 'One of the places where time wobbles.'

He gave the pole another sharp twist. 'You see, 'tisn't only bad memories that 'ave power. Objects or places with good memories like this beacon, things that were designed to 'elp people, they can be used too.'

He glanced around to ensure that they weren't being observed, gave one final twist and commanded, 'Stand back!'

The beacon's flashes grew faster and it began to hum.

Rozen watched open-mouthed and hung on to her falcon.

In Tamar's pocket the watch ticked excitedly. It could feel time thinning and wobbling and it wanted to join in but it felt Michael's deep, calming words and slowed its ticks.

Then Gawain leant forward, pushing his grisly memories away, and examined the far side of the crossing. Because, illuminated by the yellow glow, something was materialising.

'No way!' Gawain looked at Michael and slowly shook his head. 'Please tell me I'm seeing things.'

But the beacon continued to flash and the hum increased and the shape solidified.

And just as Tamar had learnt that teachers don't necessarily know everything, Gawain was beginning to grasp that the world didn't always work according to the laws of science. (Although really, ever since Nick's dragon had changed from stone to a living creature he'd known that.) Because now, right in front of his eyes, Kitto Cornish was taking shape under the yellow glare of the beacon. The blurred impression of his uncle was becoming more solid by the second, turning into the Uncle Kitto he'd known all his life.

'Wait,' Michael ordered, his hand on the boy's shoulder. 'It isn't safe yet. He 'as to be allowed to walk to this side. If you interrupt him 'is molecules could be disturbed and who knows what damage may be done!'

Rozen's eyes were huge. She'd seen some unusual things on her travels with her dad but this topped them all.

They watched the figure's wobbles slow down (although he was round, Kitto Cornish wasn't usually *quite* that wobbly) and become more solid as his molecules settled.

Arthur whispered in Gawain's ear, 'Hey mate, I knew your house was weird but I never guessed it was that weird!'

'Neither did I.' Gawain's colour matched the snow. Even though he'd lived with self-opening books, met supposedly long-dead knights and had a friend with a dragon – and been on a time-travelling train – he still wasn't prepared for this.

'This is one of the gates where time is particularly thin. There are a few of 'em scattered around Cornwall,' Michael remarked. 'I believe you were guided through one, Tamar.'

Tamar nodded, remembering travelling back through the centuries when she'd been guided under an arch in Porth Pyra, but it had been much simpler than this. She hadn't had to wait for her molecules to settle down. She tried to concentrate on what was happening to Gawain's uncle but nothing, not even this, could distract her from thinking about Nick and Dragon.

Kitto Cornish's molecules appeared to have stabilised and he shambled towards the little group waiting on the other side of the road.

Grasping Michael's hand, he pumped it up and down. 'An honour to meet you again Michael. Never ceases to amaze me how that works.'

He pushed a pair of half-moon spectacles further up his nose. 'Every time I have to travel I wonder if I'll be in one piece when I arrive.'

He turned to Gawain. 'Hello, my boy. Had an interesting day?' He tucked a woollen scarf around his neck, unaware of the irony hidden in his question. He blew on his hands and rubbed them together. 'Just had time to grab my coat and scarf but I didn't get to my gloves, they're still sitting on the chair by the door at home.'

Snowflakes perched on the rim of his spectacles and settled on his head. 'Could have done with my hat too,' he beamed.

Arthur really wished Nick was here, he would have been blown away by this. In fact, he thought miserably, he just wished Nick was here.

Kitto Cornish smiled kindly and exclaimed, 'Of course! You haven't seen me travel like this before, have you?'

Gawain shook his head as Arthur offered, 'Actually Mr Cornish, I don't think that any of us have seen *anyone* do that before.'

He glanced questioningly at Rozen but, judging from her expression, he guessed he was right. Then looking at Tamar, he asked, 'Except you maybe?'

Tamar nodded as she recalled her fellow prisoner's departure from the Ice Lady's ship. She remembered Hairy Face dissolving and his reassuring toothless smile as he told her that there was nothing to be frightened of. That it was just the 'Calling'.

However, Michael was already turning towards the field. 'Come Kitto, they've got the boy and the dragon, we 'ave little time for conversation.'

Finally Tamar looked at Michael properly for the first time. Deep worry lines were etched across his brow and his usual healthy complexion was almost grey. She'd been so busy shouting at him that she hadn't seen how upset he was.

Kitto Cornish's good humour faded and his voice trembled. 'They've got the dragon's minder?'

'They 'ave, Kitto.' Michael confirmed grimly.

'Oh, dearie me,' Mr Cornish shook his head and began rubbing the snow from his glasses. 'Oh dearie, dearie me.' His eyes glistened.

'The dragon and the boy?' he asked again.

Michael nodded and Kitto Cornish's shoulders slumped.

'Then you're right, this is no time for minor conversation. We must make haste.'

A particularly violent gust of wind whipped across the field, seizing awnings and lights.

Both men surveyed the field with its stalls and carol singers. Uncle Kitto licked his finger and held it up.

Feeling the direction of the wind he glanced at Michael Jolly, and Arthur caught a snippet of deep words being exchanged before the walls went up and the words were hidden.

***

Beyond the island a sailing ship dropped anchor.

A woman, dressed from head to toe in black velvet, stood on the deck. Icy squalls swept the wooden boards, brushing the snow into tiny drifts. The woman appeared to be unaware of the weather or the cold. Thoughtfully she contemplated the castle on the island's crown and her gloved fingers gripped the rail.

'Not long now.' She breathed a frosty breath. 'Soon all will be as it should be. What do these people say? Ah yes, *comero weeth*, take care … Well, it is a little too late for that.'

She smiled, monitoring a small boat detach itself from the island. She watched it turn and edge away from the island and towards her ship.

Clutching the handrail she studied the island's outline from its foot to its crown. It might be dark but she knew the land inside out. Soon, very soon, she'd be setting foot on its waiting stones. She'd step in Queen Victoria's footsteps. The monarch's visit had also been unexpected. Apparently the housekeeper had had to show the queen around the island and castle. But her visit wouldn't be so brief, although it would be equally surprising.

Now it was time for the island to be accorded the honour it deserved: its own queen.

And from there Cornwall was only a step away.

'Oh yes, my friends, it is certainly too late for care to be taken of the dragon and his boy but the island will be in safe hands.'

And turning from the rail she smiled to herself before calling into the darkness, 'Make ready.'

Chapter 12
Ticking Through Time

Later that evening, Tamar pulled the blanket up to her nose and smothered the pocket watch's ticks with her pillow. The Time Keeper's dress was lying beside her, hidden under the sheets. As soon as Wenna was asleep she'd be ready. In the meantime she lay still and made a list in her head:

1. Don't forget the watch.

2. Put on dress.

3. Look out for Angela.

4. Find Sir Dinadan.

5. ...

Well, five depended on how co-operative the knight was, and whether there would be someone there to help her.

This was her first planned time expedition. She'd always imagined this moment would be super-exciting, but she was too worried to be able to enjoy the prospect of her trip. She wasn't particularly worried for herself; it was more about whether she'd be up to finding a knight who would help Nick and Dragon.

She ran over the decisions they'd made an hour ago.

***

There had been the six of them, plus two dogs and a falcon, crammed into the seats on either side of the antique caravan. Michael and Uncle Kitto had made straight for it as soon as Nick's kidnapping had been discussed – although there had been that one odd moment when Mr Cornish had stopped and peered at something peeping out of the snow.

Tamar considered the way he'd adjusted his glasses to get a better look and picked it up, before raising an eyebrow and muttering, 'Roman, definitely a Roman coin …'

The men had looked at one another and their frowns had deepened but Tamar couldn't see why that had bothered them.

Immediately Michael had announced, 'Even more reason to hurry!' and had set off at a brisk pace, the rest of the group jogging after him. Interestingly quite a few cats had appeared. One or two had been sitting next to a hedge and Tamar had noticed a black tom sheltering beside the candyfloss stall. There had been others prowling in twos or threes and dodging people's feet. And then she'd seen Cathe. He'd mustered his forces.

Once the caravan door was shut they'd drawn the curtains and very soon there had been an overpowering fug of wet dogs.

Tamar had been aware of her watch doing its best to contain its excitement. It was unusual to encounter so many important people in one space. Usually it was enough for the little timepiece if just Arthur was there, but to have him and all the others squeezed together was almost too much for it.

And Rozen had had her own difficulties with her falcon.

It was clearly unused to this sort of situation and refused to settle, flapping and making high-pitched alarm calls. So for everybody's safety, and the bird's sanity,

Rozen had lodged it on her head under her top hat. Apparently it felt safer there.

Then, swiftly moving on from Kitto Cornish's unusual travel arrangements, Arthur, Tamar and Gawain had brought Michael and Kitto up to speed on everything that had happened in the last couple of days, finishing with the grim re-telling of Nick's abduction. None of them could banish the picture of Hagarawall's arm around their friend's neck, or Dragon dangling between those pale fingers.

'So now we must decide 'ow best to help Nick and his dragon,' Michael had begun. 'Storming the castle at night is perhaps the best way. Take the Lady by surprise.' He'd rubbed the bridge of his nose as if he was trying to rub the worry away.

'But they'll see us!' Arthur had protested.

'Maybe, but with the right folks on our side we'll be strong.'

Arthur had frowned. 'Strong enough to get on to the island and up the path to the castle? We'll be sitting ducks!'

Kitto had nodded. 'Art's right Michael. That castle has been a stronghold for centuries.'

'But not against the sort of folks we'll have with us, Kitto. Think on it; consider who we 'ave at our side.'

Kitto Cornish had sighed. 'You may be right but I'm very much afraid that someone will have to pay the price for the boy's freedom.'

And Tamar had felt her heart sink. If anyone paid for it, it would be her fault. She was the reason they were having this discussion.

Gawain guessed her thoughts and surreptitiously, and a little awkwardly, slid his hand over hers. She blushed but didn't pull her hand away.

They sat, hand in hand, listening to the discussion until eventually Michael Jolly had announced, 'So these are our options. What do you say Arthur? You are Cornwall's king – you must decide.'

Tamar's heart had leapt. Please let her do something to help.

Arthur hadn't disagreed; he'd sort of been expecting that he'd have to make the ultimate decision. At least this time he was trying to save Nick and Dragon, not asking them to put themselves in danger as he'd had to last summer.

Tamar watched him rest his head against the wooden wall and examine a spot on the ceiling before closing his eyes. What she couldn't see was the panic rumbling through his brain until Michael sent encouraging deep words: 'Sire, you'll find the right answers. Think on Excalibur.'

And then the wind dropped as Arthur's fingers reached for the golden sword around his neck and even the watch quietened its ticks.

At last he'd opened his eyes and sighed and pushed the tip of his forefinger into the furrow between his brows, smoothing his forehead. Then he'd turned to her and her heart had begun to thump.

'Tamar,' he'd begun. 'You can refuse, but I think Michael and Kitto are right, we're going to need someone else to help us.'

Their gazes met, two pairs of brown eyes locking out everyone else. Tamar's stomach flipped and she drew her hand out of Gawain's grasp. It wasn't just what Arthur was about to ask her – she had a shrewd idea what that was going to be – it was something else too. There was a sliver of something in the way he looked at her, as if they were more than just old school friends, and then he cleared his throat and the moment slid away. He swallowed. 'Are you up for fetching Dinadan?'

This knight had been suggested by Michael as the man most likely to add to their cause and the one best suited to cope with the rigours of time travel. Arthur hadn't any choice. Here he was again, having to ask a friend – a very good friend – to do something he wouldn't wish on his enemies. He was asking her to make a dangerous, solo trip back through the centuries.

But Tamar was more than up for it. She'd do anything to help Nick and the sooner she could get on with it the better. And, banishing the thoughts of the last few seconds, she'd smiled, relieved that at last she could do something.

'Of course!' she'd agreed straight away. 'You know I am.' And the watch's cogs had whirred.

As soon as that decision had been made, others had quickly followed.

'Michael, could you go with Rozen to see her dad and talk things over?'

Michael nodded. Rozen had to have her father's consent. No matter what she thought, her usefulness would be weakened without his approval. (Rozen hadn't been told that her mother had died while fighting for Cornwall's freedom; that the memory of his wife's death still haunted her father.)

Finally Arthur had stated, 'And Mr Cornish, Gawain and I will go to Oakwood Manor. We'll wait there until everyone is ready. Maybe there'll be time for me and Gawain to learn how to use a sword.'

He'd looked at Michael, wondering if he'd made the right decisions, and was rewarded by the deep words, 'Worthy choices, sire.'

***

Her caravan door opened. Tamar took a breath and clamped her eyes shut and hoped that her sister would think she was asleep.

Morwenna had struck up a friendship with another stallholder: a boy with the blue-eyed, chiselled-jaw look that was her trademark boyfriend. If Tamar was awake she knew that Wenna would want to spend hours discussing him, and she hadn't got hours. She steadied her breathing and crossed her fingers but Wenna was obviously not ready to sleep and began tidying up.

For goodness sake, why do you have to do that now? Tamar barely managed to contain herself.

She heard the shuffle of papers being sorted into piles and magazines being stacked, there was the tell-tale rattle of the key turning in the door (at least it didn't matter if the door was locked!) and then the jangle of the hangers on the rail. Wenna would never leave her clothes to get crumpled, especially when a new boyfriend was in sight.

Tamar had to stop herself cheering when her sister finally climbed into the bed on the other side of the caravan.

She waited for the tell-tale 'click' of the light being switched off and nearly sighed with relief when she heard it. She'd been afraid that Wenna would prop herself up to text all her friends about the boy, telling them how drop-dead gorgeous he was, or relaying every word they'd exchanged. She resisted the temptation to open her eyes. Instead she waited and listened because, although Wenna denied it, she snored. And sure enough, within minutes the air was vibrating.

Tamar had never been so grateful for her sister's snores.

At last it was safe.

The caravan wasn't in complete darkness. A helpful orange glow fed through the loose weave of the curtains from the lights decorating the stalls. Tamar tugged the dress from under the sheets and sat up, taking care not to make any sudden moves. Wenna's snores continued.

One cautious foot at a time, she edged out of bed until she was standing up. Keeping watch on her sister, she put a note on the pillow explaining that something had come up and she wouldn't be able to help out with the stall. Then she crept over to the door and turned the key. Although she didn't need it unlocked, she had to make her exit look as normal as possible.

Holding the watch in one hand, she picked up the Time Keeper's dress; the wool was smooth and warm between her fingers and, even in the gloom of the caravan, the embroidered stars shone.

Keeping a watchful eye on her sister she slowly lifted the full skirt until it was hanging above her head and then allowed it to drop. The watch whirred. It knew where it had to take her.

And Tamar Tamblyn was no longer in the tiny caravan but high in the night sky, far above Cornwall. She was right. She didn't need to unlock the door.

Stars whisked past, pin-points of light in the deep blue of the heavens. She'd wondered whether she'd have the courage to keep her eyes open but the view was hypnotic. She had no idea whether she was really seeing these things or whether it was just a sort of mirage, but the air felt unusually fresh. The planet seemed to spin beneath her, night to day and back again. Gradually city lights disappeared to be replaced by forests and fields.

She was travelling back through the centuries, seeing Earth restored to the planet it had been designed to be before man and 'progress' had taken over.

My history teachers would love this!

No more satellites in the sky or factories belching smoke: no more cars or planes or trains; no roads tearing through the woods and forests. Earth was just land and sea with the occasional settlement and relatively small town.

Tamar was as close to enjoying the view as was possible when she caught the distinctive outline of Britain.

A second later and Cornwall was looming closer. She was nearing the end of her time-flight. And then she *did* close her eyes; she preferred to avoid the sight of the ground rushing towards her. She felt a *woomph* and heard twigs snapping and smelt the undeniable scent of earth and rotting leaves.

***

The woman hurried towards the wood. She'd seen a flash of colour high in the sky; emerald green and gold. The Time Keeper was on her way.

A rabbit bounded out of her way and a hedgehog opened an eye and followed her progress from its shelter in the undergrowth.

'Darn skirts,' the woman remarked to herself breathlessly. 'Style over substance.' And she picked up her darn skirt and began to run towards the particular part of the wood where she expected to find the girl. Her blonde hair escaped from its tidy plait, a strand clinging to her sticky neck and a trickle of sweat dribbling between her shoulder blades.

She'd been sceptical about this way of travelling and had had to be persuaded that it would work – that the dress's design really would act as a safe method of travel and that the girl's journey through the years would be sufficiently controlled to ensure a safe landing. The woman had been less than happy about this choice of travel for the young Time Keeper; none of the other Keepers had journeyed like this. But to be fair all the others had been men and few men would wear skirts (although there were always the Scots, they were man enough to be happy in kilts). Anyway, she doubted that any of them would have possessed this girl's courage. Although that was one opinion she'd kept to herself.

She hurried along the earth path winding through the thickets of bramble and hawthorn. No doubt it was sensible to choose somewhere generally left to the animals for the girl to appear, but it didn't make her task any easier. Another decision made by men, she thought grimly.

Swiping a low branch out of her way she rounded a bend and arrived at the clearing to find the girl lying, unmoving, on the ground.

The woman's heart raced. 'Blast!' she exclaimed, and ran towards the inert form. Somewhere in the distance a blackbird called, answered by another closer to hand.

'Oh my, they've done it this time.' She puffed, her hand on her chest as she gazed down. And then the girl's eyes opened.

'Angela?' Groggily, Tamar propped herself up on one elbow and, out of habit, checked that the pocket watch was still in her hand. She wiped her hand across her face and looked at the woman. 'I can't believe it's you!'

The woman breathed out. 'You're all right! You had me worried, Tamar. Don't try to get up; you'll be dizzy an' we can't 'ave you hurtin' yourself when you've only just arrived. My word, but you've done well.' A note of pride crept into her voice. 'They told me 'ow you saw off the Ice Lady last summer. *Your* summer I mean.'

Angela's smile grew. 'The last time we saw each other must 'ave been on Bodmin Moor in your time – the night you were commissioned.'

Tamar nodded, still trying to accommodate the concept of this younger Angela.

The woman peered at the girl. 'The first female Time Keeper. Now that's what I call progress.' She picked a dried leaf off Tamar's dress. 'And now you're 'ere.' Angela looked at the sky through the hole in the wood's leafless canopy. 'I'm glad you made it safely.'

'*You're* glad!'

Angela chuckled. 'Did you recognise me when the tent popped into the fair at Trezion?'

'Course I did. Once seen, never forgotten.'

Angela smiled again. 'It was decided that it would be good if you caught a glimpse of *someone* who was on your side.' Her smile faded. 'I gather that as you're here, events must 'ave taken a turn for the worse.'

Tamar nodded miserably. 'They have.' She glanced at Angela. 'They've got Nick and Dragon.'

Angela's expression said it all. She drew a square of fine cotton out of her sleeve and wiped her neck.

'Is Brane involved?'

Tamar nodded, overcome by another wave of despair. 'Yes, and Hagarawall – you know the pale guy. And that woman …'

'The Lady of Clehy?'

'Yeah her … well I think so, although I haven't seen her yet. And there's a creepy, weird boy too. He's got silver hair. I think he's called Cador and he hates Christmas.'

Absentmindedly, Angela removed a twig caught in Tamar's hair. 'I don't know what you 'ave to do Tamar, we're never given the whole picture. Are you 'ere to collect someone?'

'Yes,' Tamar sighed. 'As quickly as possible. I know that time is sort of warped but Michael said that it still keeps ticking. It doesn't exactly come to a stop.'

'He's right,' Angela agreed. 'Who's been suggested?'

'Someone called Sir Dinadan.'

'Ah, one of the king's knights.'

Overhead a buzzard floated on the thermals, defining lazy circles in the blue sky. Occasionally it gave an extra flap. A field vole exited from beneath a bramble bush and disappeared down the path through the dead leaves. It was winter here too. There was no snow but the air was cold and the branches were mostly bare. The trees shivered in a sudden gust.

Tamar began scrabbling to her feet and Angela cupped her elbow. 'The king's court is here for the winter – that tent you saw me in is one of 'is.'

'Does he know he's got a travelling tent?'

Angela shook her head and smiled a quick smile. 'I doubt it.'

Tamar brushed herself down and tucked the watch into its custom-made pocket as Angela added, 'I tend to keep my distance. As far as anyone 'ere knows I'm merely one of the women who cooks – liberation is a long, long way off! Come now lass, 'tisn't far.'

And beating at the brambles and branches that dared to get in her way, she led Tamar through the woodland towards King Arthur's court and the knight who would be making the most unexpected journey of his life.

Chapter 13
The Gathering

The Writer had documented Nick's abduction.

She'd witnessed Michael Jolly's reunion with Arthur, Gawain and Tamar, and she'd sent Viatoris to the fair. He'd sent deep words informing her of Kitto Cornish's arrival.

'He's arrived by the gate at the crossing, ma'am,' he'd informed the Writer, and at this point she'd decided she needed to see for herself what happened next.

She'd found a particularly warm and nondescript coat and accessorised it with a baggy scarf and a woolly hat. She was a stylist's nightmare but a spy's dream. No one would give her a second look, or probably even a first look with her flat shoes and thick tights. She'd congratulated herself. Nobody took any notice of old people and they certainly wouldn't take any notice of her.

She'd been lingering near the ancient caravan. The crowds had swirled around her with no one even glancing her way, until a couple of boys had raced past. Unfortunately for him, the boy doing the chasing knocked into her as his friend sped ahead.

The one in the lead had shouted impatiently at his friend. 'Come on Jack! Bet I beat you.'

Jack had been laughing, but as he looked into her eyes his laughter had died and he'd blanched.

He'd swallowed. 'Sorry, I didn't mean to …'

The Writer tried to resume her little old lady look but the boy had seen beneath the mask.

This was no ordinary old lady.

'Um, very sorry …' He couldn't drag his eyes away.

His friend was still challenging him but Jack's legs wouldn't move.

'Perhaps you'd better go,' she said quietly. 'But be more careful from now on won't you?' Never had such a mild request sounded so *forceful*.

The boy almost bowed. 'Yes, yes I will … I promise.' He was gibbering.

'*Good.*' The word spun and expanded. 'You'd better go then,' she commanded.

He started backing away, his eyes still on hers until his friend ran back to him, grabbed his arm and ordered, 'Come *on*, Jack. We'll miss it!'

And Jack was dragged down the field, his feet stumbling and his mind reeling.

The Writer watched them go. Little boys sometimes needed a lesson in manners. Then she resumed her watching.

It was only a few minutes later that the caravan's door had swung open and the young Time Keeper emerged. She'd watched Tamar cast a quick look around the field and over the crowds before darting down the steps. Even from here the Writer could feel the watch's excitement.

She'd dug her hands into her coat pockets and waited for the rest of the company to exit the caravan.

It was barely a minute after Tamar had disappeared into the crowds that the door re-opened and Michael, Fly and Rozen appeared. Michael had swept his scarf around his neck and said something. The girl hadn't replied but she'd nodded, lifted her head resolutely and placed a hand on the top of her hat. The Writer had smiled a little sadly as she watched Michael lead Rozen towards the bottom of the field. She knew that Rozen wouldn't be dissuaded from her decision. She was also aware of the resolution Rozen's father had made when her mother had died.

How he'd promised his dying wife that he would protect her daughters against any and every danger.

The Writer could imagine his reaction when he heard that his daughter had thrown in her lot with the Guardians. There would be no sitting on the fence for that young woman. It might break the poor man's heart. He would know just how dangerous her choice was.

But the Writer's musings had been interrupted by the last of the caravan's occupants appearing at the door. She'd observed Kitto Cornish, Arthur, Gawain and the dog file down the wooden steps, and watched Arthur lock the caravan door. She'd seen them sweep the field for any sign of Brane or Hagarawall – but the Guardians' enemies were long gone. They'd won their trump card.

Her mind turned to her own team and Servo observing the boy and his dragon – hopefully he wasn't being tempted to intervene. He knew the Rule. She sent firm words to Viatoris to remind him of his duties and tramped her way across the field.

The Writer cast a look towards the sky. Thick, snow-bearing clouds blotted out the stars and the moon, and the snow was falling even more heavily. She heard snippets of conversation from concerned adults as their children shouted and lobbed snowballs. Very soon this part of Cornwall would be cut off from the rest of the peninsula and the Ice Lady would be able to set foot on the island with little or no opposition.

She was turning towards the gate in the hedge when a tiny 'pop' stopped her in her tracks.

She scoured the snow blanketing the field. Her sharp eyes were looking for anything out of place and fixed on a bronze-coloured disc in the snow at her feet. She bent and picked it up, laying it in the palm of her tatty, beige glove.

It was a Roman coin.

Her mouth set in a grim line.

If things continued at this pace there'd be more than mere coins popping up; very soon Roman memories would be swarming out of the frozen ground. Not only inanimate objects that had never been alive in the first place, but fragments of the people who'd lived here so long ago … and they'd certainly be more than just inert skeletons.

She looked up to find the top-hatted automaton on the barrel organ watching her.

As if it had been waiting for her, the moment she looked at the machine the music started and the automaton came to life. With the handle of the organ turning, the automaton bowed and began its routine, drawing the unsuspecting crowd. It was as if the Ice Lady was parading her control over ordinary people. Demonstrating her power to those who knew her.

The Writer sighed and shook her head and turned towards the hedge. She had to get back to the cottage.

A barn owl floated overhead, largely unnoticed by the crowds in the fields, but the woman saw it and her serious expression softened. She walked to the top of the field. Ahead of her, Kitto Cornish and the young king and his friend hurried through the deepening snow.

***

When they'd first left the caravan none of the trio had spoken a word, they were too aware of the possibility of listening ears. Arthur and Gawain silently retraced their steps over the snow-covered cobbles between the rows of cottages standing sentinel on either side of the lane while Kitto Cornish trailed behind them. They hadn't slowed until they'd turned the corner and reached the wooden door set into the wall bordering the grounds of Oakwood Manor.

Despite Merlin's words, Arthur wasn't sure that it would let him in. But Gawain's uncle gestured towards the door. 'It will know you.'

And he was right. Arthur had barely touched the handle before the door creaked open.

'You see? It recognises you. Marvellous!' Even in the face of all that had happened, Gawain's uncle was irrepressibly delighted.

Arthur and Gawain entered the tunnel with Lightning at their heels. Kitto Cornish was about to follow when he caught sight of the Writer making her way towards the cottage. Kitto recognised her despite her disguise. He performed a quick bow and a couple of deep words were snatched before he was interrupted by his nephew urging him to hurry.

'Come on, Uncle,' Gawain was saying. 'The door wants to close.' The door was straining on its hinges, determined to secure the tunnel.

Kitto shot a hasty farewell to the Writer and squeezed through. The door swung back, the key turned in the lock and the latch fell into place. They were back in the stone and earth tunnel they'd exited such a short time before. They watched the candles in the niches flicker into life, shadows dancing on the walls, and smelt the warm, fusty air.

'Have you been here before?' Gawain asked his uncle. 'I mean the Manor – not the tunnel.'

'Once, a long time ago lad, but not by this route.'

Arthur touched the rope anchored into the stone wall. 'Hold on to that then Mr Cornish. The tunnel gets steeper further on but you should be okay.'

Arthur sent Lightning ahead and hastily followed. He and Gawain saw, much sooner than they expected, a small grey arch illuminated by candles, which indicated the stone door at the top of the tunnel. Kitto Cornish was breathing heavily by the time he caught up: he'd never been one for exercise.

Lightning stretched and stood on his hind legs, leaning his fore legs against the stone of the door. Immediately it felt the touch of his pads it opened, flooding the tunnel with amber light.

'Fascinating,' Kitto Cornish panted. 'Quite fascinating. I must ask Falco how he instructs his gates in the art of admitting welcome guests. It would be most useful at home.'

Gawain drew a breath. Their shop and cottage was unusual enough without having doors that recognised people.

'No, let's leave that to Dr Columbarius,' he said quickly. 'I don't think we really need it.'

But Kitto Cornish was already deep in thought, considering just how it could be applied to his shop and how handy it would be to be able to admit only the desirable customers.

'*Gothewhar vaze*, Kitto. Still intent on using the ancient arts in your cottage?'

Silhouetted in the arched doorway Merlin extended a hand towards Mr Cornish as he bid him good evening, and helped him over the threshold into his home.

'Falco!' Kitto bowed but didn't say anything else out loud and within seconds the two men were engaged in a carefully hidden, deep conversation. However, watching their expressions, especially Kitto's, Arthur knew that they were greatly worried. Merlin's face was as near to neutral as it could be but his eyes were troubled.

Finally Falco Columbarius nodded, bringing their discussion to a close; aloud he said, 'Kitto, it might be easier for everyone if we resume the use of Merlin. It's my usual name and I believe that Michael told those who needed to know.'

Kitto nodded. 'It came up in conversation in the caravan. Of course Arthur knew and I believe Miss Tamblyn had already met you. My nephew had wondered, the books and one or two other things had alerted him to your ... um, unusual origins. And Rozen, of course, is quick and appears to take *most* things in her stride.'

But Gawain wasn't listening to their conversation. He was shaking Arthur's arm and mutely pointing at the ceiling. Briefly, their focus on Nick's plight was diverted because it seemed that the library had undergone a radical transformation. The ceiling, which had been white with plaster mouldings, was now vaulted like the ceiling in a cathedral or castle.

Arthur stared. The apex was so high it was shrouded in shadow.

On each of the ceiling trusses carved owls and stars mingled with painted wooden shields. Where the top of the walls met the inner roof-edge, wooden beams stretched from side to side. And on each of these beams plaster angels brandished trumpets, spears and swords. Arthur was reminded of the statue in Porth Talant churchyard and the angels on the Jollys' clock. Perhaps these ceiling angels came to life too.

Perched between two of the statues Tyto fluffed her feathers and stretched her wings; presumably she was used to her surroundings changing.

A piece of furniture stretched the length of the room. It was the longest table either Arthur or Gawain had ever seen.

Arthur had visited some castles around the country. His dad had a particular interest in anything to do with Britain's past, which too often had meant trailing around dusty houses and castles listening to a guide churn out a list of facts which nobody but his dad had found interesting. The number of times he'd felt his heart sink as his dad had clasped his hands behind his back, rolled on the balls of his feet and asked the guide for more details.

But in all those mind-numbing visits Arthur had never seen a table like this.

It was highly polished oak and a name was carved in the table top in front of each chair.

Gawain ran his fingers over the engravings. He could make out some of the letters but not a whole word. Until he came to one.

It began with a capital 'G' followed by 'a' and then 'w'.

His name was waiting for him.

I wonder what other names are here, he thought; but a sudden crash from the hall doors being flung back interrupted his examination. A pair of elderly knights strode in simultaneously with the tunnel door swinging open to admit Michael Jolly and Rozen.

Without ceremony, one of the knights, flung his cloak over the nearest chair and boomed, 'We heard your call, Merlin,' and stamped his feet, dislodging snow. 'The weather slowed us. That blasted woman is up to her old tricks again.'

It was Lancelot and Bedivere.

Merlin greeted his guests. 'Come in, come in!'

Taking Bedivere's cloak, Merlin embraced both men. 'You're no later than Michael and our other guests.'

The wind howled and rattled the windows, gusting down the chimney and bending the flames in the fire.

'The snow is falling deeper by the hour,' Bedivere observed. 'Her ship is moored off the island.'

Their host nodded. 'I know, Bedivere. Tyto has been keeping watch.'

High above them the owl screeched and a dead mouse dropped between them.

'Tyto!' Merlin exclaimed mildly. 'Kindly keep your dinner in your talons.'

Bedivere approached Arthur and executed a swift bow. 'We meet again, sire.' His eyes bore into Arthur and took in the others scattered around the room. 'The boy and his dragon?' he asked.

Arthur nodded. The last time he'd seen either of the knights had been at the lake when the Lady had given him Excalibur and the old King Arthur had bequeathed him Cornwall's care. He was desperate to have time to talk to Bedivere but every time they met it seemed to be in a crisis.

'How long has he been gone?' Lancelot asked.

'A few hours,' Arthur replied quietly.

'And your other friend, the Time Keeper?'

'Tamar? Um … she's travelling.'

'Is she now!' Lancelot slapped his thigh. (Arthur had only ever seen people do that in a pantomime.) 'The young Time Keeper travelling. She's a brave 'un.'

Merlin beckoned to Rozen, standing nervously just inside the door adjusting to her new world. (So far this evening she'd seen a man appear through a portal and now here she was in the company of the legendary Merlin and two old guys dressed in weird clothes.) 'Gentlemen, let me introduce you to Rozen, another brave ally. May I suggest that the bird stay close to you my dear? Tyto has never encountered a merlin at such close quarters.' He smiled wryly. 'Well, one of the feathered variety at least.'

But his smile vanished as another windy squall howled and shrieked around the house and the flames dipped and the shadows in the roof grew. A couple of candles flickered and were nearly extinguished before they felt the heat of the wise man's stare.

The Lady of Clehy was making her presence known.

Chapter 14
Captive

Hagarawall and Cador were triumphant.

They'd propelled Nick down the narrow alley and over the deepening snow with Hagarawall clutching the tiny dragon by his snout.

Dragon hadn't struggled. He'd just hung limp and defeated with his tail and legs swinging as his captor strode down the hill. He'd never looked so pathetic. The group had marched in silence, their footsteps deadened by the snow-carpet. Not a door or a window had opened and they hadn't passed a single person. The only one to speak had been Brane, with a terse, 'Down damn dog!' when the hound had snapped at Dragon.

But as soon as they'd left the village behind them, Nick felt them relax.

They were steering him towards the beach where a boat waited in the shallows with a boy holding a rope to stop it floating away. Brane's crow flew ahead of them and settled on a rock.

They slithered down the icy bank and onto the snowy sand. Occasionally the moon would peep out from behind a cloud and briefly illuminate the sea and beach, but then another cloud would scud across the night sky and plunge them into darkness.

Cador leant into Nick's face and sneered, 'So where are your friends now, Dragon Boy?' He cupped his hand above his eyes and slowly turned a full circle. 'Oh, aren't they here? That's strange!'

Hagarawall grinned at Cador and joined in, their animosity momentarily forgotten. 'Of course we mustn't forget the famous Michael Jolly, must we Cador? But fancy that … he isn't here either!'

'Oh dear,' Cador continued, 'it seems that you're all alone. None of your friends could be bothered to help you.' He sniggered. 'Not so big and strong now, are we?'

Nick clenched his fists. 'Be careful what you say about my friends.'

Cador sniggered. 'Why? What are you going to do about it?'

Hagarawall's fingers dug under Nick's collarbone as he whispered, 'What was it that you said about me? Oh yes, now I remember …' His grip tightened. 'You said, "I wouldn't like to meet him on a dark night!"'

'Yeah, but that was ages ago.' Nick refused to show his fear.

'Oh was it?' Thrusting Dragon towards the Crow Man, Hagarawall said, 'Here, hold this thing for me Brane,' and wrenched Nick's arms behind his back. A bolt of red-hot pain exploded in Nick's shoulders.

He groaned but still managed a defiant, 'They're more powerful than you lot!'

Cador let out a high-pitched giggle. 'More powerful than us? I don't think so.'

Nick tried to ignore the taunts and focus on Dragon. The Crow Man had clamped his fist over Dragon's jaw.

'You mustn't hold him like that, you'll hurt him.'

Brane gazed, incredulous. '*You* are telling *me* what to do?'

The crow cawed and hopped off the rock.

Cador shook his head in mock disbelief. 'Not the wisest of moves, Dragon Boy.'

Hagarawall's grip on Nick tightened. 'Perhaps we should show him who's boss.' And heaving a rope out of the boat he began to thread it round his prisoner's wrists, every coil scraping and gouging the skin. Eventually he tied the last knot and grunted with satisfaction as a trickle of blood seeped under the rope and Nick groaned again.

However, the Crow Man had tucked his hand under the dragon's body and even kicked at the dog when it dared to sidle up. Perhaps the Ice Lady had instructed that Dragon should be brought in alive. A spark of hope flickered in Nick's muddied mind.

'Make yourself useful Cador, pass me that sack,' Hagarawall ordered.

'Make myself useful?' Cador echoed as he reached into the boat. 'If it hadn't been for me we wouldn't have got any of them!'

'Of course not!' Hagarawall replied scornfully. 'Especially as a couple of girls had you whimpering with their talk about *Christmas*.'

Nick didn't hear Cador's reply. He was watching Brane swing a black metal chest out of the boat and kick the lid open. He held his breath. Dragon was dropped into the box, his tail pushed down and the lid slammed closed. The Crow Man turned a key in the lock. And then Hagarawall dropped a sack over Nick's head.

'Now Dragon Boy,' Hagarawall sneered through the sacking as he tugged it tightly over Nick's face. 'Let's see how big and strong you are without your dragon ... and your powerful friends.'

Dust filled Nick's nose and mouth and he swallowed.

'Maybe,' his jailer continued, 'you're not as brave as you think you are. Can you feel this?'

There was a pause and then a vicious blow, landing somewhere in the region of his kidneys, sent Nick staggering over the sand.

'Or this?'

There was a fresh bloom of pain as Hagarawall's steel-toed boot cracked into Nick's knee cap.

'And how about this?'

Nick stumbled as Hagarawall's fist crunched through the sacking into his jaw and blood filled his mouth.

'Welcome to our world Dragon Boy!'

Nick swallowed the rising bile and braced himself against the next blow but the Crow Man's voice cut in. 'That's enough Hagarawall. You've made your point. We've got to get to the island; she'll be waiting.'

Nick suspected that Hagarawall's blows and kicks could have been much harder, he was thankful for Brane's intervention – whatever the motivation.

There was the swish of a wave sweeping up the beach over the pebbles and the scrunch of a boat being dragged on to the sand.

'Get him in.'

And Nick was being pushed towards the waves.

Hagarawall needn't have worried that he would have tried to escape: he could barely walk and he wouldn't have gone anywhere without Dragon. Even if they carried on beating him he wouldn't leave.

Nick fell into the boat. The wood creaked and the wind sang but he caught a few words.

'See,' he heard Cador say, 'if we'd waited we wouldn't have got any of them.'

'It wasn't your idea,' Hagarawall bickered.

'Maybe not, but none of it would have happened unless I'd taken them on.'

'Taken them on?' Hagarawall asked, unable to believe his ears.

'That's enough!' Brane growled. 'We've got work to do.'

The argument stopped. It was clear who was the boss.

Before the sack had been thrown over his head, Nick had caught a glimpse of a spotty boy not much older than him, waiting by the boat. But then the snow clouds had drifted in front of the moon, dragging the beach and sea into deep night. He was fairly sure that apart from the boy nervously clutching the oars, no one else was around. The villagers were probably all at the fair or in bed by now. In the summer people walked along the beach well into the evening, but not on a cold night in winter.

Blood dribbled down the back of his throat. He ran his tongue around his mouth checking for damage. His jaw ached but all his teeth were intact.

He attempted to marshal his thoughts. It sounded like they were taking him to the island. Perhaps this is what Rozen's sister had been talking about. He tried to remember what she'd said. It had been something about the owners being away and the island being unhappy. Perhaps the Ice Lady was there already, waiting for him. His pulse raced. The physical injuries inflicted by Hagarawall were nothing compared to what she'd done in the summer without even touching him.

***

Servo Watched the antics of Nick's captors.

He'd winced with every kick and punch and felt a tightening in his chest when the tiny dragon was dropped and locked in the metal box. This was a bad business. The dragon wouldn't last long if he was separated from his master. Neither would he cope with the cold. And if the dragon died, what would happen to the boy? Servo had

had plenty of experience of dragons and their keepers and one rarely lasted without the other.

Already the creature's glossy green scales were losing their luminosity. Just like the coat of a dog, a dragon's scales were an indication of its health. Servo sighed. This dragon was unusually attached to the boy. It could be just a few hours before it wasted away altogether if it was left alone in its metal prison.

A lament rose from the box. Even from the inside of the tin chest the notes carried over the sea.

Servo gritted his teeth and tried to block the song, but the keening sawed its way into his mind, continuing inland, towards the village. The notes glided, sliding under front doors and through the slimmest of window openings. They drifted up the hill, coiling around chimneys and over the roof tops, until they arrived at Oakwood Manor.

Merlin stood by the fire as the song filled the room and his knuckles whitened.

'They've separated the boy and the dragon,' he muttered. He closed his eyes and gripped the stone mantelpiece.

And on a garden wall a cat stirred. Cathe's ears flattened. He stood and stretched. He would have to make a careful selection from his army for what was to come.

Chapter 15
Sir Dinadan

Angela hurried ahead of Tamar. They didn't speak. There wasn't time for conversation.

They were heading towards the castle perched on the cliff top, close to the water's edge. A flag flew from its mast. Tamar's mind buzzed. She'd seen this castle before but only as a ruin with a few low walls and an archway or two; nothing like this building.

Tamar pinched the soft skin on the underside of her arm. *Ouch!* This was for real then.

They'd reached the settlement spreading inland from the foot of the castle. Narrow, rutted streets wove between roughly built houses topped with thatched roofs. Some appeared to double up as shops with large picture signs swaying over open doorways.

Angela hurried past a door displaying cloth and another packed with animal skins and furs; one had hay-filled crates in its entrance piled with glistening fish. The next house was a smithy and it was here that Tamar caught her first glimpse of a knight. *A real, live knight!*

He was holding his helmet under his arm with his blue and gold shield propped against his leg on the dirt floor. The blacksmith was sweating and swinging an enormous hammer at the anvil. Orange and yellow sparks flew as a young, soot-smeared boy worked a pair of bellows to keep the fire burning. Noise and heat billowed from the doorway.

Tamar stopped to watch but she was pulled from her thoughts by Angela shouting, 'Come on Tamar, quickly!' and disappearing down a tiny alley.

Tamar picked up her skirt (it wasn't just mud in the road), and ran after her guide and past a pig snuffling and rooting in the earth. A doorway opened and a bucket of something unmentionable was thrown into her path. Only the best houses had toilets.

'Eeugh!' She skipped sideways, narrowly avoiding the bucket's contents.

She hurried after Angela through the warren of streets, passing a viciously bruised man trapped in wooden stocks; dodging scuttling rats and a woman covered in running sores. But much worse was the blond-haired boy.

She saw his feet first. They were bare and covered with dirt. He'd probably never worn a pair of shoes in his life. His trousers were brown and thin and patched, held up by a piece of twine tied around his thin middle. But it wasn't the state of his clothes that caught her eye, it was the fact that his feet were at eye level … because he was dangling from a wooden gibbet. She stopped dead in her tracks. From his height and build he could have been only about thirteen or fourteen – about her age – although it was difficult to tell. She swallowed.

'Tamar!' Angela's shout shook her out of her trance as a woman thrust a tray of steaming grey meat under her nose. 'Sheep's foot m'dear? 'Tis fresh this mornin'!'

Tamar stepped away and shook her head. 'No, no thank you.' She retched and clamped her hand over her mouth and ran after Angela.

Catching up with her, she swallowed. 'This is horrible!'

Angela glanced at her. 'Seen the boy 'ave you?'

'What's left of him.'

'There's a lot of growin' up that needs to be done afore they learn true justice and compassion – if they ever do.'

The woman looked hard at Tamar. 'This is your first real taste of 'ow other people work isn't it?'

Tamar nodded.

'I'm sorry to say it, but there'll be other more shockin' sights on your travels. This is mild compared to some.' She gave her a squeeze. 'Remember why you're 'ere. Come on.'

Tamar's fingers strayed to the sword hanging around her neck, she took a deep breath. 'Okay.'

'Good girl! Now then, there's a tournament today. I'm certain we'll find 'im there. He's a bit of a show-off, never takes life seriously, an' he's somethin' of a ladies' man. Better not let 'im too near your sister!'

Tamar started. How did Angela know about Wenna's steady stream of boyfriends?

The woman smiled, 'In my line of work 'tis always good to have a grasp of the details.' And without elaborating she gestured to a hill. 'Can you see the tops of those tents? That's where they're holding the tournament. If we get separated make for there and ask for Sir Dinadan.'

'But I can't get him back on my own!'

'Who said anything about you being by yourself? You'll 'ave the right help at the right time.' Angela tucked her hair back into its plait. 'An' if we don't happen to see each other again today, I'm sure there'll be other meetings.'

'Let's not get separated then!' Tamar said.

They pushed through the crowds. Past laughing men brandishing tankards of ale, and irritable mothers shrieking at their children, and young boys fighting and rolling in the mud. (Why do boys have to fight?) It was a whirl of bodies, noise and smells: mostly sweat and beery breath with more than a tang of urine thrown in.

At the side of the field, falconers were exercising their birds, swinging a tempting lure on a long string in wide loops. Other birds were perched on their owners' thick leather gauntlets with tiny hoods pulled over their heads to calm them. Tamar briefly wondered about Rozen and her bird; maybe she did this too. But then they burst out of the crush of sweaty bodies and Tamar realised that they'd arrived close to the pavilions similar to the one that had appeared at Trezion's fair.

The pavilions bustled with activity. Knights and squires, stable men and medical attendants (judging by their blood-stained aprons) hurried in and out of them. Horses and pages trotted up and down the field's edge. Knights joked and talked. And facing the pavilions on the other side of the field was a grandstand just like the one in her history book. Ladies dressed in fine clothes giggled and whispered behind their hands while noble men leaned back in their seats and chatted.

But the most arresting sight was in the centre of the grandstand.

A young, dark-haired man and his wife were sitting on gilded chairs, warmed by fur-edged cloaks. The man wasn't wearing a crown but it was clear who he was.

Tamar was seeing King Arthur and Queen Guinevere in the flesh. Seeing them before everything went wrong and his life was turned upside down. This was the king who'd lived so many centuries before and had become a legend even before he'd died. Tamar watched him turn to his beautiful wife and whisper something in her ear. She saw the queen smile and look at him. Their marriage was a happy one for now.

A shout interrupted her thoughts and she turned.

She didn't need Angela to confirm that the knight leaning against a fence with his shield at his feet was Sir Dinadan. She remembered a book she'd borrowed from Gawain. Nick had been joking about Gawain having a coat of arms and she'd drawn one on a T-shirt for him. Gawain's had been a weird two-headed eagle. Oddly, Dinadan's coat of arms had stuck in her mind too. Maybe because it was a black lion standing on its back legs – a lion rampant or something.

She whipped around. 'That's him isn't it?' but her words faded.

Angela had gone.

'Angela?'

There was no sign of her.

A woman pushed past balancing a baby on one hip and trailing a toddler clinging to her dress.

'Excuse me,' Tamar gripped the woman's arm. 'Have you seen a lady called Angela? She's got blonde hair and she's wearing a sort of browny dress – a bit like yours.'

But the woman was staring at the stranger's wrist. *Blast*, Tamar thought as she followed the line of the woman's gaze. *I'm wearing my watch!* Tamar never took her wrist watch off. Ironically she'd always liked to know the time; it had given her a sense of control. Funny really, she'd never felt less in control than she had since she'd been made the Time Keeper.

'Sorry,' Tamar said, letting her hand drop.

The young mother cast a nervous look towards the symbols on Tamar's bodice and another towards the wrist watch and crossed herself. She backed away, dragging the toddler with her.

Tamar sighed. 'If only you knew.'

Her finger ran over her sword and chain, it was warm which must be a good thing. The watch ticked in its woollen pocket but the ticks were getting louder. She took a deep breath. Angela had gone, maybe pulled somewhere else, and she had to get on with it.

Tamar clutched the pocket watch. 'Looks like it's just you and me ... again.'

The watch whirred happily.

'And somehow we've got to get Sir Dinadan to Trezion and our – well, my – century.'

The metal casing sat in her hand and the cogs twirled.

'Any ideas?'

Unhelpfully the watch merely ticked.

Tamar attempted to still her thoughts as she contemplated her quarry. How was she going to do this? She could hardly stroll up to the knight and calmly explain that he had to accompany her to another time and that they'd do it with the aid of a pocket watch. She knew these people believed in magic, but they also believed in witches; and those tended to encounter a rather grisly death and she wasn't ready to experience any form of dying – grisly or not.

'What do they say? Keep calm and carry on. Bet they weren't thinking of taking a medieval knight to another century when they said that!'

She watched Sir Dinadan. He was deep in conversation with another knight but then a younger man, a squire or a page or something, approached and bowed and led the other knight away.

'Right then Tamar Tamblyn come on; it's time for you to kidnap your first knight.'

She composed herself and strolled towards him while she tested a few phrases. It was important to sound convincing. She was a short distance away when she heard him shout to a servant leading a grey, white-maned horse up the field. 'Here boy, can you not see me?'

The boy led the horse towards the knight. Tamar didn't know much about horses but even she could see that this was a thoroughbred stallion. It tossed its mane, gave a little whinny and trotted towards his master, dragging the unfortunate boy with it. The horse and the man met and she saw the animal flick its ears and heard him snicker as Sir Dinadan rubbed its neck and nose. Then the knight turned to the boy and pointed towards a pavilion; it looked like he'd forgotten something important, and immediately he was running back towards the tent.

'Now's your chance, Tamar,' the Time Keeper instructed herself. 'Get on with it.' And clutching the pocket watch she approached her prey.

'Really could do with you here, Angela,' she muttered. 'I really don't want to do this by myself.'

She could have been only about twenty paces away when screams cut the air and everyone freeze-framed.

'Dinny, Uncle Dinny, come quickly.'

A couple of children were charging towards Sir Dinadan and a little girl shouted, 'We've seen a magic horse.'

Seeing that the source of the noise was merely a couple of excitable children, the crowds resumed their chat, but Tamar sidled closer.

'Come and thee,' a little, barefoot boy enthused.

'Have you two escaped from your mother again?'

The children ignored this comment as the girl, all tousled hair and big blue eyes, repeated, 'Come on Uncle Dinny, it's magic!'

'Yeth,' the boy lisped. He was just past toddler-stage, about two or three years old. 'It'th magic, ithn't it El'nor?'

Tamar saw a smile creep across the knight's face.

'Well, it must be true if Elinor says it is!'

Elinor surveyed the knight seriously. 'It *is* true Uncle Dinny. It was white and it had a ...'

Her brother chipped in. 'It had a big white ...' but then was lost for words, so his sister took over.

'It had a horn!' Elinor finished triumphantly. 'On its head.'

Dinadan's smile was replaced by a frown. 'A horn?'

He crouched down and, face to face with Elinor, said, 'You know it's very bad to tell untruths, Elinor.'

But Elinor said, 'It's not an untruth Uncle, it's a true.'

The smile crept back.

'Well, maybe if it's a true we should go and see it together.'

But something in the man's tone annoyed the girl. She might only be little but she could sniff out a patronising manner a mile off. 'It *is* a true. We did see it. It was by the lake.'

Dinadan stood up. 'Do you want a ride on my horse?'

The children began to bounce. 'Oh, yes please, Uncle Dinny!'

'Perhaps we can go and find this magic horse together.'

'No they can *not* Dinadan!' A young woman burst out from between two pavilions and folded her arms: the female war stance.

'Lowenek has been looking high and low for these children and you have had them here all the time. When will you grow up?'

Sir Dinadan opened his mouth to protest but the woman carried on. She was beautiful and petite, but with those two spots of angry colour on her cheeks Tamar was reminded of her sister when she'd been crossed.

'This will not do Dinadan. You must take life more seriously. They could have been drowned or injured. Poor

Lowenek has a hard enough time looking after them without you making life more difficult for her.'

Again Sir Dinadan began to speak just as the little girl said, 'Uncle Dinny is taking us to see the magic horse.'

'Yeth,' her brother agreed, 'it'th in the woods.'

'Oh no, he is *not* taking you to see a magic horse. He's a very naughty man.'

Tamar witnessed a knight wilting. A rare phenomenon.

'Marya, I …'

'No excuses, Dinadan.' Marya turned to the children. 'Come along. Lowenek is waiting for you. She's in tears, the poor girl.' She shot a severe look at the knight. 'Her job is already difficult, having to look after you two, without making it worse by disappearing like that. You are not permitted to run off. That was very bad.'

Scooping up her son and holding out a hand to her daughter, Marya turned to the unfortunate knight. 'Next time Dinadan, perhaps you will have a thought for others.' Her eyes bore into him. 'I beg you to consider the consequences of your actions and what effect they have on those around you. Maybe it is time for you to find a wife to keep you in order!'

And with that threat ringing in his ears, Marya stalked off leaving Dinadan standing alone and forlorn with his horse.

Tamar watched him as he ruefully exchanged a wave with the little boy now hanging over his mother's shoulder and heard him turn to his horse and mutter, 'Me? Get a wife? Never!'

He swung himself onto his mount and called out to his page who was just returning, sweating and panting, with a brightly painted lance. 'Boy take care of my weapon until I return. I'll be but a moment.'

The page bowed but Tamar saw his eyes roll and

guessed that his master changing his mind was not unusual.

Sir Dinadan dug his heels into his horse's side and set off at an angry trot.

'Oh no!' Tamar exploded under her breath, and hurried after the errant knight. 'Don't go.'

She picked up her skirts and ran after the unsuspecting knight. 'Come on then my trusty time companion.' The watch allowed its cogs an extra turn and a couple of quick ticks. 'We'll trap this man if it's the last thing we do.'

The page watched his knight disappear into the woods – followed by a girl who appeared to be talking to herself.

***

The woods were cold and dark. The winter sun barely penetrated. Trees grew close to one another, knitted together with ivy and brambles. Tamar had a flashback (or a flash-sideways) to her first piece of involuntary time travel when she'd landed in a snowy wood. Was this the same winter before the snow came, or was it another one?

A narrow path wound through the trees.

On a moss-covered branch above the path a squirrel gnawed a hazelnut. Closer to ground level a robin hopped onto a twig. It watched the knight and his horse pass followed a few minutes later by a girl. The robin flew to the top of the tree, tilted its head and began to sing. The notes rose and spread and swept towards another robin perched in the heart of an old oak. This second bird listened for a few seconds before puffing out its red breast and relaying the song, note for note. The message spread from branch to branch and tree to tree. At ground level a few dead leaves stirred and at the forest edge the wind sighed. The knight and the girl were nearly there.

Tamar had her head down, preoccupied with attempting to avoid the worst of the brambles, so she walked straight into the man standing in her path, his hand on his horse's reins.

'Now, why are you walking in my steps, I wonder?'

His blue eyes searched hers. They weren't tolerant. He'd had enough of women for today.

Tamar was lost for words.

'Do you think that I'm blind, that I failed to observe you as you watched me and the children and Marya?'

'Um …'

'Well? Answer me girl!' His eyes were cold.

'Well, um, the thing is …'

'What 'thing'?'

'No, not an actual thing. The, um, the situation is …'

The knight tutted and looked heavenwards.

She sighed and tried to come up with a plausible explanation. Really there was only one way – and that was to tell the truth.

Taking a deep breath she began. 'I've been sent to present a quest to you.'

An eyebrow rose.

She continued desperately. 'It's true. It's a quest to rescue someone who's been captured.'

The other eyebrow joined in.

'And to conquer an island that's been taken over by an evil queen.'

The eyebrows all but disappeared under the thatch of blond hair. The girl's ramblings sounded like an over-the-top fairy tale. First of all he'd had his niece and nephew telling him stories about a horned horse and now here was this girl, a stranger, babbling some nonsense about a quest. No knight in their right mind would believe these stories.

But her mouth just kept on. 'And the person who's been captured by this evil queen, he's a good friend of mine and he's got a dragon.' Her face twisted, and she tried to choke back the tears, but one escaped and rolled down her cheek. 'And it might die if we don't sort out this horrible woman!'

The knight scrutinised the girl. Was she mad?

However, perhaps fortunately for Tamar, a movement in a clearing behind the knight stalled any other words.

She wiped her damp cheek and peered past her interrogator.

The faintest breeze slipped between the twigs and branches. Dead leaves eddied. Dinadan's horse whinnied and pawed the ground and, wide-eyed, pulled on its reins.

In Tamar's pocket the watch began to stir and in her brain words and pictures tumbled over each other as the illustration from a children's picture book came into focus.

The shape in the clearing moved and looked directly at her.

'Um …' She pointed to the clearing at Dinadan's back.

His frown reappeared but to give him credit he didn't ignore his horse's strange behaviour. Instead he slowly turned to follow the direction of Tamar's shaking finger.

The shape shook its mane and lowered its head.

A unicorn, a real unicorn, was standing a few paces from them: pure white, almost silver, with a long, tapering horn at the centre of its forehead.

Dinadan shook his head and whispered, 'Those children were telling the truth.'

He gazed at the creature for a few moments before shaking his head again and slowly turning his horse so that it might see its distant relative.

In Tamar's pocket, the watch ticked enthusiastically.

Dinadan didn't take his eyes off the beast as he quietly said, 'It is well known that no man can touch such a creature; only the sight of a maiden will tame him.'

But Tamar wasn't about to try and tame him. She didn't think that was the reason for the creature's appearance.

For some minutes neither of them spoke. The unicorn was much larger than she would have imagined – if she'd believed in unicorns. It was probably the height of a shire horse and its eyes were sapphire blue. She longed to stroke it but somehow that would have been just plain rude (rather like trying to give the queen a hug). Tamar guessed that a unicorn demanded rather more respect than an ordinary horse.

She speculated on the reason for its appearance and remembered that the last time she'd seen one, although nothing more than a stone statue, had been at Dr Columbarius's, or Merlin's, house. She attempted to organise her thoughts. Perhaps it had come so that she could grab Sir Dinadan. But in the middle of these thoughts a couple of slender trees on the opposite side of the clearing shook … and another shape emerged.

Crystals of frost inched over the ivy. Tiny particles of ice crept over the earth and snaked up gnarled trunks. They swarmed along branches to the twig-ends and within moments icy stalactites had grown and hung, glittering, above the forest floor. It could have been a beautiful Christmas grotto except instead of a red-robed Father Christmas appearing, the emerging figure was dressed in black.

Tamar's throat dried. 'Oh no.'

'So, my little Time Keeper, we meet again.'

The woman's words curled mockingly in the cold air. The Ice Lady had returned. Somehow she'd sniffed out the Time Keeper. It looked like she, too, could travel through time.

'What …?' started Sir Dinadan.

The Lady of Clehy was wearing her signature black velvet and, as usual, her hair was piled on top of her head. But this time she looked paler, less *solid*, than she'd appeared on their last encounter. There was a translucent quality about her, as if she'd left a few molecules behind.

'Now, I wonder why you've been sent. Why you should be here in this particular century,' the woman ruminated. The words, although quietly spoken, coiled through the cooling air, filling the clearing.

'Who …?' attempted Sir Dinadan.

The woman placed a gloved finger thoughtfully under her chin. 'Why should you be so close to the time of that particular king? He is handsome is he not? And his Queen Guinevere is beautiful. They are happy. For now.'

She paused and fiddled with her collar. 'But how easily can even the best be brought down! It will take such a little effort to divert them from their proper course.'

The woman smiled a self-satisfied smile. 'It can be just a matter of seconds for the wrong path to be chosen and for a life to be changed forever – but you know how their story ends don't you?'

She didn't expect an answer, instead she watched a stalactite icicle stretch and grow. Wherever her gaze fell another icy needle took root until every branch and every twig was bending under their weight.

'How …?' whispered Sir Dinadan.

'So much more appealing than summer.' She looked sharply at Tamar. 'Of course, that was when we last met wasn't it?'

She stroked the trunk of the nearest tree and watched the frost grow at her touch. 'Ice and dark is so much more attractive than sun and light. Don't you agree?' She studied her gloved fingers and her face darkened, recalling the damage inflicted by the pocket watch on their previous meeting. 'My hands are covered; they will never again see the light of day,' she mused. 'However, this time I'm prepared. Your mechanical companion won't harm me a second time.'

A twig snapped and an icicle fell to the ground.

'Oh,' said Sir Dinadan, his usual eloquence lost.

The unicorn shook its mane and took a couple of steps towards the centre of the clearing, positioning itself between the Ice Lady and the girl and the knight. A yellow cone of sunshine flicked on and the unicorn was in the spotlight. Tamar and the knight and his horse stood on rising ground on one side of the clearing and the Ice Lady stood on lower ground directly opposite them. The middle ground was occupied by the unicorn.

The Ice Lady frowned and remarked, 'It would seem that you are not alone in your travels.'

She flicked a suspicious look at Tamar. 'Maybe Merlin is up to his old tricks. That man is always dabbling in matters that don't concern him.'

'And you are ...?' managed Sir Dinadan.

'A. Very. Evil. Woman,' Tamar answered for the Ice Lady, pulling the words together. Every syllable was an effort.

'Ahhh!' a frosty exclamation escaped as the Ice Lady examined the man and his mount. 'Maybe you too are to be enlisted.'

'Enlisted?' Sir Dinadan repeated.

She tilted her head. 'Perhaps they feel that more warriors are needed to prop up their pitiful defences.'

Tamar remembered the Lady's hands freezing her with a single touch.

The woman said, 'If I were you, sir, I would leave before your future is forever changed.' Her eyes slid over Tamar and narrowed. 'Before this little witch has the opportunity to make life more than a little complicated for you.'

The woman's fingers itched in their velvet gloves. The scars from her last meeting with the girl hadn't faded. The young Time Keeper and her timepiece had wreaked lasting damage on her hands. Her skin should be young but now it was withered and translucent and it was all the fault of the girl and her watch. 'Before she can inflict unspeakable horrors.'

Sir Dinadan turned towards Tamar. 'Who *are* you?'

But through the despair filling Tamar's mind, a tiny corner was still hers and she wasn't going to stand for this. The Ice Lady smiled and it was that superior smile that finally did it for Tamar and un-did the Ice Lady's work. The pocket watch whirred encouragingly and the unicorn turned to face Tamar, lifted its head and gazed deep into her eyes. The ice retreated, melting as fast as the Lady of Clehy could spin it.

'Those are all lies.' Every word was a struggle against the woman's power but Tamar wasn't going to have her character tarnished. 'None of that is true.'

Sir Dinadan was rooted to the spot, unable to move as he listened to the conversation. Even his horse was still.

The Lady of Clehy smiled again. 'Do you think he cares who tells the truth and who lies?' She looked at Tamar, her head on one side and blinked. Tamar had the uncanny feeling that at any moment the woman could take flight and swoop and seize her and tear her apart.

But the unicorn had turned its back on the Lady of Clehy and had begun to walk towards Tamar.

The knight stirred and passed his hand over his eyes as if he'd been dreaming. Tamar opened her eyes wide, willing herself to stay awake. She was drowning in drowsiness. She took a long breath of icy air and ordered her feet to move. They felt like lead but, bit by tiny bit, the blood began to pump. Pins and needles jumped in her toes as she wriggled them and edged towards the knight. She would have to have enough willpower for them both. Her hand was ready in her pocket. 'Are you ready to begin the quest, sir?' she whispered, ignoring the weight pressing down on her eyelids.

'Quest?'

'To rescue a boy and a dragon and to release an island.'

The woman took a step into the clearing but Tamar had her hand on the pocket watch. She would have loved to discover whether the Ice Lady was as well protected as she claimed, but she had other priorities.

'Hold onto your horse, sir.'

The unicorn was close, its warm breath dispersing the icy crystals.

The Ice Lady began to stride towards them, twigs cracking like gunshots under her feet, but the unicorn was in front of her and now the Ice Lady showed her true colours.

'Out of my way beast!' She raised her hand, but hesitated.

'Quickly, hold a strand of the unicorn's mane sir,' Tamar instructed the knight. 'Whatever you do, don't let go. Hold onto your horse with your other hand.'

The knight wearily raised his hand, it was such an *effort* and it felt so heavy, but the unicorn sidled closer to the knight.

The Ice Lady's hand hovered close to the unicorn's silky tail. She had to get past but the creature was blocking her way.

'You won't escape, you foolish girl. The only power you have is borrowed from that jumped-up timepiece.'

The pocket watch's ticks grew louder.

It didn't appreciate name-calling and it hated bullies.

'And you think that your power is stronger?' Tamar asked as she slid her hand under the knight's arm. 'Remember what happened last time you tried to challenge me and my "jumped-up timepiece"?' Unicorn, knight, girl and horse were primed and ready to go. 'Or has your skin healed under those velvet gloves?'

The Ice Lady's eyes darkened and a crow cawed. Muttering black words she stretched out bony, but velvet-protected, fingers just as the young Time Keeper whispered an imperative, 'Now!'

The watch geared its cogs and readied its hands and in the branches the robin sang as the world began to spin. A furious shriek filled the woods, launching flocks of birds and sending animals for cover.

And an icy touch brushed Tamar's neck and wrist.

Chapter 16
The Plan

The unicorn stepped into the snow.

Sir Dinadan was still holding the creature's mane and Tamar still had her arm threaded through his. The watch had quietened as it usually did after a trip, satisfied that all had gone to plan and that its Time Keeper had been delivered to her destination. It had been aware of the cooling of its mistress's skin at the very last moment, and the Ice Lady's scream had momentarily interfered with its cogs, but not enough to stop them turning. It allowed itself a celebratory chime and resumed its normal time keeping.

Tamar dropped the knight's arm.

'We're safe now.'

Her neck and wrist stung like nettle stings, but much, much deeper.

'You can let the unicorn go.'

But the knight wasn't listening. 'What alchemy is this?' Sir Dinadan was having trouble adjusting to his different surroundings – a wood still, but this one illuminated by moonlight filtering through bare branches on to drifting snow. Somewhere far off an owl called.

Tamar was so very tired and her skin hurt. The Ice Lady had inflicted her own form of injury. But it wasn't the external hurt that bothered Tamar so much as the dark shafts of pain and despair lodged deep inside her. They would be harder to heal.

The unicorn turned and walked slowly towards the Time Keeper and lowered its head. Sapphire-blue eyes framed by long curling lashes held hers.

Hesitantly she reached out and touched its velvet nose. 'Thank you for coming,' she whispered. 'You know, you're very beautiful.'

The unicorn breathed warmly on her cheek and neck and the stinging in her skin faded.

'I don't know what I would have done without you. I think she would have caught me.'

But before she had time to dwell on the alternative outcomes, the unicorn turned and trotted into the woods, leaving hoof prints in the snow.

Tamar looked at her captured knight. His colour had deserted him.

'I think I know where we are, but to be on the safe side let's follow the unicorn's tracks; they should lead us in the right direction.'

'The right direction,' the knight repeated. He was in shock.

'Yes, we've got to get to Dr Falco Columbarius's house.'

'Falco columbarius … a merlin.'

'That's right,' Tamar agreed. 'A Merlin.'

She took the horse's reins from the knight's hand and led it through the wood with Sir Dinadan sleep-walking at her side.

The white wood was still. Animal prints chased across the snow, weaving under thickets of hawthorn and hazel, and another robin appeared. It hopped onto a twig where the trees grew less closely together. Tamar turned the horse's head and walked towards it. The robin flew to the next tree and continued to sing as it fluttered on to a branch a little further away.

A gentle snow began to fall, settling on the brambles. The scent of wood smoke weaved between the trunks and a light glimmered through the thinning trees.

Tamar led the horse and the dazed knight and followed their guide. A few more paces and the trees thinned some more and parted to reveal a house – with a stone unicorn standing on the edge of its slate roof.

The oak door opened and a white-haired man, wearing a long, blue cloak and leaning on a staff, stood framed and waiting for his final guests. Tamar led the knight and his horse out of the tree cover and towards the house. Last time she'd approached this building it had been with Arthur, Gawain and Nick … and Nick had been making them laugh as usual. Her eyes filled.

The knight stared. 'Merlin?'

Merlin held out his hand. 'Dinadan, we've been waiting for you.'

He glanced from the knight to Tamar and he smiled. 'You've done well.' But then the smile faded. 'However, we haven't much time.'

Tamar's stomach lurched. 'Nick and Dragon?'

The man nodded and Tamar saw worry lines reassert themselves.

'Do you know where they are?'

Another nod.

'Has *she* got them?' A thought raced after the question. 'But how can she? We've just seen her.'

Merlin replied, 'In the same way that you can be here in this century my dear.'

He stood to one side. '*Deeo agye*, come in, Dinadan, your horse will find his way to the stables.' He took a step towards the knight standing, still dream-like, at the foot of the porch steps.

'I know this must appear a little strange my friend, but

I can assure you that very soon it will be easier to comprehend … well, a little easier perhaps.' He smiled briefly. 'Worlds spin and turn but the constant is friendship and love for those we may not even yet know.' He caught Tamar's eye. 'Care and love can transform even the most timid of souls.' The smile grew. 'And I am in the presence of two of the bravest souls.'

Tamar shook her head. 'I'm not brave.'

'I'm not going to argue the point with you Miss Tamblyn, we haven't time, but I would merely ask you to examine the evidence of your own actions.'

Tamar wiped away a treacherous tear. Any form of praise was dangerous right now.

A shout echoed from inside the house. Merlin glanced over his shoulder and then towards the knight and the black-haired girl at his side; her dress was witness to her travels. 'Come in Dinadan, we're having tea while we lay our plans. You can meet some old friends.'

The knight mounted the steps as his horse trotted to the side of the house. Merlin put his arm around Dinadan's shoulder and led him towards the library. Tamar followed them through the candlelit hall with its mosaic floor and sweeping staircase, and on down the corridor past the armoury.

The library doors swung open and a blast of warm air and light reached out and an owl screeched a welcome. Tamar noticed a hedgehog bustle past as her attention was drawn to the humans in the room.

Michael Jolly was sitting quietly in an armchair. How weird that she'd seen his sister hundreds of years away. He held up a hand in greeting. The worry lines were still forged across his forehead but he was less pale than he'd been when she'd left. It seemed impossible that only a few hours had passed since that discussion in the caravan. A few hours and she'd travelled to another century full of knights and rats and muddy tracks. She wished she could wipe away the angry words she had aimed at him.

But then her attention was drawn to Kitto Cornish, immersed in a book which appeared to be turning its own pages.

He glanced up. 'Hello my dear. Had a good trip? I'm learning about how our molecules reassemble after travelling through time and portals. Very helpful.' He returned to studying the book as it turned a page.

But perhaps strangest of all was the sight of two elderly knights wielding fearsome swords against her friends.

As she watched, Sir Bedivere was lowering his sword, protesting. 'You expect too much of them Lancelot. Time is not on our side. We can only instruct our young friends in the rudiments of sword play.'

But Lancelot was objecting. 'Old friend, it is vital they learn as much as we are able to teach them – we face a deadly enemy.'

'I'm aware of that Lancelot, but perhaps a few moves well learnt are more use than several poorly learnt.'

And Arthur was raising his sword, asking, 'Can we go through how to parry again?' He was only too aware of how little time they had.

Rozen (who'd now acclimatised to Bedivere and Lancelot's presence) was holding a sword with both hands. 'Gawain, how about you try the middle-guard move. You know, the one where you sort of hold the grip near your stomach and point the blade at my face, and I try to defend myself.'

'Are you sure?' Gawain asked. 'These things are dangerous.'

'No kidding! Come on, we've got to have some idea of what we're doing.'

Rozen was attempting a defensive stance, her feet planted on the rug, when she glanced towards the library door and exclaimed, 'Tamar!'

Arthur spun around, his sword in his hand, forcing Bedivere to leap back with a yell of, 'Art! Your sword!'

And immediately, blushing at his error, the young king was grabbing the sword's scabbard and crossing the room and crushing Tamar in an immense bear hug.

He smelt of wood smoke. Tamar closed her eyes. She felt his heart beating and for the first time that day – whichever day it was – she felt safe.

He stepped back and held her by the shoulders. 'You look done for.'

Tamar didn't trust herself to speak. Tears were too close and that hug had been too welcome.

Arthur wished he could use deep words to talk to her so that they could speak without anyone else overhearing them. A confusing mixture of emotions welled up. Awkwardly, he ran his fingers through his hair and twisted the miniature sword hanging around his neck.

They looked at one another for several seconds before there was a discreet cough from Merlin. 'Our young Time Keeper has done well, has she not, sire?'

Arthur nodded, 'Very well,' and took in the knight at Tamar's side.

Whereas both Bedivere and Lancelot were white-haired, Dinadan, having been snatched from his own century, was blond. He was tall and broad-shouldered and ramrod straight. And very good-looking. In fact he was everything anyone would imagine a knight to be.

As far as Arthur could tell he hadn't been about to fight because he wasn't wearing chain mail or heavy armour of any sort, just a sort of robe or cloak over his other clothes.

But the knight was unaware of Arthur's scrutiny. Nothing could explain this house and its strange inhabitants, with a pair of elderly knights calling each other by such familiar names. Bedivere and Lancelot? He'd jousted with both only that day. But they hadn't resembled these two elderly men with their white hair.

He passed his tongue over his lips and whispered to the man at his side, 'What kind of wizardry is this, Merlin?'

A frown settled on Merlin's forehead. This was a tricky one to explain. If he wasn't careful Sir Dinadan would be too traumatised to be of any help.

Lancelot opened his mouth but Merlin shook his head.

The clock ticked in the corner and the candle flames on the Christmas tree sank before flickering back into life.

'Arthur, maybe it's time for refreshment from your exercising and learning. Perhaps we could all benefit from a plate of Mrs Beswetherick's famous cake and a glass of something to fortify us. There's a bottle of mead warming by the fire.'

But his deep words were telling the other deep thinkers, 'This poor man is confused and on the edge of reason. Lancelot, you must give him time to adjust. He has travelled over many centuries in order to be with us.'

Lancelot closed his mouth and Bedivere put down his sword, exchanging it for the mead.

The others understood what was going on and quietly moved towards the fire and a low table loaded with home-made cakes, biscuits and scones.

'*Deeo neaz than tane*, come close to the fire, Dinadan. You look tired.'

Merlin grasped the puzzled knight by the elbow and led him towards a chair and nodded meaningfully towards some sparkling glasses.

'A glass of mead my friend.'

Arthur took the bottle from Bedivere and, exchanging a quick look, filled a glass and handed it to their host.

Merlin smiled. 'I think it would be helpful if perhaps we all had a small glass, we may need to be fortified against the night that is to come.'

Bedivere and Arthur passed the glasses round. In a corner close to the fire the hedgehog had rolled herself into a spiky ball while Fly and Lightning stretched themselves in front of the flames, warming their stomachs. Tamar had taken only a single sip of mead when part of a mouse, the tail end, dropped at her feet. She looked up. On a beam high above her, Tyto glared down at the half-eaten rodent. Tamar noticed the new ceiling and her mouth dropped open.

Arthur handed her a piece of lemon cake. 'Impressive isn't it?'

'How did he do it?'

He shrugged. 'No idea.'

Pushing the earlier emotions away he said, 'It was like this when we got here. To be honest we really haven't had time to think about it. We've been too busy learning how to use a sword.'

'Have you got Excalibur?' She looked around hopefully.

He shook his head. 'Nope, apparently I'll find it at the right time – whenever that is. Although it seems to be leaving it to the last minute. Anyway, what about you? Was it all okay?'

Tamar shoved a wedge of cake into her mouth and wondered how the housekeeper's preparations for Christmas were going. She'd almost forgotten about Christmas Day. The warm fire and soft candlelight should have been comforting but she was too aware of the absence of Nick and Dragon.

Arthur waved a hand in front of her face. 'Hello. Earth calling Tamar.'

'Sorry, yes it was okay' ... *apart from a boy hanging from a gibbet and me nearly being caught by the Lady of Clehy* ... 'Yes, it was fine.' Later she'd tell him about meeting Angela and seeing the boy and the Ice Lady. Sometime she'd tell him about the unicorn, and she might even have a go at describing her time-journeys, but not now.

Instead she asked, 'So what's the plan?' because every second was valuable.

A flame shot up and a log crackled.

Merlin walked towards the fire, picked up a log and weighed it in his hand before throwing it onto the grate. It hissed and spat but he gave it one of his stern looks and it settled down.

He turned and surveyed the assembled company.

'The plan, Miss Tamblyn?' He stroked his short beard and surveyed the room just as Rozen's top hat stirred and a feathery head peered from under the brim.

'Perhaps first we should consider the problem and the talents we have gathered.'

Tamar dug her nails into her palms. She was desperate to be on the move but Merlin glanced at her with a look that said, 'Wait.'

Silence, punctuated by crackles and hisses from the sappy piece of oak filled the room. At intervals sweet-scented wood smoke drifted from the granite hearth. On the wall the clock ticked, its pendulum marking each passing second of Nick's imprisonment. And at the back of the room, dwarfed by the now-vaulted ceiling, the Christmas tree twinkled.

Michael Jolly and Kitto Cornish (Kitto was still coming to terms with being one of such an illustrious company), Sir Bedivere and Sir Lancelot – the four deep speakers – waited. They had many years' experience of their old friend's wisdom.

Merlin took off his spectacles and polished them with his sleeve. Dinadan had begun to stir as if he was waking from a dream, and was looking curiously at the elderly knights.

Merlin began. 'Dinadan, I imagine that all of this must be a puzzle for you: this house and these people. But you will have to trust me when I tell you that we need you. A young boy and his dragon are in peril.'

The knight cast a quick look towards Tamar. 'The girl was telling the truth?'

Tamar nodded. 'Just like Elinor and her brother.'

Dinadan wiped a hand over his eyes. 'Elinor …'

'You'll see them again,' Merlin reassured him. 'You are with us for a while, no more. Your time in that century won't be cut short.'

'That *century*?'

Merlin rested a hand on the stone mantelpiece and ignored Dinadan's outburst.

'So, we have three knights,' he bowed towards Bedivere, Lancelot and Dinadan.

'We have Michael Jolly and Kitto Cornish.' He exchanged a small bow with each of the other two wise men.

'And we have Gawain with his sword cane, Rozen with her falcon and Miss Tamblyn with her mighty timepiece.' The watch ticked enthusiastically. 'And of course we have our sire, who is yet to be reunited with Excalibur.'

At the mention of a sire and Excalibur, Dinadan again looked confused but Tamar, focusing on her kidnapped knight, leant across and put her hand on his arm. 'We'll explain later.' She felt partially responsible for his confusion but he nodded as a tiny smile tugged at his lips. 'Maybe you have an older sister Miss Tamblyn?'

She coloured at the implied compliment and shook her head. 'She's got a boyfriend.' Her heart thumped at the possible complications of Wenna and this handsome knight meeting.

'Dinadan!' Merlin scolded, but he smiled. The knight's personality was reasserting itself.

'So we have our team and now we have our quest.'

Dinadan glanced at Tamar and arched his eyebrows and Arthur felt the tiniest of jealous tugs.

Merlin gathered himself. 'There is no doubt that the Lady of Clehy is determined to rule the island, the Little Mount, and in turn to take Cornwall.'

Gawain's grip on the sword cane tightened.

'We must not underestimate her power. Although it is based on shifting sands it is strong, and of course she has the dragon and Nick.' He hesitated. 'Furthermore I have reason to believe that they, Dragon and Nick, have been separated.'

Kitto Cornish's head jerked up. 'Separated?'

Merlin nodded. 'I'm very much afraid so.'

Michael Jolly looked grim. 'Bad, very bad.'

Rozen and Gawain looked at one another and Arthur, watching Tamar, saw her colour fade. He knew what she was thinking. In her mind this was all her fault. He wished he could reassure her but the only thing that would make it better would be the rescue of Nick and Dragon. And now, at last, Merlin began to outline his plan.

Chapter 17
The Queen of the Castle

The boat thumped against the harbour wall. Under its hull the sea swelled and fell away. The spotty boy steered it close to the steps, killed the motor and leapt over the side.

The Crow Man surveyed the empty harbour. Satisfied that no one was on hand to observe them, he ordered, 'Take the sacking off the boy. He can't escape … unless he can swim with his arms tied.'

The sack was lifted and at last Nick was able to take a dust-free breath but Hagarawall yanked at the ropes binding his wrists and a fresh shell of pain exploded. Nick swayed.

Cador sneered, 'Can you climb the steps, Dragon Boy?'

Nick swallowed, he wasn't about to say or do anything that might put Dragon at risk; they could mock him all they liked. He glanced at the spotty boy straining on the boat's rope. Their eyes met but the boy's nervous gaze slid towards the Crow Man. It was obvious that there was no way he'd risk his own safety.

The Crow Man picked up the metal box containing its precious cargo and stepped out of the boat and onto the harbour steps. Nick followed his every move.

Cador's eyes narrowed. 'Maybe you care too much for your creature?' The Ice Lady's son considered their prisoner. 'Why not give the box to me Brane? I'm certain that our friend would like to see whether his pet can endure complete immersion.'

And before the Crow Man was able to react, he'd

snatched the metal chest out of his hands and was holding it above the inky water.

'Maybe I should carry out an experiment: do dragons like water or do they drown?'

Nick's stomach knotted.

Cador pretended to slip but the snowy steps were more slippery than he'd anticipated and the pretence became a reality. He wobbled precariously and his eyes widened and the box slid through his fingers.

'No!' Nick screamed, unable to contain himself. The box tumbled towards the sea.

The Crow Man leapt forward yelling, 'Are you mad Cador?' and grabbed the spinning tin. A split second more and it would have disappeared.

The Crow Man stepped back from the water's edge and shook his head in disbelief. 'You might be her son, but you know what your mother would do if she learnt of your stupidity.' Drying the box against his coat he muttered, 'I had my doubts about you and you've proved me right. You're still wet behind the ears, nothing more than an apprentice.'

Cador coloured and opened his mouth but the Crow Man growled, 'Say nothing boy! Save your blustering. Your actions could have cost us dearly.'

The Ice Lady's son glowered but swallowed his words.

Nick's heart pounded. He would never have thought that he'd have reason to be thankful to the Crow Man.

But as if he could read his thoughts, Brane turned on Nick and leant close to his face and breathed, 'For myself, Dragon Boy, I wouldn't trouble if your dragon drowned.' He tightened his hold on the tin. 'Think yourself lucky that we have orders to deliver it to the Lady.'

He turned, muttering, and mounted the steps, his coat brushing the stones and his crow hopping ahead of him.

Nick's mouth was dry. He didn't care one jot what Brane's motives for saving Dragon were. He'd saved him and that was all that mattered. His legs shook and his heart thumped as Hagarawall pushed him up the steps.

'Get a move on.' He shoved Nick between his shoulder blades. 'She's waiting.'

The spotty boy was busying himself with the boat, making a show of winding in the slimy rope; anything rather than meet Nick's eye. He didn't dare to say or do anything that might anger the Ice Lady or her allies. He'd dared once – before he'd realised what he was dealing with – and the result had been painful. He wasn't about to try it again.

Nick managed a sarcastic, 'Thanks for the help!' before Hagarawall propelled him over the last step and onto the snowy cobbles and past a row of cottages at the foot of the island's hill. Lights glowed behind their curtains and smoke rose from the stone chimneys, but all the doors remained resolutely shut.

***

Servo and Viatoris Watched the procession: Brane holding the now-quiet tin box, Hagarawall driving his prisoner forward, and a sulky Cador bringing up the rear. They Watched the crow take flight and swoop up the hill towards the castle's turrets as the white dog chased up the winding path. And they noted a group of horses, each as black as night, tethered on an open stretch of grass behind the cottages.

Normally Viatoris could be relied upon to use their meetings to boast about his youthful prodigy, crowing about the boy Leonardo's latest invention or artistic endeavour, but tonight he was silent.

Both Watchers were horribly aware of Dragon's plight.

The creature would be cold; which was never a good thing for a dragon. He would be hungry; young dragons needed regular feeding. And he would be lonely. It was a dangerous combination. It was clear that although Brane was fulfilling his mistress's wishes he was doing it with the minimum of care.

Servo shook his head. 'Brane had better hurry if the dragon is to be delivered alive to the woman.'

Viatoris sighed. 'And even if it is still alive, how much longer will it survive if they are separated?'

'I calculate there are only hours left.'

The other Watcher nodded. 'I agree. The dragon is young. It imprinted the boy as its parent. The dragon's minder was the first to hold it and the first to care for it. As far as it is concerned, he is its parent.'

'We have to hope that the boy's allies are ready.'

Viatoris glanced at his companion and voiced the unthinkable. 'How I wish for the gift of intervention.'

Servo looked around nervously as if their boss, the Writer, might appear at his elbow. 'We both know that no such thing is permitted.'

'And yet,' Viatoris continued, 'and yet we both have broken The Rule.'

Servo didn't say anything. His memory of pulling Arthur into an earthy hideaway and screening him from the scrutiny of the skeletal highwayman was still fresh. He shifted guiltily.

But Viatoris didn't try to prove any superiority. Instead he stated, 'And it was I who briefly removed the young Leonardo to this century, only for him to witness the miracle of flight.'

Ruefully he added, 'His idea of man's ability to conquer the air has always been attributed to his genius, but it was my tampering with time that was the root of his belief.'

Servo cast an astonished look at his colleague. In all their years working together – and it was *many* years – he'd never heard Viatoris admit to making a mistake. He could almost begin to like his time-travelling companion.

'But now we have to Watch,' Viatoris continued. 'Does the Writer know what is happening?'

'I believe she does. She is close to the Manor. She waits for Cornwall's Guardians to assemble. The Time Keeper has travelled but I'm certain that she will be back before the night is over.'

Viatoris sneezed and pulled his cloak around him as an icy squall blew in from the sea. A cloud slid in front of the moon and a wave surged against the harbour wall. Flakes of snow settled on the Watchers, reducing their invisibility. It was just as well that no one came out of the cottages. They might have been freaked out by two snow-covered but, apparently, hollow shells of people standing on the harbour wall.

***

Hagarawall pushed Nick through the low doorway and watched him stumble and fall onto the stone floor. He checked the room. The only window was set high up in the wall. It was small, no bigger than a computer screen, and secured with iron grills.

His eyes darted around the room.

'Come on Hagarawall, she'll be waiting,' Cador called impatiently. He'd recovered his spirit. 'And you, Dragon Boy, you'll have this room all to yourself.' He looked at the stone cell. 'I don't think you'll be leaving here in a hurry.'

But Hagarawall frowned. Last summer the girl and her friend had escaped from a seemingly secure prison. Somehow they'd tricked their way out of the ship's hold and had even organised a waiting boat to carry them to land.

He thought of that toothless old man who'd been shackled in the hold with his dog; even he had vanished into thin air.

Another shout echoed down the stone stairs and along the low, rounded roof of the corridor.

'That's Brane,' Cador informed Hagarawall helpfully. 'Come on. Just lock it. He won't be going anywhere.'

Hagarawall didn't reply. As far as he could see there wasn't a way out of the cell and, anyway, the boy's arms were tied. He swung the door shut and turned the key in the lock and dropped it in his pocket.

Nick listened to their footsteps echo and fade along the corridor.

A single candle burned in his cell. There was no furniture. Not a chair or a rug, nothing. Just a cold stone floor and white-washed walls. He'd never felt so hopeless.

He thought of the treacherous path leading from the harbour, the barred castle door and the windowless corridor. The outside door had been locked and he'd heard the key turn in the door of his cell. There was no hope of escape.

'I've had it.'

He shuffled to the corner facing the door, wedged his back against the wall and slid down.

'Dragon, how are we going to get out of this one?'

His head bowed. Even if he could escape he couldn't run. He was in no fit state to take on one of his enemies never mind all four of them.

***

A couple of floors up, two men and a boy stood in front of a woman. She'd installed herself in the blue drawing room.

The crimson library had been too cosy and the great hall had too many reminders of the ancestry of this castle, with its shields and coat of arms, and she was still smarting from failing to capture the Time Keeper and the knight. By now the pair of them would be with that man. She avoided even *thinking* his name.

A couple of candles flickered pathetically in the corner and the ashes in the cold grate stirred. The woman preferred the minimum of heat and light.

The Lady of Clehy shot a glance at the metal box.

Her skin had a glossy, marble sheen. Brane observed her from under the brim of his hat. She'd been travelling again. Every time she travelled she appeared less solid. Hiding his thoughts he held the box and waited.

'We got it for you!' Cador began enthusiastically but withered under his mother's gaze. She hated enthusiasm.

'And who secured the prize?'

'It was my idea to take them on …' Cador began, but trailed away. She had a nose for boasting.

Brane stepped forward and offered the tin box.

'Put it on the table.'

Silently the Crow Man placed it on the table. The albino hound raised its nose and sniffed.

'Open it.' Her fingers itched inside their gloves.

Slowly Brane prised the lid up and let it fall open and the woman peered inside. Dragon lifted his head. His scales had darkened from a vivid green to a dull olive green. His wings drooped and his tail lay flat on the bottom of the box. He looked up but his eyes were lifeless. An expert on dragons would recognise the warning signs, but the Ice Lady was no expert.

She frowned. 'Is this the beast?'

'It is, ma'am,' Hagarawall confirmed. 'The Dragon Boy is in the locked room.'

She placed a velvet forefinger under Dragon's chin and tipped his head back. Then she picked up the tip of his left wing and pulled it out until it was fully stretched. The skin was translucent and every vein was visible; rather like her hands.

The dragon didn't protest or struggle. His breathing was shallow and he'd begun to shiver.

She frowned again. 'A dragon should be a fearsome beast.'

Cador craned his neck to get a look at their prize. It certainly didn't look very scary.

'Maybe it needs a fire,' he offered helpfully, but one look from his mother stopped him. She hated heat.

Brane had a shrewd idea of what was wrong with the dragon but he didn't care. What was it to him if it died?

Hagarawall organised his words before speaking. 'Whether or not it is fearsome, ma'am, it's separated from its keeper and their allies.' Her cold eyes examined him. He waited before continuing. 'And, ma'am, surely they will all be weakened when they try … when they make a foolish attempt to take this place and rescue their friend and his dragon.'

The wind whistled around the castle. The woman's gaze slipped towards the tin box with its pathetic dragon and then to the window. Her finger and thumb plucked at a velvet-covered button. Brane waited.

'We could have it killed, but …'

In the box Dragon's golden eyes had begun to mist over and his head had drooped to the floor. He was tired and his master had abandoned him. He didn't have any reason to care or to fight. There was nothing left worth fighting for.

The Lady of Clehy walked to the window and peered through the leaded glass to the dark sea and sky. She looked beyond the sea to the land. Even in this light she could make out the lane winding up the hill from the village towards the house.

'But they are a weak and sentimental people. The creature alive may be more use than if he is dead.'

The Lady of Clehy smiled and pressed her gloved fingertips against the cold glass and watched the crystals form. She had the dragon and the boy, and her army was assembling.

In the depths of the sea a pale hand moved and the flesh rippled. On an ancient path a tree shivered as a shadow rushed past. At the edge of the cobbled causeway an almost-complete figure pulled himself onto the stones and slowly stood to face the castle.

On the harbour wall two snow-encrusted figures Watched the tall silhouette at the leaded window, while on the harbour steps a spotty boy tugged his coat around him and waited.

And somewhere an owl screeched.

Chapter 18
Ready, Steady …

In the brick-built stable adjoining Oakwood Manor, Lancelot and Bedivere were working their way along the wooden stalls; they both had an eye for horses.

Arthur and Gawain, Tamar and Rozen waited at one end of the sweet-smelling stable and watched the men run careful hands over the animals' spines and legs. The knights' horses were stabled there, but there were others too. One was dappled, another was grey and there was a chestnut stallion in a stall beside a black mare.

Gawain nudged Rozen and whispered, 'Watch Merlin!' because he was moving from horse to horse, stroking their necks and whispering in their ears.

'What's he doing?'

Rozen watched. 'I think he's trying to calm them.'

They followed his progress. Most responded but a couple still snorted and pawed the ground.

Gawain nudged Rozen again as Merlin stood in front of one particularly nervous horse and tapped his staff twice on the ground.

'Brilliant!' Gawain said, as a shower of white sparks flew from the staff and the horse steadied.

'That's amazing,' Rozen agreed, impressed. This was horse whispering at its most magical.

Tamar had also been watching Merlin but noticed Dinadan heading straight for his horse. She watched the knight stroke the horse's neck. *He's okay then. That's something anyway.*

Gawain nodded towards the merlin perched on Rozen's arm. 'Will it be all right on a horse?'

'Yeah, she should be fine,' Rozen said, checking the bird's jesses. 'Sometimes when we're on the road I ride our horse, Ned, and she rides with me. I was training her to be part of my act for the fairs. I do a bit of falconry and if I do it on horseback it makes it seem more impressive.'

'D'you like travelling and performing and all that?' Gawain was intrigued. He'd lived all his life above his uncle's shop.

'Mostly, but sometimes I'd just like to be like other people – go to school, have friends, go on holidays.' She stroked the bird's head with the tip of her finger. 'Dad's always on the move. I think he's scared, although he always makes out that it's just time to get to the next fair.' She shook her head, her red curls rippling. 'He's always sort of looking over his shoulder.'

Gawain nodded. 'Yeah, I got that impression when we met him. It was like part of him was dead pleased to meet us but the other part was scared.' He shot a look at Rozen, wondering if he'd offended her but she was nodding.

'And I know what you mean about wanting to be normal,' he continued. 'Until this lot came along I was pretty much a loner. Being brought up by an eccentric uncle hardly helps when you want to hang out with friends.' He twiddled the top of the sword cane. 'Perhaps if I'd known about the time travel and stuff, I wouldn't have tried to fit in.'

He glanced at Tamar. She was checking the pocket watch while Arthur leant against the wall beside her.

Judging from the young king's preoccupied look he was probably engaged in some sort of deep conversation. Arthur didn't say much, but they all knew about it. 'Now we're just a bunch of weirdos together … maybe it's all about finding your own people.'

Rozen nodded. 'Yeah, you're probably right. Find your own particular brand of geek and everything else will be fine!' She sighed. 'I wish Dad had been happier about me coming here though.'

'Was he angry?'

She shook her head. 'Not angry, no, Dad hardly ever gets angry. More sad. That made it worse. He said he'd let me come with you guys, but just this once.' Rozen thought about Michael and her father. There'd been an undercurrent of something else going on but neither of the men had said what. 'It would have been easier if he'd been cross.'

Gawain was silent. Going on past experience Rozen's dad had every reason to be worried.

'But I didn't really have a choice, did I?' Her wide grey eyes were solemn and Gawain was reminded of her little sister. 'Just like you guys didn't have a choice. I could have lived all my life in the shadows and played it safe but I can't live like that. It hasn't made Dad happy and it wouldn't work for me.'

She kicked at the straw and shot Gawain a brief look. 'Live dangerously, eh?' She grinned wickedly and dimples appeared. 'Anyway, what about you with your sword cane? Will you be able to handle *that* on a horse? Someone told me that they can be dangerous.'

Gawain rolled his eyes. 'I'm never going to be allowed to forget that am I?'

'Mmm, probably not.'

Gawain looked at Tamar leaning desolately against the wall. It was obvious what was on her mind. 'Tamar do you think it's fair that I make one crass remark and it's never forgotten?'

Tamar drifted over.

'What crass remark?' she asked vaguely. She pulled the watch out of her pocket again; it was winding itself up. She flipped the lid open and inspected its face, wondering whether it would show her anything useful. Rozen looked at it curiously.

'Is that how you get about?'

Tamar nodded, distracted. 'Yeah it's nothing to do with me. It's all about the watch.'

'Hang on!' Gawain said. 'Whose name is on it, Tamar? You were the one chosen to be the Time Keeper weren't you? Not me, not Nick; you!'

'Yeah I know, but it's not like I have special powers or anything.' She grimaced. 'Except for getting one of my best friends captured by some of the worst people I've ever met.' Her voice wobbled dangerously. 'Perhaps you could call that a special power.'

Arthur had been idly stroking Lightning's head while he watched Merlin and the knights. He'd seen Bedivere talk to Lancelot before joining Dinadan at the far end of the stables. Then he'd watched Merlin draw Bedivere to one side and engage him in earnest conversation.

But Tamar's comment cut through his thoughts. 'You're wrong,' he said firmly. 'They would have got Nick somehow. It wasn't your fault.' He pushed himself away from the wall. 'You've got to stop beating yourself up.'

'Yeah, but you've never done anything like that have you?'

Arthur didn't miss a beat. 'Remember that day on the moors, the day we met Michael and Angela the first time?'

'And?'

'*And* it was me that nearly got us all caught by the Crow Man, wasn't it?' That day was one of his recurring nightmares.

She sniffed and slid the watch back into her pocket. Since when had she turned into this emotional wreck? She couldn't stop crying and it was driving her mad.

Merlin's voice interrupted their conversation. 'Sire, your horse is approaching.'

Arthur looked up. A white stallion had appeared in the stable yard. It was Argo, the horse that had been instrumental in helping him to save Cornwall last summer. Immediately the young king ran out into the snow.

'It's so good to see you!' Arthur rubbed the great horse's neck. He sent deep words, capable of expressing so much more than the spoken word, and was rewarded by a thickly accented deep reply. 'And you, sire.'

Tamar joined the horse and his king and leant against the creature's side. 'Argo!' She breathed in his scent and for the first time dared to feel a flicker of hope as the horse responded with a snicker.

They were ready, or at least assembled, to storm an almost impenetrable castle on one of the coldest nights on record.

***

Inside Oakwood Manor, Michael Jolly and Kitto Cornish were making their own preparations.

Before he'd left, Merlin had returned the library to its former state, replacing the arched and beamed ceiling with white plaster. He was concerned not to upset Mrs Beswetherick if she should return unexpectedly.

'The great hall may yet be required,' he'd said to Michael and Kitto, 'but for now it's safer this way. Mrs B's a treasure and I couldn't do with scaring her and her cakes away.'

Kitto had nodded fervently, a crumb lodged on a shirt button. 'Quite so, Merlin, quite so!'

So now the room was quiet and not a great hall but a library again. The fire still burned in the grate and the candles still flickered on the Christmas tree (Merlin had given them a good talking-to about fire hazards). And the clock, with the engraving of Tamar's name, was ticking normally until suddenly the ticks increased. Michael and Kitto looked at one another.

'It's time my friend,' Michael said, pulling himself out of the leather armchair and reaching for his coat.

'It is indeed,' Kitto replied, as he tucked his scarf around his neck.

They faced each other and gravely shook hands.

'*Comero weeth*,' Kitto said quietly, bowing and blinking.

'Please, no bowing Kitto, we're equals! *Tereba nessa.*' Michael responded before turning to his dog and commanding, 'Come Fly, we've work to do.'

Kitto watched his old friend open the stone door at the side of the mantelpiece and step into the tunnel with his dog at his side.

The door closed and Kitto Cornish stood beside the fire and surveyed the room. The curtains might be drawn across the windows but he knew what was waiting for them. The creatures may not be able to penetrate Merlin's cleverly guarded house and grounds but they'd be waiting.

He picked up a slice of chocolate cake and took a bite. 'Ah, Mrs B, what a treasure you are, fortifying the soldiers before they go into battle.' He chuckled grimly to himself. 'It is to be hoped that you never have to witness the apparitions gathering on our shore.'

Brushing the crumbs off his coat, he picked up a book and waited while it turned its pages, one gold-edged leaf after another, until it arrived at the right place.

He adjusted his glasses and peered at the book. 'Ah, yes, I was hoping you might show me that.' He examined a set of instructions.

Closing the book with a 'Right then!', he tucked it under his arm, lined up his heels at the edge of the granite hearth and, counting his paces, walked to the centre of the library.

'This should be it.'

He blinked a couple of times and waited, and then it started. As he began to shimmer he muttered, 'Straight there, mark you. No shilly-shallying. We haven't time for that.' And then he disappeared.

In her place beside the fire the hedgehog opened a button-eye, yawned a tiny, pink yawn and scuttled towards one of the shelves to disappear beneath it and reappear in the snowy night.

Chapter 19
Go

The Writer saw the arched door open and Michael appear. Their eyes met and deep words were briefly exchanged but then he was on his way, striding down the lane with his dog at his side. He muttered quiet words, not to Fly but to the cottages. He was locking doors, ensuring that no curtains opened or one shutter unfastened. No villager should be allowed to see what was to follow.

Minutes later a procession emerged through the snowy darkness. Standing in a cottage doorway against a red-painted door, the Writer meticulously noted the riders and their horses because this would all have to be written.

At the head was Argo with Lightning running at his side – which was as she would have expected – but the great white horse was trotting beside a chestnut stallion. Her eyebrows rose. Arthur was riding beside the Time Keeper. Despite the enormity of the situation the Writer smiled a small smile. *So, the Time Keeper wishes to be on equal terms with her king.* They made an arresting picture: the young king on his white mount next to the raven-haired girl on her stallion. Merlin must have spoken to the horses because it appeared that all the riders, whether or not they were accustomed to riding, rode as if they were born to it.

The Writer squeezed herself further into the doorway and watched the rest of the procession pass.

Next to follow was a handsome blond-haired knight, trotting on a grey horse. To his right a red-headed girl, dressed from hat to toes in grey, rode with a falcon on her shoulder, while on the knight's left was the boy that the Writer knew as Gawain. His back was straight and the sword cane swung at his side. The Writer nodded to herself. The boy's ancestry would soon be revealed.

And then towards the rear came the two old knights, Lancelot and Bedivere. She looked for Merlin but he wasn't there. She frowned. *What can be the reason for his absence?*

At the very back was Cathe. He prowled, his black coat shining against the white of the snow and his vast paws leaving deep imprints. His tail twitched and he turned to her and blinked a green eye and purred. He was no longer the ginger tom cat but the great wild cat, and it felt good. He was itching for a fight.

But Cathe wasn't alone. A range of ordinary moggies strolled behind him. One was ginger; another was a particularly grubby white. Others were black or tabby or dirty grey. But what they all had in common was that they were quite clearly battle-hardened. Each one sported scars of past fights: a torn ear or a limp, a missing tail or a scarred nose. Cathe had assembled an army of battered warriors.

She watched the procession trot down the lane in the steadily falling snow towards the sea and sent word to her Watchers. Then she turned and slipped through a dark door between two cottages.

Once inside the door she removed her knitted gloves and tucked them into her old coat pocket. Then she picked up an oil lamp which flickered to life at her touch. She was standing at the top of a tunnel.

The Writer looked down at her feet.

The sensible, leather shoes disappeared to be replaced with a pair that would have made any shoe designer proud. *That's better.* She began her walk, following the path leading under the cottages towards the sea bed. Further down the tunnel her coat was exchanged for a dress and the wool hat disappeared and long hair tumbled down her back. She was young again. Her dress was a midnight-blue silk creation studded with stars; and her hair wasn't grey but dark, dark black. Cathe wasn't the only one to shake off his disguise.

***

Above ground the procession made its way down the winding lane.

No stars were visible. An occasional street lamp lit the swirling snow and shone just enough light to illuminate their way. Arthur considered what lay ahead and Merlin's instructions. They'd all assumed that he'd be coming with them but Merlin had insisted on staying behind.

'My place isn't with you,' he'd said.

Lancelot had protested, 'What! Not join with us? Why not?'

Merlin had leant on his staff. 'I've taken vows Lancelot. This battle isn't my battle.'

Arthur had been dumbstruck and judging from Tamar's face she was horrified too.

'What do you mean, old friend?' Lancelot had persisted, his blue eyes fierce. 'Of course you must come. We need you at our side.'

But Merlin had met his unbelieving gaze evenly. 'No Lancelot, you don't need me.' He'd glanced around. 'You may think you need me but you are equipped for battle. You all have gifts; use them wisely and don't be unsettled by the enemy. Remember her power has its limits. Its basis is weak.'

Rozen and Gawain had glanced at one another.

It looked like Rozen's wish to live dangerously was going to be put to the test.

Lancelot had been about to protest again but Merlin had held up his hand.

'No more discussion,' he'd said firmly, his eyes dark beneath his brow. 'Find Nick and Dragon and return the island to its people.'

Later Arthur realised that Bedivere hadn't uttered a word, and when Lancelot had turned to him to enlist his support, the old knight had merely shaken his head. 'He's right Lancelot, this is not his battle – it's ours. We must do what we've been called to do ... whatever the cost.'

So here they were, approaching the stony causeway and the island. A motley army of two old knights, a younger time-travelled knight, four teenagers, a bird, a dog and some cats. *And*, Arthur thought, *I haven't got Excalibur*.

The wind whipped Tamar's hair across her face and shot icy blasts at her skin. The moment they'd broken out of the shelter of the village it had unleashed wild screeches, beating the sea into a churning mass of foam and salt spray. The Time Keeper slipped her hand into her skirt pocket and felt the comforting metal of the pocket watch and its gentle ticking as the cogs synchronised to her heartbeat.

Arthur shouted above the wind. 'It's a low tide, the causeway's clear.'

He had to gather his breath to make himself heard. 'We have to cross the beach and follow it round to that rock there.' He pointed to a jagged rock maybe ten metres high, growing out of the sand. 'The causeway's just beyond it.'

Rozen's falcon was hooded but it sat hunched miserably against the driving wind and snow. She glanced at it and wiped the hair out of her eyes and studied the silhouette of the castle. How on earth could they attack that? Until now she hadn't really thought about the enormity of their task but the granite castle perched high on the island's peak brought it home to her.

Gawain, to the other side of Dinadan, felt a shiver run down his spine and turned to see a stranger riding on his outer flank carrying a shield bearing a coat of arms.

The man turned and smiled and Gawain caught a glimpse of kind eyes and a warm smile. But then the man and his horse were gone. Gawain peered into the darkness but no one was there. He swallowed and turned to Dinadan, wondering if he'd seen anything, but the young knight was staring straight ahead, preparing himself for the fight.

Gawain chewed his lip. He had the ability to pick out stuff that was happening to other people but this had most definitely been for him, and he hadn't a clue what it was about.

However, both Lancelot and Bedivere had seen Gawain's visitor. They glanced at one another and Bedivere nodded. It wouldn't be long before the boy knew his true lineage.

***

Inside the castle a shape shimmered outside a locked door and muttered to itself as it waited for its molecules to stabilise.

'Come on, come on,' Kitto Cornish murmured impatiently. 'Time is of the essence.' His scarf settled, closely followed by his coat and shoes until finally he was ready to spring into action. (Although 'spring' might be putting it a little generously.)

One of the arms of his spectacles had become dislodged, allowing his glasses to hang diagonally across his face with the metal bridge lodged under his nose. He rearranged them, quickly looked around and examined an empty metal hook sunk into the stone wall, where the key to the cell should be. His face dropped. 'Hmm, a locked door and no key, just when I can't risk any further disassembling.' He patted a pocket. 'My molecules have had quite enough disruption for one day.'

He glanced at his watch and sighed. 'Well Kitto, you're just going to have to do the best you can.'

With a decisive sniff Gawain's uncle tucked the book firmly under his arm, dug into his pocket and drew out a rat and several balls of grey fluff. 'You've made it then,' he said, addressing the rodent. 'Well, at least we can put *that* part of the plan into action.'

Kitto balanced the rat on his palm and, puffing, bent down and deposited it on the stone floor at the base of the door. 'Now, you know what you've got to do.'

He examined the gap between the bottom of the door and the floor. 'Just enough room for a tiny body; off you go now.'

The rat looked at him and squeaked but Kitto Cornish shook his head. 'Of course you can! *Comero weeth* little friend.' The rat appeared to pause and consider the space beneath the door before flattening itself and squeezing underneath.

'Right then Kitto, not a minute to waste, onwards and upwards.'

And scuttling along corridors and up spiral stairs, and pressing himself into corners and doorways, Mr Cornish hung onto his book and hoped.

Higher up in the castle in a blue-painted room a tiny dragon lay alone in a cold, tin box. Its eyes were shut and its scales were no longer olive green but a dull brown. Its sides barely moved. It was on its way out.

***

Servo stood on the shoreline and Watched a figure, dripping seaweed, emerging from the stormy sea as, further along the beach, another half-formed shape pulled itself onto the sand. The Ice Lady's army was assembling.

A shout cut through the wind's shrieks and the Watcher turned. Gawain had seen something.

'Art,' Gawain was pointing at a rock. 'Look, in that crevice!' The young king's horse halted. The Watcher waited.

Arthur squinted into the darkness. At first he couldn't see anything. Then a ruby-red spark winked – and hope blossomed.

'Excalibur!' Arthur shouted, steering Argo towards the rock.

Servo Watched the horse and the boy as they broke away from the rest of the party and the stallion galloped, hooves drumming, mane flying, over the sand. The horse's canter was slowing to a trot as Arthur leapt off his back and began scrabbling over the icy stone.

But Bedivere had seen something too. Despite his age the old knight's eyes were sharp. The wind whipped his white hair as he leant forward and muttered a quiet, 'Blast!' before bellowing, 'Sire, take care!'

Because a figure had materialised just a couple of metres behind Arthur ... and it wasn't on his side.

Arthur's stomach flipped. A remnant of a man was standing on the rock. Its skull gleamed bright white and although traces of muscle and flesh hung to its arms, it was mostly bone. And it didn't look friendly.

On the night Excalibur had first been given to him, Arthur had encountered creatures like this but then they hadn't been interested in him; this one, it appeared, was.

The creature sidled closer, bones rattling, and Arthur heard its voice in his head.

'The sword,' it said, the words creeping inside Arthur's skull. It stretched out longing fingers. 'The sword,' it pleaded. 'Must have the sword.'

Arthur licked his lips and shook his head.

The creature advanced.

Its tone changed. 'Must have the sword,' it demanded. 'Mistress says I must have the sword.'

Its eyeless stare fixed on the crevice in the rock. 'Must have the sword,' it repeated wistfully. Arthur shook his head again. His speech had deserted him. But then there was a sharp bark and the creature's sockets darkened as a flash of black and white and wide open jaws took a flying leap and knocked it to the ground.

Bones jerked and a hip bone was dislodged and Arthur's enemy literally had his legs taken from under him. The sword-seeking skeleton was just a heap of bleached bones.

'Thanks,' Arthur said, and Lightning wagged his tail. Attacking skeletons was no big deal.

Arthur attempted to ignore his pounding heart and scrambled, legs wobbling, through pools and over slimy seaweed as Excalibur's hilt glittered in the rocky fissure. But as Arthur slid towards his sword a fleshless hand reached over the rock and grasped his ankle.

'Go away,' his voice quavered. He tried to shake off the bone fingers. 'Disappear, won't you?'

But the creature was determined. 'The sword, mistress wants the sword.'

'Does she?' Arthur responded, more bravely than he felt. 'Well, she can't have it. It's mine.'

'The sword ...' The creature tugged on Arthur's leg.

'I know; you've told me,' he said through gritted teeth, kicking out. 'She wants it.'

There was a cry as the hand, and presumably a good part of its body, slithered down the rock and Arthur dived towards the sword.

'Hi Excalibur,' he whispered. 'It's good to see you.'

He slid his hand into the familiar hilt and, just as it had done many centuries before, the sword allowed itself to be released from the stone. Without time to consider the echoes of history Arthur turned to face another, decidedly skinny, opponent.

'Don't tell me,' Arthur said to the figure, trying to overlook its lack of flesh and the seaweed draped between its ribs. 'Your mistress wants the sword.'

He leapt forward, Excalibur's hilt in his hand, and yelled, 'But she can't have it!' And in one deft move slipped the sword between the creature's empty ribs, neatly slicing the seaweed in two.

'Cool move Art,' he congratulated himself as the pile of bones hit the rock and a femur rolled on to the sand. With Excalibur at his side he was feeling better already.

Arthur turned and yelled, 'Did you see th–?' but the words died on his lips because, advancing along the causeway and mounted on nervous horses, were the Lady of Clehy, the Crow Man, Hagarawall and Cador. The albino hound trotted at the Lady's side and the blue-black crow flew above his master.

This would have been bad enough in itself but to add to it, the Lady of Clehy had enlisted her own army ... a battalion of long-dead men and women. Arthur watched them with growing horror as they hobbled and shuffled and limped and moaned behind her.

Their purpose was clear, they wanted the sword.

Chapter 20
Reunited

Nick leant against the damp stone wall. Every time he moved a part of him hurt, and his arms were still pinned behind his back.

The stump of the single white candle spluttered and hissed as a dribble of wax dripped on to the floor, narrowly missing a woodlouse. Nick watched the insect navigate the white-washed cell and thought about Dragon – he loved woodlice. Nick bit his lower lip and tried to think of something other than Dragon being forced into the box.

He couldn't imagine life without Dragon. He tried to swallow the lump in his throat but it wouldn't budge, and then a voice outside the cell pulled him from his thoughts.

Maybe his captors had come back and were going to have another go at him.

I don't care. It was true. He really *didn't* care.

But instead of the door swinging open to reveal Cador or Brane or Hagarawall, a whiskery face appeared under it, followed by the rest of a small hairy body. It was a rat. It sat on its haunches cleaning its whiskers, then it scuttled over the stone floor and sat at his feet.

'What do you want?'

It squeaked.

Nick shook his head. 'Sorry, can't help you mate. I don't speak rat.'

The rat made what could only be described as an exasperated squeak and scurried around Nick's legs to his back. After some urgent scrabbling it hauled itself onto his wrists and began gnawing at the rope.

'Oh right, I've got it!' He shuffled out from the wall. 'You're my rescue party.'

The rat squeaked again.

He had a funny feeling that it was saying, 'Yes, obviously!'

Until a year or so ago he would never have believed this. Although to be fair he wouldn't have believed in dragons either. A rat coming to his rescue was just one more weird episode at the end of a long line of weird episodes.

***

Meanwhile, Kitto had climbed to a couple of floors above the cell, but before he went any further he had to consult the book he'd brought from Merlin's library. So, tucking himself into a convenient cubby hole under a flight of stairs, he swept a couple of spiders out of the way and extracted a candle stub and a box of matches from his coat pocket.

Peering down the corridor, Kitto Cornish listened intently, waiting for footsteps to shatter the castle's silence, but there was nothing. His frown faded and his shoulders relaxed. He struck a match. It flared and went out.

'Come on, come on,' he muttered dropping the match on to the stone floor.

His hands were shaking.

He breathed in and struck a second match but it was a dud.

'Blast it!' he muttered, and rattled the box. There were only two matches left. Why on earth hadn't he checked before he left?

He took a deep breath and dug out the second-to-last match and wished he'd brought a torch instead of a candle. The Lady of Clehy had a hatred of light and heat; he should have been better prepared. All in all he wasn't doing very well.

He struck the match against the side of the box and it sparked into life and flickered against the candle wick. The candle spluttered and Kitto shielded the flame with his hand and watched it anxiously. Little by little the flame grew. Finally, he breathed out and tried to listen to the castle's sounds above his thumping heart.

'Come Kitto,' he scolded himself as he turned his attention to the book, 'calm down.'

Mr Cornish pushed his spectacles up his nose and leant forward. 'I need to know where Dragon is,' he informed the book and watched it flip open; it had chosen a floor plan of the castle. But instead of there being just one floor, several floors had been drawn on top of one another. You couldn't see where one floor ended and another began.

He peered at the pages. 'I can't see what's what!'

Maybe the book agreed, or maybe someone else heard Kitto's complaint, because the book creaked, the spine and the cover pressed themselves down and the floors and the walls inched up until they were a three-dimensional model of the castle.

Every detail was perfect. The library's shelves were stacked full of books and a lamp sat on a polished side table besides an arm chair. In the kitchen a pan sat on the cooker, while on the back of a bedroom door a dressing gown hung on a hook. And in the bathroom three yellow rubber ducks lined the side of the bath.

Kitto blinked. 'Was that you Merlin?'

No one answered.

So saving his questions for later, Kitto Cornish examined the model and nodded as he committed the castle's layout to memory. Now he knew where he had to go. A 3D model was much easier to understand. 'Thank you,' he said and watched as the walls and floors and shelves flattened and dissolved into a 2D map.

'Brilliant, quite brilliant,' he commented, closing the book and sliding it under his arm. 'So, to the library first, I think.'

He dusted a sticky cobweb off his lapel and stood up. A grandfather clock ticked and somewhere a mouse darted over the stone floor.

'Come on,' he instructed himself, and headed towards the living quarters, carefully opening one door after another. However, it was quickly becoming clear that the castle was sparsely populated. So, picking up speed, Kitto darted through the crimson, book-lined library and on through the banqueting hall and a room with paintings hung on every wall.

He paused and pulled a red and white cloth from his pocket while he waited for his heart to steady.

'Really ... should ... get ... more ... exercise.'

Wiping his brow he listened, but still there wasn't a sound.

'Good,' he wheezed, 'it must be here somewhere. Think, Kitto, think!'

He leant against the wall and closed his eyes, visualising the model. His lips moved, listing the castle's rooms, and then his face cleared. 'Of course ... the blue room, where it will be coolest – that's what she'd like!'

Thrusting his handkerchief into his pocket and wedging the book firmly in the crook of his arm he half ran, half crept, up a short flight of stairs and along a wood-panelled corridor. The door to the blue drawing room was directly ahead of him. Mopping his brow, he tip-toed forward and placed his ear against the old wood. Not a sound. Holding his breath he cast a cautionary glance behind him and leant on the iron handle. The door creaked and swung inwards and finally Kitto Cornish smiled. In the corner of the room a candle stub still burned, and on the table a tin box waited.

***

The rat squeaked. Nick pulled his wrists apart, and the ropes fell off.

'Thanks' Nick said, flatly. 'Kind of you.'

He examined his wrists. They were covered in welts and raw skin and drying blood. He knew he should be more grateful because the creature had worked really hard to help him, but what was the point? A rat and a boy against his kidnappers and their leader – and Dragon was probably dead by now anyway.

Which was when he heard the scrape of a key and the rattle of it turning in the lock and saw Mr Cornish's anxious face peering round the door.

'Nick!' Kitto elbowed the door open, shouldered it and pushed his way in. He was holding a metal box.

'I would have been here sooner,' he began, 'but it took a little while to find the key. These people have no idea of how to look after a castle.'

Nick sat up dry-mouthed. Mr Cornish was holding the box – the one they'd put Dragon in – with a book balanced on its lid. 'I think they've all gone ...' he began. 'No one seems to be around.'

Kitto Cornish shuffled forward and laid the box at Nick's feet.

'Rat has done his work then,' he stated.

An outraged squeak from floor level.

'Sorry, sorry,' Kitto burbled. 'Of course I didn't doubt that you could do it, Rat.'

Another squeak and another apology but Nick had tuned out of the man/rat conversation. He lifted the book off the box and put it on the floor and looked at Kitto Cornish.

Gawain's uncle nodded towards the tin answering the unspoken question. 'I don't know lad. You look.'

Nick's heart pounded. What if Dragon was dead?

Sliding his fingers under the lid he prised it open and gently removed it.

Dragon lay in the box.

Nick peered in, his heart hammering, and tentatively drew his finger along Dragon's spine. Usually this would have the animal doing his little dragon purr but he didn't make a sound.

'Well lad?'

Nick slid a hand beneath the creature's belly. A faint beat pulsed against his palm and an eye opened. Nick breathed out and nodded.

Kitto puffed out his cheeks, whipped off his glasses and vigorously polished the lenses. 'Well, that's a turn-up.' His face broke into a broad smile.

Nick lifted the dragon out of the tin and balanced him on his open palm, holding him at eye level. 'He'll need to warm up.'

'And,' Kitto added, 'stay close to you.'

Nick stroked Dragon's back. 'You're going to be all right mate.' He glanced at Mr Cornish. 'But we're going to get our own back.'

Dragon's other eye opened and his tail twitched and Uncle Kitto passed Nick a small brown paper bag. 'I took the precaution of bringing these.'

Nick delved into the bag. 'Thanks, that's brilliant!'

Dragon's eyes widened as he caught a whiff of the dried spider in front of his snout. He barely moved but within a millisecond the spider had disappeared and Nick was grinning from ear to ear.

'Welcome back mate.' He looked at Kitto. 'Thank you again.' He paused. 'Are you up for giving the opposition a taste of their own medicine?'

Kitto Cornish coughed nervously and pushed his glasses up his nose. 'D'you think that's wise?'

'Probably not, but I'm not known for wisdom.'

Mr Cornish smiled. 'Maybe for bravery?'

Nick shook his head, 'Not that either.' He rummaged in the bag and chose a dehydrated woodlouse. 'Can you show me the way out of this place? There's bound to be a fight going on somewhere and if there's not one yet, there soon will be.'

Kitto Cornish pulled himself to his feet. 'In that case I'd be honoured to be your guide. Sadly we'll have to leave by more conventional means than the way I entered. However, the place appears to be deserted so it shouldn't be difficult.'

'Right little fella,' Nick said to the dragon. 'I'm sorry about this but you're staying inside my shirt.' He pulled his sweatshirt open and slid Dragon into a pocket in his T-shirt. 'You've got to stay warm and it's cold out there.' The dragon curled up and closed his eyes. He was back with his master.

Nick hauled himself up. Bits of him hurt. Lots of bits. Cuts and bruises littered his body but he shut out their complaints and grinned at Gawain's uncle. 'Lead on then Mr Cornish. I think it's time to get even.'

Chapter 21
Let Battle Commence

On the causeway below the castle, battle lines were being drawn. Viatoris and Servo were about to have their work cut out. Servo was Watching from the shore and Viatoris from the island. (But much to the Writer's exasperation neither would be able to give a complete description of what was about to follow. It would all happen rather quickly.)

Both Watchers observed Arthur, armed with Excalibur, swiping at any partial bodies attempting to block his path. Servo Watched Arthur scramble on to Argo's back while Viatoris shivered and thought longingly of Italy.

Slipping Excalibur into its scabbard which had been lying in another rocky crevice, Arthur muttered an urgent, 'Ready!' to the horse and galloped towards Tamar. She was very pale.

'Are you okay?' he asked.

'Yeah,' she replied with a determined nod, but her face was ash white. This was worse than she'd imagined. 'What about you?'

Arthur raised an eyebrow and flashed her a brief smile. 'What do the Chinese say? May you live in interesting times!'

She shook her head and mumbled something impolite about him and his sayings.

'Have you got the watch ready?' he asked.

'Of course.' Her brown eyes met his and, for a third time that night, everyone else was locked out. She cleared her throat and thought of Nick and Dragon. 'I'm ready.'

The King and Excalibur, the Time Keeper and her Watch, were poised for battle.

But the Ice Lady was ready too.

The wind gusted and the snow fell and Arthur's enemy concentrated.

Icicles stretched from the castle's walls. Stone gargoyles froze. And deep underground the Writer listened to the waves thunder above her.

The two sides advanced. There was a swish of swords being drawn but the snow was getting heavier and the wind was strengthening. Bedivere and Lancelot exchanged glances. This wasn't good – the Ice Lady was in control. They'd hoped to take their enemy by surprise but she'd succeeded in setting the pace.

And then Arthur groaned and rolled onto Argo's neck and clutched his head and Tamar's horse stopped in its tracks.

The Ice Lady narrowed her eyes, funnelling every ounce of her dark energy into the boy's brain. Razor-sharp words sliced his mind, black syllables sneaked into his ears. She was harnessing her power, summoning all the deepest, darkest words at her disposal. Previously Arthur had experienced only snatches of phrases but now the Lady was painting pictures with her words.

Heavy nightmares stole into the space behind his eyes. Dark apparitions sneaked into his mind.

His heart pounded. He was running, falling, running again. His feet were slipping from under him. Something was behind him, its breath hot on his neck – meat-infested breath. Claws ripped his shirt, teeth sunk into his flesh.

Then the creature was re-forming and a long-fingered, black-eyed witch was propelling him towards the edge of a bottomless mineshaft – and she was laughing. The witch was Matearnas and this time she was winning. This time she'd be Cornwall's queen.

Arthur, Cornwall's king, lay crumpled on the great horse's back and moaned and dry-heaved and dreamed his nightmares.

The Ice Lady was hurling every last spark of black energy at his helpless brain, summoning all her dark thoughts, pulverising his mind. Every word was finding its target. Lancelot and Bedivere knew what she was doing but she was blocking their thoughts. She'd been planning this for too long.

'You're no more than a boy.' The woman punched words deep into his head. 'What can you do against me?'

She laughed a low, deep laugh. Arthur lay slumped helplessly over the great horse's neck, the real world lost to him.

Behind her the Crow Man, Hagarawall and Cador waited.

The Crow Man's dark eyes glinted and Cador smiled. It was good to see his mother at work. He sat on his horse a little straighter and pulled up the collar of his silver jacket and flicked the snow off his shoulders.

The woman's eyes darkened, her pupils dilating as she smelt victory. She nudged her horse forward. 'You're just a boy,' she breathed, 'with a ridiculous toy sword.'

Cador allowed his mount to take a step but Hagarawall leaned over and laid a warning hand on the boy's arm. 'Your mother knows what she's doing, boy,' he growled, his eyes unreadable.

Cador took one look at his mother's henchman and pulled back on the reins. He never quite knew where he was with either of these men. Instead he satisfied himself with watching the effect his mother was having on the imposter king.

Arthur's hand had begun to shake. The sword felt so *heavy*.

'You see,' the woman continued smoothly. 'It's too much for you isn't it?'

She glanced at the rest of the company; no one was moving. She smiled.

'It would be so much easier to give it to me. After all, you know that it's mine really, don't you?' Her words were deep ... and so persuasive.

Arthur struggled to hold the sword and to block the words.

Out loud he said, 'Not ... too heavy,' but every word was an effort.

The woman advanced. They were a long way apart but she didn't want to rush it and risk losing control.

Tamar shot a worried look at Arthur. His colour had deserted him and he'd begun to shiver. She glanced around but both Gawain and Rozen were frozen and Dinadan and the old knights were unmoving. Why weren't they doing something! This terrible woman had immobilised them. Maybe it was her recent brush with the Ice Lady that had immunised her, or maybe it was that famous Tamblyn anger, but whatever it was Tamar felt a spark ignite. 'Come on girl,' she told herself.

The Ice Lady's attention was fixed on the sword and Arthur as closely as her motley army were watching their leader. None of them paid attention to Arthur's allies.

Tamar flexed her fingers, slipped her hand into her pocket and grasped warm metal. Enthusiastic ticks greeted her fingers. Pulling the watch out, she whispered,

'Right my little time companion, let's see what you're made of.'

She stretched out her arm and flipped the emerald case open with her thumb so that the watch's face could see the Ice Lady.

The Crow Man caught the movement and leant forward. What would his mistress do now? The albino dog barked but he hissed a vicious, 'Quiet hound!'

The Ice Lady stopped in her tracks but her reaction took Tamar by surprise. She'd expected her to back off, or at least show a little respect, but the woman didn't falter. Not even for a moment.

Instead she merely smiled a condescending smile and shouted above the wind. 'Oh my little Time Keeper, I might have been touched by your timepiece once before …' the wind howled and the watch ticked, '… but as I told you, it can't touch me again.'

She held up her hands and arms. 'Look! I'm prepared.' The Lady of Clehy held up her head. Not only were her hands covered, but not an inch of her skin was exposed. Velvet sleeves met velvet gloves and a black velvet collar covered her long, white throat. A veil was pinned to her hair by an ebony clasp, floating over her tall forehead and her hooked nose to below her chin. The watch ticked despondently.

But that split second of divided attention was enough for Arthur's allies. It was just the lifeline they needed. The second the Lady of Clehy focused on the watch rather than Arthur her hold had loosened.

The wind fell and Bedivere gripped his sword and shouted, 'Sire, use the words and the sword together. Defend with one, attack with the other.'

And Gawain, feeling the hold on his mind ease, rubbed his eyes and blinked. Hagarawall was on his horse, lank-haired, a few metres from him. Without stopping to consider the consequences he brandished his sword cane and yelled, 'All for one!'

Tamar smiled briefly. They were more than just the three musketeers now. She flicked her hair out of her eyes and tucked the watch back in her skirt pocket. 'Don't worry,' she whispered to the timepiece as Dinadan roared past with the Crow Man in his sights, 'you'll have your chance.'

And finally the night was a confusion of swords cutting air, flesh and bone, and metal bouncing off metal, and all hell breaking loose.

Tamar tightened the string inside her pocket and considered her next move. There really wasn't any choice. Drawing herself up she tucked her skirts under her legs and commanded, 'Go!'

A heartbeat later her stallion was ripping towards the Ice Lady and scattering the opposition. Tamar was determined and angry. Very angry. There was no sign of Nick or the dragon and Tamar knew that the mind behind their capture was this woman. The men might have carried out the kidnapping, and the dragon-napping, but the woman would have ordered it.

She screamed as she charged, oblivious to the shouts from Lancelot and Bedivere. At that moment she really didn't care if she lived or died. She just wanted to get even. And a Tamblyn woman wanting to get even is a very dangerous thing indeed.

Fortunately for her, the knights were practised at horsemanship and Lancelot was quickly at her side. She glanced at him and for the briefest of moments thought, *I'm on a horse with a knight riding beside me. Morwenna would never believe me.*

She heard him command, 'Bedivere, you take the left flank – I'll take the centre ground.' Then she concentrated. This was no game. It was life and it was dangerous.

She had a glimpse of Rozen slipping the falcon's hood off but she didn't have time to watch the air fight between the dark-feathered crow and its tiny opponent as they rose and spun and swooped and dived above her. Nor did she note the moment the falcon was joined by a pale owl, but she heard its screech as it plunged towards its mortal enemy.

She didn't observe the advance of Cathe and his troops as they prowled towards Cador with their ears flat against their skulls. But she did hear Cador's scream. It looked like he would have other things to terrify him apart from Christmas.

And then her life did that thing she'd heard about but never experienced. It flashed in front of her eyes (which was quite distracting), but then Arthur was at her side (which wasn't). Although he was a pale shade of green he was resolute.

'Lancelot,' he shouted. 'I think Rozen might need your help!' Brandishing Excalibur he added, 'There's a load of old bones which need your attention. Let me deal with their charming leader.'

Lancelot nodded and steered his horse towards their newest recruit.

Meanwhile Servo was observing Sir Dinadan and Brane.

He saw the blond-haired knight skilfully wield his weapon, first flipping the Crow Man's hat off his head with the tip of his sword and then running the blade from the collar to the hem of his enemy's coat, ripping off all the buttons.

The knight announced, 'Sir, you are undressed!'

But Brane whipped his sword towards the knight's horse. Servo saw the animal skip back, its neck tensed, and heard its shocked squeal as the tip of the Crow Man's sword pierced its flesh just enough to distract its master.

The Watcher winced as the blood ran and he heard the rage in Dinadan's voice as he shouted, 'What kind of coward are you, sir, that you maim animals?'

And Brane's reply: 'The winning kind!'

The gloves were off.

Meanwhile Lancelot, following Arthur's instructions, had fallen back to support Rozen against the skeletons. She'd turned down Merlin's offer of a sword in favour of taking her merlin into battle but now Lancelot threw her a weapon. 'Just a touch will do it Miss Tregenza,' he barked. 'These creatures don't like pure-forged metal.'

'Right!' she yelled, catching the sword's hilt (it was fortunate that she was well co-ordinated), and whipped round to face one that might have been a pirate.

A bubble of hysteria rose in her chest. *When I talked about living dangerously,* she thought as she lunged forward, *I didn't expect to be fighting a skeleton wearing a hat!*

Lancelot glanced over his shoulder as he dispatched a see-through opponent to find that Rozen had already demolished the once-upon-a-time pirate and was now turning towards a skeleton clutching a bottle of brandy. He watched her swipe at it and saw it fall apart with a rattle and the tiniest of grateful sighs (maybe *now* it would be allowed to rest). Lancelot smiled. *The red-heads are the ones to watch. Great fighters!*

On her coal-black horse the Ice Lady took in the mayhem.

Her main ally, Brane, had lost his hat and was engaged in fighting Dinadan – who'd made it to this century despite her best efforts. While Cador ... she took in her son and her mouth twisted. She'd placed such high hopes in him and yet here was her silver-haired son cornered by some cats. Meanwhile Hagarawall appeared to be defending himself against a boy and a sword cane!

She screamed against the wind and the shouts and the clash of metal on metal, 'Go to it fools! We will not be defeated a second time,' before whipping round to face a fully recovered Arthur and a furious Tamar.

They were bearing down on her, Excalibur glinting in the young king's hand, when the night air was torn by a desperate shout from Bedivere. And Argo came to a skidding halt, narrowly avoiding hurling his rider to the ground.

'What the hell are you doing?' Arthur shouted, clutching the horse's mane.

But Tamar, whose horse had also skidded to a stop, had seen what Arthur hadn't.

'Look!'

Arthur glanced to his left as Gawain dived, sword cane raised, at Hagarawall. But the pale-haired man was lunging, his sword dangerously low, towards his young opponent. It was clear who was the most experienced.

And Bedivere was clamping his knees into his mount's side and shouting again, 'Gawain, no!' because the boy was no match for Hagarawall.

He just had time to think, *I hadn't wanted to leave young Art before his battles were won,* as he dived between Gawain and Hagarawall. And pain, which had nothing to do with his body but everything to do with his mind, exploded.

The others saw the old knight charge between Gawain and Hagarawall but they didn't see the point of Hagarawall's sword penetrate Bedivere's cloak, skin and muscle to puncture his heart. Nor did they hear the knight gasp as the sword found its mark. But they all saw him slide from his old horse and hit the stones.

It felt as though the earth had stopped spinning: time washed around them. A star appeared, pulsing and waiting.

And then Dinadan was dashing the Crow Man's sword to the ground in one swift stroke and Lancelot was groaning, 'Bedivere!'

Rozen glanced around. One skeleton with a little more muscle than most, but very little skin, had frozen mid-stride. Another, wearing a torn frock-coat and carrying a rusting firearm, cast a look at the fallen knight and dropped his weapon while a third creakily took a step backwards.

And the watch deep in Tamar's pocket missed a beat … and it *never* missed a beat.

Hagarawall and Gawain faced each other across Bedivere's inert body and the colour leached from Gawain's face.

'No!' Arthur shouted, as Bedivere's blood pumped into the snow. He slid off Argo's great back and tumbled to land beside Bedivere's crumpled body.

'No,' he whispered again and slipped a hand beneath the knight's head. The star blinked. Bedivere's horse nuzzled his master's neck.

The knight's eyes flickered open. Managing to lift a hand to lay it against his horse's face, he focused on his young friend, the true king of Cornwall; a ghost of a smile drifted across his lips. 'It was time, sire.'

Blood trickled from the side of his mouth. 'You will need your friend.' Bedivere coughed red bubbles.

The old knight gasped. He was losing blood fast.

'But I need you too,' Arthur whispered, a sob stuck in his throat.

Bedivere's eyes closed but he forced them open and licked his lips.

'Sire,' another gasp, 'you have work to do here.' His breath rattled. 'Your friend has his own destiny. He must live … his story must be fulfilled.'

Bedivere's eyes were heavy. He was so tired. Arthur leaned in close. Bedivere was telling him something. 'I can hear the Calling, sire … for me and my old horse. Our time is over.'

Arthur shook his head but the old knight nodded again and his body began to relax. He sighed. 'This won't be the last battle, Art; there will be others. You must never give up. Remember, Cornwall's fate lies in your hands.' His eyes were open but unfocused, staring somewhere to the left of Arthur's ear.

A tiny cough and a bloody smile, 'I'm so proud of you.' And his head lolled sideways and his eyes finally closed.

A tear rolled down Tamar's cheek and Gawain swallowed hard. Bedivere had been involved right from the beginning. None of them had spent much time with him, but with someone like Bedivere you didn't need to.

No one spoke or moved. A flicker of starlight hesitated over Cornwall and then made its mind up and began to blaze with unabashed confidence. And somewhere in the Cornish sea a dolphin swam and leapt.

Rozen looked up from watching the man and the boy. The Ice Lady was paces from them. She could have attacked but for some reason that Rozen couldn't understand the Lady of Clehy hadn't advanced. The eyes of the woman and the grey-eyed girl met. Rozen sat up in the saddle and straightened her top hat as her falcon dipped and landed on the grey cloth of her right shoulder. Girl and bird regarded the hawk-nosed woman. The short sword itched in Rozen's hand but she waited and watched.

She took in the scene. The Crow Man had clearly come off worse in his fight with Dinadan. He had his hand pressed over a gash in his sleeve which, judging by the red stain spreading between his fingers went a lot deeper than the wool coat.

Cador was trying hard not to snivel but was clearly failing – and was clearly terrified. In the fighting, he'd slipped from his horse and was now pinned against a rock by Cathe. The great cat's tail flicked as he surveyed his prisoner. Whenever Cador shifted, even by a hair's breadth, Cathe emitted a low don't-even-*think*-it growl with a backing chorus of growls from his feline army.

To an outsider it would seem as if Hagarawall at least had won his fight. Bedivere had died. However, Rozen was beginning to understand.

Of course!

Bedivere had died willingly. There was no way the Ice Lady could stand against that. Bedivere's deliberate death had made Arthur strong. Already the wind was dropping and the snowfall was lighter.

Hagarawall crowed, 'One down …' but was interrupted by his leader screaming, 'Fool. Don't you know what you've done?'

Because Bedivere's body had begun to shimmer.

Gossamer light lapped over his face and hands and feet and a breeze swept around him. The removal was beginning. The solid was being swapped for the distinctly translucent. The snow-covered pebbles were actually becoming visible through his body. His old horse gave a little whinny of pleasure and its ears pointed forward as it, too, lost definition. Wherever it was going, Bedivere's horse was clearly happy to be on its way.

249

The Ice Lady's horse danced, feeling the pull of that other place. 'Quiet!' she ordered, and leant forward, her eyes narrowed. 'I will not be defeated a second time. I'm the one who should rule Cornwall.' The woman took in the wounded Crow Man and her son cornered by the cats.

Bedivere's sword fell to the ground and his body, and his shadow, disappeared. All that was left was a vague impression and pink-stained snow.

Arthur stared at his own empty, blood-stained hands.

Lancelot creakily dismounted and reverently picked up Bedivere's sword.

'He won't be needing that where he's going,' he said sadly as he wiped the blade.

Slowly he knelt in the bloodied snow beside his young king. Then Dinadan slid off his horse and, bowing his head, joined them.

A movement along the causeway, behind the Ice Lady's back, caught Rozen's eye. The girl held her breath and squinted through the gloom. Then, despite everything, she smiled.

'Tamar,' she said in a low voice. 'Tamar, look.'

The Time Keeper looked up from the bloodied snow and wiped her face with the heel of her hand. Another tear traced her cheek and she sniffed but then she blinked. Rozen glanced at the Ice Lady. Fortunately she hadn't seen what they'd seen. She nodded towards Cador and Tamar understood: it was pay-back time.

Swallowing a hiccup, Tamar slowly manoeuvred her mount until she was beside Rozen and they were facing the Ice Lady's son. She cast a look over her shoulder but the Lady of Clehy was watching Arthur and his knights. She risked another quick glance along the causeway and brushed away a tear. Nick was hobbling towards them trailed by Kitto Cornish, but more importantly his left hand cupped something squirming inside his jacket. The beginnings of a smile grew. Her friend and his dragon were both alive. Her heart beat a little faster as she turned to Cador. Justice would be done.

Side by side, the Time Keeper and the falconer nudged their mounts towards the Ice Lady's son.

'You see,' Tamar whispered to her watch. 'I promised you there'd be another chance.'

'How about snatching a couple of hairs?' Rozen suggested. She'd been filled in on Tamar's first meeting with the boy. 'His deoxyribonucleic acid should be interesting.'

'His *what*?'

'His DNA.'

'Oh right.'

'That would be satisfying. Besides we don't need to lower ourselves to their level.'

'We don't?' Tamar wanted to do more than snatch a couple of hairs but Rozen was right. They had to preserve the moral high-ground, but there was no reason for Cador to know that.

Nick took in the little group around Arthur and wondered what had happened. He saw their adversaries: Brane bleeding, Hagarawall looking at the ground and the Ice Lady concentrating on a spot in front of Arthur. But then he saw Cador hemmed in by cats and the girls advancing on the boy. He waved Uncle Kitto to a stop and crept forward, completing the girls' pincer movement.

'Okay Dragon, our hour has come.'

Tamar saw his face clearly for the first time and winced. It was black and blue. His jaw was swollen and one eye was nearly closed.

'Perhaps more than a couple of hairs,' she whispered to Rozen and ducked her head towards Nick.

'Boy!' Rozen exclaimed softly. 'Yeah, maybe several more.'

Tamar extracted the excited watch and held it up and leant forward, holding the timepiece above her horse's twitching ears. The watch ticked and glowed, and played a little of Cornwall's anthem, and Cador looked up – and screamed.

'Not that!' He shrunk back against the rock, the cats forgotten, and his mother spun around.

Tamar glanced over her shoulder and shouted, 'You may be protected, but your son isn't.'

The Ice Lady spat, 'You wouldn't dare!'

'Don't you believe it!'

The woman made to move but Tamar continued, 'Come any closer and your darling boy won't look so pretty.'

'Pretty? That's stretching it!' Rozen grinned and calmly leant down and pulled Cador's hair. He yelped as she observed, 'Yuck! It's covered in gel. Never mind, it'll still be useful.'

Hagarawall took a step.

'Stop fool!' the Lady commanded.

The white hound snarled at Brane's side but the Crow Man ordered, 'Stay.' He knew that despite her poor opinion of her son, if anything happened to Cador at their hands, frost would invade their bodies.

Nick took a couple more steps and the cats parted to make way for him. Cador was well and truly trapped. He had the rock towering at his back, the girls to his left and in front of him, and Nick to his right.

Cador's eyes darted from the timepiece to Nick and took in his injuries and a hint of swagger built. Despite his perilous situation he couldn't resist sneering, 'Looks like Hagarawall did a good job.'

And Nick's resolve to remain in control melted and there was a satisfying crunch as his knuckles hit Cador's jaw, closely followed by a squeal from the Ice Lady's son.

Nick shook his head. 'You really are a prize idiot.'

Cador clutched his jaw and snivelled. Blood trickled from a split lip but he didn't move – or say anything else. The timepiece was now inches from his face.

'Good one,' Rozen remarked.

'You retreat and I'll let Cador go,' Tamar ordered the Ice Lady and her crew. 'But one false move from any of you and he gets to meet the watch. Tick – tock.'

Cador's eyes switched to his mother.

'You've ten seconds,' Tamar added. 'One … two …'

'Mother …' Cador said.

The Lady of Clehy snarled at Tamar: 'You'll pay for this.' It wasn't so much her son's predicament that angered her, but her own humiliation at the Time Keeper's hands.

'Three … four …'

Arthur and his knights watched, and Servo and Viatoris waited as the power shifted while, far below, the Writer listened.

'Five …'

'Mum,' Cador pleaded.

'Six … seven …'

'Mummy!'

The Ice Lady swung her horse around and snarled again. 'Brane, Hagarawall, take the hound and go.'

She shot Tamar a poisonous look. 'Believe me girl, you will pay. This is not the end.' She tugged on her horse's reins, turning it. A ship drifted into sight and her mount took a couple of steps along the causeway.

'Keep going,' Tamar commanded. 'Don't try anything. I'm still counting.'

Arthur swung himself on to Argo's back and Gawain picked up his sword cane.

'I'm ready with the watch,' Tamar informed Cador. 'Don't let your mum try anything.' The timepiece ticked, agreeing. The Time Keeper watched the woman and her henchmen retreat and checked that everyone on their side was ready should the Ice Lady attempt anything. She needn't have worried. Apart from Nick and Kitto they were all armed and not one Memory remained. 'Okay, go.'

Cador snivelled and opened his mouth but Nick leant in. 'Look at my face, mate. D'you fancy looking like me?'

The Ice Lady's son closed his mouth, slid from between the Guardians – Tamar couldn't resist a final 'Happy Christmas!' – and ran after his mother.

The Guardians and their king, armed with Excalibur, monitored the withdrawal. Both Lancelot and Dinadan had their swords at the ready and Cathe waited, every muscle tensed. Lightning stood, ears pointing forward, watching his white counterpart trail after the Ice Lady's horse with his tail between his legs. The crow cawed once and took off, swooping towards the waiting ship.

Tamar swallowed as she observed their enemies' withdrawal. Brane was still bleeding and the Lady of Clehy didn't turn, even to see if her son was with them. Hagarawall cast a brief furious look at his enemies but followed his leader to the waiting ship.

Cornwall's king watched the retreat. Deep words leached into his mind.

'Sire, you must let them go.' Lancelot had been observing the young king; detecting the jumble of emotions. 'Bedivere died to preserve your lives.' Arthur heard him sigh. 'Besides, your allies are exhausted and would be unable to fight. You must allow them to rest.'

The young king closed his eyes. Every bone in his body wanted revenge.

'Look at them, sire.'

Arthur flung his head back. He wanted to howl at the moon. Bedivere had died and their enemies were getting away.

'There will be other times, sire.' The deep words were purple interlaced with grey but a hint of silver rippled through the purple, and a thread of gold ran through the grey. 'And a great king always looks after his troops.'

Cornwall's king opened his eyes and looked at his friends: Nick's face was a bruised mess, Rozen was white with exhaustion and Gawain could barely hold the sword cane. Lancelot was right. Now was not the time.

Finally Arthur turned to Tamar. She was watching him, waiting, her eyes grave. A breeze picked up, lifting her hair and their eyes met.

And then they felt it: a rumble of settling stone. The sand shivered and the sea rippled, then the rumbling stopped and the beach and the sea were still. The island was free and Cornwall was safe, and very soon the Little Mount's keepers would be home. If an island could be content, this one was.

Arthur breathed out. 'We did it,' he said. 'We did it, didn't we Tamblyn?'

Tamar nodded, although the Lady of Clehy's threat still echoed in her brain, and smiled at her friend.

The Ice Lady had been banished.

For now, at least, they'd won.

Chapter 22
The Return

Merlin shouted his thanks to Mrs Beswetherick, 'And a happy Christmas to you Mrs B, give my regards to your family and have fun with your grandchildren. Thank you for popping in so early!'

A question floated back to him.

'Oh I'll be fine thank you Mrs B. What? No, I'm sure I won't be lonely.'

He listened as her footsteps retreated and the back door slammed.

Opening the library window, he leant out.

Mrs Beswetherick's slightly out-of-tune voice could just be heard as she made her way home. Strains of 'God rest ye merry, gentlemen ...' warbled along the path mingling with the church bells. The sun was only just rising, the sky was pale but the snow sparkled in the early light. Mrs B's choice of carol was remarkably appropriate. He hummed as she reached, 'Let nothing you dismay,' and closed the window.

The fire burned in the grate, the candles flickered on the tree and the presents waited. On the library's shelves one or two self-openers were especially fidgety because their specialism was Christmas. Outside, a white-antlered shadow passed in front of the window and Merlin listened to the scrabbling and then silence on the roof. The stag was back. The quest must have been fulfilled.

He glanced at the dark oak table stretching the length of the room. Gold and red Christmas crackers containing remarkably funny jokes and *really* nice presents (a miniature silver sword on a chain for one person and a perfect replica of a shield for another), lay in each place. There were crystal decanters containing wine and cola and red candles burning in holly holders. Of course Mrs Beswetherick hadn't seen any of this. Which was probably for the best.

In the kitchen a turkey and piles of roast potatoes were cooking and mince pies, chocolate cake and Christmas pudding were waiting. Everything was ready.

Merlin arranged his cloak and reached for his staff. 'Well, Tyto,' he said to the owl dozing on a shelf, 'they're almost here.' He held out an arm. 'Are you coming?'

The bird eyed him and a particularly large book shuffled.

Merlin cast a stern look at the tome. 'Not yet. Your heraldic secrets have to remain undiscovered for now.' He ran a finger along its spine. 'I will let you know when your mysteries can be revealed to young Gawain.' The book's pages settled.

'Good,' Merlin nodded. 'Wait for another day. Christmas isn't the time.'

The bell rang and the owl swooped and landed on Merlin's shoulder as he strode along the corridor to the front door, but before he'd quite reached it, the handle turned itself and the door creaked open. It would do that only for familiar friends.

Michael was waiting, hollow-eyed, on the step.

Without a word Merlin gestured Michael and Fly in and the suit of armour clanked to attention.

Merlin took in his friend's hunched shoulders and the deep lines between his brows and sighed. 'Bedivere?'

'You knew?'

'In a way … yes.'

Michael looked wretched. 'It might 'ave helped if I'd been told.' It was the nearest thing to a reproach. 'Bedivere … did he know it was going to happen?'

Merlin nodded. 'He had an idea.'

'Was it the only way?'

'No' Merlin replied slowly. He closed his eyes and pinched the bridge of his nose between his finger and thumb and shook his head wearily. 'No, it wasn't the only way.' He opened his eyes. 'It depended on how the battle was played out.'

'Ah,' Michael nodded. He swallowed. 'I'll miss him.'

'We'll all miss him, but ultimately it was his choice. He asked that no one be informed in case it ended differently.'

'I see.'

Merlin closed the door and Michael unbuttoned his coat and flipped his hat at the rounded wooden post at the bottom of the stairs. They watched the post lean towards the flying hat, ensuring it landed on target.

'Hat trick,' Michael murmured.

The two men stood side by side, silently contemplating their old friend.

'He was a good man,' Michael observed. 'A noble man.'

'One of the best.' The world was going to be a different place without Bedivere. Merlin blinked back a tear. Saying that final goodbye never got easier.

The suit of armour creaked uncomfortably.

Merlin murmured a barely audible, 'At ease,' and the suit of armour relaxed. Its owner drew out a large handkerchief and blew his nose. He coughed and steered the conversation away from Bedivere's death. Grieving would come later.

'And how did it go with Rozen's father? Will he permit her to join the Guardians?'

'No, Merlin, he won't.' Michael replied. 'There was no turning 'im. Peder Tregenza is ruled by 'is fears.'

Merlin's mouth tightened.

'And before you say anything Merlin, it wasn't your fault. What befell 'is wife was an accident. No one, not even you, could 'ave foreseen it any more than you could 'ave foreseen what would happen to Gawain's parents.'

Michael thought of his conversation with Peder Tregenza. The man had been like a cornered dog. No matter how quietly and reasonably Michael had argued the case, Rozen's father had refused to even meet his eye, repeating that Rozen's place was with him and her sister.

Tyto flew to the balustrade overlooking the hall and Fly yawned and flopped at his master's feet.

Michael continued, 'But I can't imagine that this will be the end of young Rozen's involvement. She 'as 'er mother's blood!'

A commotion on the wall halted their conversation. A couple of the paintings shuffled up making room for a shield. Merlin flicked a glance towards the panelled wall. Bedivere's coat of arms had arrived.

Michael added, 'Although I did manage to persuade ol' Peder to allow Rozen to dine with us. It might be the right time to explain Bedivere's actions.'

Tyto launched herself off the balustrade and flew back along the corridor and into the library, and Fly pulled himself up and made for a warm rug and fire.

'I'll wait for you in the library, Merlin,' Michael was bone-weary. Life had its mountain-tops but it certainly had its valleys too.

Merlin nodded. 'A little soul-food might help; Mrs B has left a tin of home-made biscuits and a flask of hot chocolate by the fire. I suggest you help yourself.' He watched Michael make his way along the candlelit corridor to the library, then he turned and opened the door.

A minute later a dark-haired boy, mounted on a white stallion and accompanied by his dog, appeared leading his wearied allies: Rozen and Gawain barely keeping their eyes open; Cathe padding between the two knights; and Nick sharing Tamar's stallion and lolling against her back. It had been a long night.

***

It took a while before the horses were stabled and everyone was settled, but eventually, with the early morning sun slanting through the library's leaded panes, Merlin positioned himself in front of the fire and turned to face his guests.

Lancelot and Dinadan leant side by side against the library wall, while Kitto Cornish and Michael Jolly and the rest of the company occupied chairs or cushions or rugs. Tamar had wedged herself between Arthur and Nick, her oldest friends, and was watching Nick feed Dragon a selection of dried spiders and beetles.

Merlin cleared his throat. 'Congratulations are in order.' He opened his arms, encompassing his audience. 'Last night you fought a courageous battle and secured a great victory.'

Tamar concentrated on Dragon, she guessed what was coming. No matter what anyone might say she still felt responsible for everything that had happened.

Merlin looked at her. 'Tamar, that woman would have engineered a battle somehow. None of it was your fault.' He repeated sternly, 'None of it. You must let it go.'

Tamar took a shaky breath.

He pinned her with an unwavering look. 'Today you have helped to gain Cornwall's freedom and Nick and Dragon are restored to us.' Dragon clung to his master's shoulder. His scales had recovered a little of their shine but his eyes were dull.

Merlin added, 'And I gather that you and Rozen succeeded in securing a trophy.'

With a little smile Rozen held up a few silver hairs, 'Just for analysis.'

Merlin returned the smile but then he looked around and it faded and a silence grew. 'However, we also mourn a gallant ally.'

Arthur swallowed.

'A brave and noble knight.'

Lancelot whispered a, 'Hear, hear!'

'There are ancient laws in place which dictate how a battle should be fought and certain things are not allowed.'

Arthur frowned.

Merlin read his expression. 'Sire, if you will permit me to explain, this is pertinent. It's important that it is understood why we weren't all directly involved in last night's battle.'

Rozen's falcon bobbed her head and stretched and began preening.

'Indeed magic could be used – and was used by the Lady of Clehy – but for a fight to be won cleanly it has to be won fairly. Courage must win the day. Not subterfuge. So there were some of us who, despite our own wishes and if we were to remain true to our vows, were barred from the fight.'

Michael nodded and stroked Fly's soft head.

'Although we were permitted to assist in other ways.'

Kitto folded his left hand over the fist of his right hand and rested his chin on his knuckles as he considered his unorthodox entry into the castle.

'So your victory was a clean victory.'

Tamar glanced at Dinadan and wondered how his inclusion could be counted as anything other than magic. But Merlin, catching the thought, explained. 'And as for our noble friend, Sir Dinadan,' he bowed towards the knight, 'it's true that his journey to join us was unusual, but his swordsmanship was untainted. That is allowed as laid down in the Ancient and Royal Cornubia Decree.'

Nick looked at the young knight. He still had no idea how he'd joined them.

'The whole story will be unveiled to you later Nick,' Merlin said, intercepting his thoughts. 'Suffice it to say that without Tamar's courage, Dinadan wouldn't have been able to join us.'

He turned back to Arthur. 'This brings me to our very noble friend and ally – Sir Bedivere.'

A log blazed in the grate and several Christmas tree candles sparked and flared. Merlin pulled his staff towards him and began to trace invisible symbols on the floor with the staff's tip. Restorative music was necessary.

'Bedivere knew what he was doing.'

Arthur's eyes misted and he bit his lip.

'Even before he left here he had an inkling of what waited.'

And Arthur recalled the previous evening in the stables and Bedivere's quiet conversation with Merlin.

'He knew it was the only way to stop her.' Merlin paused and glanced back to the invisible cyphers inscribed on the floor.

'The Ice Lady could be defeated only by something she knows nothing of – that is, love. Bedivere loved Cornwall and he loved all of you and he knew the rules. He too was bound by The Vow. The Vow which dictates that we defend the defenceless, and promote harmony and justice. Ultimately that is what you all fought for last night. You fought for love: love of Cornwall and her people; you fought for justice and you defended your land.'

But an unsaid word hovered in the space between them.

Sacrifice.

Gawain thought, *But he died saving me!*

Merlin regarded Gawain sympathetically. 'Gawain, you mustn't blame yourself. Bedivere wouldn't want that. To ensure our victory Bedivere died willingly. He knew that the moment his life-blood hit the snow, the Lady would be defeated.'

Merlin passed long fingers over his eyelids and stared into the fire. Then he considered the symbols drawn on the floor and tapped a full-stop.

'And although our friend's absence is a great sadness, it is he who secured the final victory. He is the one who overpowered the Lady of Clehy and he and his horse have gone to a good place. Even now the celebrations are beginning.'

And dragging the staff's tip along the length of the invisible phrase he announced, 'So it is only right that we, too, celebrate. Arthur, you led your small army courageously. Bedivere would be proud of you; he wouldn't want us to be using Christmas Day to mourn his passing. This is a day for fun and feasting. He would be upset to find that it had been ill-used.'

He raised the staff's tip with a flourish, dragging the musical phrase into the air. And, as a conductor raises a baton, he signalled the music to begin, banishing the hurts and sorrows and fears; the Ice Lady's dark threat would be evicted from Tamar's mind and Nick's injuries would start to heal. And although Arthur's grief might not disappear, it would be softened.

He'd borrowed Mrs Beswetherick's song; 'God rest ye merry, gentlemen, let nothing you dismay,' filled the room.

'Mrs Beswetherick has prepared a feast, although she had no idea just how many she would be feeding,' he smiled, a mischievous glint in his eye. 'But before we eat, all weapons must be put away. Gawain, your sword cane will be perfectly safe here and Art, it would be wisest if Excalibur remains with me.'

Arthur nodded. He couldn't think how he'd explain it to his mum and dad anyway. He caught Lancelot's eye and a grin grew as he thought of the shabby house in Castle Close. 'Yeah, that's cool. I think Excalibur might be kind of out of place at home anyway.'

Lancelot chuckled and the double doors scraped open and Angela Jolly appeared carrying a tray of roast potatoes. 'For those of you who know the way to the kitchen,' she announced, 'a little help wouldn't go amiss.'

Immediately Michael Jolly was on his feet, astonishment and joy splashed across his face, 'Angela!'

And suddenly it felt like Christmas Day should feel.

Nick watched Dragon sit up and lazily eye a fly as Rozen turned to Gawain. 'Happy Christmas, Geek!'

Gawain looked up, torn from his thoughts, and smiled, 'It takes one to know one!' and his smile grew as he leant over and hugged her. 'Happy Christmas, welcome to the club.'

And Arthur held out his arms, 'Come here Tamblyn! Merry Christmas to the bravest Time Keeper in the history of Time Keepers.'

Tamar grinned and leant into Arthur's chest. 'Thanks, but I think that some of the other Time Keepers might have something to say about that ... and you're squashing my nose.'

Dinadan turned to Lancelot and muttered, 'The young king shows wisdom!'

Lancelot bellowed a laugh and slapped his thigh (an unusual habit) and exclaimed about the younger knight being an incurable romantic.

And even Kitto was putting his books aside. Just a tad reluctantly, he re-shelved *A Beginner's Guide to the Use of Portals* (after all, it was a most useful read, especially the map illustrating the best of Cornwall's time gates) in favour of the festivities.

Merlin glanced around the room and pulled out a chair.

'Ladies and gentlemen, your attention!'

The room quietened.

'I omitted to mention that all your families have been informed that due to the vagaries of the weather ...'

Nick raised his eyebrows and Merlin smiled. 'Due to the bad weather, your families have been told that you will not be returning home quite yet.'

Did they really accept it that easily? Arthur sent the question hurtling into Merlin's mind.

The wise man chuckled as he announced, 'Apparently the unusual weather has been on the local news.' He beamed. '*Most* convenient.'

'And a message has been delivered to your sister, Tamar, that you and your friends are my guests.' A little self-consciously he added, 'I'm told that that carries some weight in these parts. So it seems you will be enjoying a double Christmas Day! However, in order to enjoy this one you will need to assist Angela in setting out our meal.

Once you have done that, please ensure that you sit in your chair. Your names are carved in the table. You will find that the gifts inside the crackers are different for each one of you.'

Fixing Rozen with a meaningful look, he said, 'Miss Tregenza, yours is particularly pertinent. Although you may be separated for a while from Cornwall's other Guardians you have proved yourself to be a fierce protector of our beloved Cornwall. Therefore your gift will, in its turn, protect you.'

He cocked his head. Laid beneath the cheerful tones of the carol, sleigh bells jingled.

'Happy Christmas everybody!'

And Now ...

Far below Cornwall, in a high-domed cavern, the Writer perches on the edge of a plinth. Carved in the stone walls of the chamber are friezes of armed knights on horses, interspersed with groups of ladies wearing sumptuous gowns. On the floor are rugs woven in the deepest reds and purples and golds.

The Writer glances at the walls, at the candles still burning in their niches, and casts a look towards the ceiling high above her. Stars glint.

She turns to the sleeping figure installed on the cushioned plinth. His eyelids flicker.

She traces a finger over the rubies in the crown.

'Your successor has succeeded, Your Majesty,' she whispers. 'Sir Dinadan will soon be restored to his proper time and Sir Bedivere has left in the noblest way. The Fair Isles will be ringing with celebrations.'

And somewhere to the west a harp begins to play. The notes twist and twirl and rise and fall and bright-shadowed figures dance around a laughing knight.

***

On the cliffs high above the hidden cavern two, mostly invisible, figures glance at the cloudless skies and then at one another.

Viatoris digs into his shirt pocket and pulls out a velvet drawstring bag, unlooses the strings and draws out a flat, round leather case. Pressing the clasp, it springs apart.

It's his compass. The machine he'd last used in the summer on the cliffs above Porth Talant. It detects more than the north and south; it has a nose for evil and good. Together the Watchers wait as it springs to life.

The inner independent circle quivers, its needle trembling. Slowly, as if it can't quite make up its mind, the needle shifts, inching over the darker portion of the outer ring towards the lighter, flower-filled half.

Servo breathes out. 'Your instrument is always dependable, is she not?'

'Usually,' Viatoris agrees.

But the needle hasn't settled. Although it leans towards the bright flowers and butterflies on its sunny half, it still trembles uncertainly until finally coming to rest above a pink and purple flower.

Viatoris clicks the compass shut and slides the leather case into its protective bag.

'It seems that the story is not yet played out here in Cornwall,' Servo states.

Viatoris slips the bag into his shirt pocket. 'That does appear to be the case … but for now all is safe.'

A gentle breeze whips at their feet. Other times and places are calling. The Watchers glance at one another and, for the first time in their history, they shake hands. A double crackle, a duplicate *woomph* and the cliff is empty.

There's Watching to be done.

***

Rozen turns Merlin's gift over and runs her forefinger over the smooth metal. She lifts it to the sky. The moon illuminates the silver's delicate engravings. On the upper side her name shines back at her, *Rozen.* She turns it between her fingers and reads the inscription, *The fifth Guardian.*

Then she takes either end of the chain between her thumb and fingers, raises her arms and, holding the clasp, fastens it behind her neck.

The silver sword falls, warm, against her skin.

The fifth Guardian is ready.

***

Meanwhile, on the county's northern shore, the bones of a ruined castle shift above a mossy sea cave. Deep in its foundations the castle's memories of dancing and feasting and jousting are stirring.

On the deserted beach below the castle, a blue-cloaked, white-haired man checks the moonlit sky and enters the cave. Setting his staff to one side, he draws a jewel-encrusted sword from beneath his mantle.

He runs his fingers over the cave wall and lifts the sword ... and slides it into the rock. And a bubble of time begins to quiver, its translucent edges expanding and stretching, as an owl takes flight and a Cornish star shines.

Notes and Thanks

Merlin's Vow is the third in The Camelot Inheritance series. *The Golden Sword* and *The Time Smugglers* are books one and two.

Many people have helped and encouraged me in my writing journey including my wonderful family, both past and present, and numerous kind friends.

My heartfelt thanks must also go to Sally Vince; an editor gifted with flair and sensitivity. Her touch enabled this story to blossom.

While Pete, my ever optimistic, positive and patient husband, has been a tower of strength. (He's also an excellent cook and makes me laugh. So many superpowers in one man.) None of this would have seen the light of day without him cheering me on.

And, as always, grâce à Dieu.

The settings in *Merlin's Vow* are loosely based in Cornwall UK, but, as with all 'The Camelot Inheritance' series, they are not quite real and all the characters are completely fictional. However, if you'd like to visit some of the places that were the inspiration behind *Merlin's Vow*, I suggest you ride on the train line between Liskeard and Penzance and visit the village of Marazion and the castle on St Michael's Mount.

Visit my blog for photo galleries related to the books at: http://rosie-morgan-cornwall.blogspot.co.uk

Or stay in touch via twitter: @WritingRosie

Cornish Words Used In
'The Camelot Inheritance' Series.

Agroas = rose-hips
Aiglets = hawthorn berries
Brane = crow
Cathe = cat
Clehy = ice
Clowas, convethas = hear, understand
Comero weeth = Take care
Deeo agye = Come in
Deeo neaz than tane = Come close to the fire
Durdathawhy = Good day
Gothewhar vaze = Good evening
Hagarawall = storm
Kernow = Cornwall
Kevrin = secret
Marth = horse
Matearnas = Queen
Me ore hedna per thaa. Voyd alebma! = I know that very
    well. Go away!
Medhegneth = medicine
Morah = one dolphin; morahas for more than one.
Myrddin Emyrs or Merlinus = Merlin
Na rewh nakevy = Don't forget
Taran = thunder
Tenestatha, comero weeth = Goodnight, take care
Tereba nessa = Till the next time
Theram cara Kernow = I love Cornwall

40113970R00173

Made in the USA
San Bernardino, CA
11 October 2016